Reviews of *The House Husband*

'Whittaker's entertaining novel about role reversal is deftly done, with lots of sly jokes at the expense of the self-styled New Man, and plenty of grittily (and stickily) realistic domestic detail'
The Times

'Very funny and moving . . . A real page-turner'   Marian Keyes

'A delightful first novel with lots of humour, a tinge of sadness and plenty of wisdom'   *Publishing News*

'Highlights the things which really matter in life. A great read!'
Woman's Weekly

Also by Owen Whittaker

THE HOUSE HUSBAND

the Godfather

Owen Whittaker

ORION

Copyright © 2000 Owen Whittaker

The right of Owen Whittaker to be identified as the author of this work
has been asserted by him in accordance with the
Copyright, Designs and Patents Act 1988

First published in Great Britain in 2000 by
Orion
An imprint of Orion Books Ltd
Orion House, 5 Upper St Martin's Lane, London WC2H 9EA

A CIP catalogue record for this book is available
from the British Library

Typeset by Deltatype Ltd, Birkenhead, Merseyside
Printed and bound in Great Britain by
Clays Ltd, St Ives plc

For my father, Harry.
My very own gentle, funny, courageous wheelie.

I miss you.

Acknowledgements

Thanks to my agent, Jonathan Lloyd for looking after me, and his assistant, Tara Wynne, for listening to me flap and panic before dealing with my traumas with kindness and efficiency.

To 'Batman and Robin', my editors, Jane Wood and Selina Walker for their hard work, and to Jane again for lending a sympathetic ear to my personal woes over lunch. Especially to Susan Lamb for championing my cause with such enthusiasm, Dallas and his team, and all in sales, marketing, and production at Orion for grafting on my behalf. 'Tis much appreciated.

Special thanks to Lucinda for her help and advice with book two. To my brother, Glyn, for ringing me to talk about football, music, sex, anything but ruddy books; and to my mother for not understanding a word I say about writing even when I waffle on about it.

To Jo and Dennis for letting me borrow their study, and leaving their small but ferocious cat on guard outside the door so I could not leave until they came home.

To Katharine Noren again, this time for locking me in an attic above Dunworley Cottage Restaurant and feeding me Moose, Reindeer, Vodka with loganberries, and a particularly ruthless Schnapps made from birch trees while bullying me to write – even if I did want to scream every time she said, 'And how many pages today, Owen?' Also, as with *The House Husband*, thanks to my friends and the good people of Clonakilty, and this time

Dunworley and Ring as well. I'll be back as soon as I've sobered up from my last trip.

To Catherine Buchanan for knocking loudly on the outside of my bedroom door on her way to work at six thirty every morning to make sure I dragged my backside out of bed and got on with the rewrites, even if I could have cheerfully strangled her at the time.

Lastly, and most importantly of all, to the blond and the redhead, my kids, Harry and his sister, Isabella. I love you both. Even though my son's bedroom looks as if it has been burgled on a daily basis, and my daughter draws identical looking pictures of Daddy, the cat, and the Teletubbies all over the pages of my manuscript in felt tip, what would I do without you?

Part One

Shock Waves

1

What's another word for onerous? Onerous. Weighing one down? Actually onerous, clever-sounding word though it is, isn't quite right. Claustrophobic? That's closer. Damn it! Another two hundred and thirty pages to go before I finish this book, and I've spent fifteen precious minutes scouring the dictionary and the spell-check on my computer for one miserable word. If I had an ounce of sense, I'd just carry on and fill it in later. The trouble is, I'm a perfectionist and the fact that I, an experienced novelist with a perfectly adequate vocabulary, cannot think of a suitable word to convey what I am trying to say is driving me MAD! If I don't think of something soon, there is every chance that my computer will be given the opportunity to discover whether or not it can fly, because I swear I am about to hurl it through the window in front of me at any moment.

Onerous? Claustrophobic?

I know about words, because I write novels. Horror stories. Intelligent ones. They're successful – bestsellers in fact. I'm the master of deep-seated, psychological terror, so I'm told. England's answer to Stephen King.

I wonder if it's worth leafing through one of my earlier books.

The word I'm searching for might be an old fave. Look through any writer's body of work, literary or commercial, and you'll find they have a favourite word or two they use over and over again. I once went through a couple of mine, and found I had used the words 'depressed', 'insane' and 'victim' at least forty times in each book. God knows what an analyst would make of that.

I pick up a paperback copy of one of my earlier efforts, *The School Room*, and leaf through it, but it's no help. I glance at the photo on the back. The clothes look dated, but I'm pretty much the same, with the exception of a few more grey hairs.

I read the biography printed underneath: 'Max Patterson shot to fame on the publication of his first novel *The Inner Scream*. Three of his novels have been filmed, the latest, *The Locked Door*, is due for release early next year. He lives alone in a Gothic mansion in West Cork, Ireland.'

He lives alone. And I do, unless you count Maeve and Eugene, and they're staff, so publishers don't.

I prefer it this way. I've lived here for ten years, now, in my Gothic mansion in Dunworley, West Cork, here in southern Ireland. Except it's Georgian, not Gothic. It's just decorated that way. It suits the image, and image, the picture you portray, is all.

I write in a tiny attic room at the top of this very large, spacious and, I'm delighted to say, rather gloomy house. My office has low, apex ceilings, yellowing walls, and is filled with tea chests, containing things that if once important are now long forgotten. I have covered them in dust sheets to assuage my guilt at leaving them to rot. Then there's my desk, computer, printer, a couple of filing cabinets and a mass of paperwork scattered liberally over what little floor space remains. I work here because it has a rather introverted atmosphere, which helps me to delve into the darker side of human psychology, a base ingredient of everything I write.

I moved to Ireland on the advice of my accountant, Lawrence, or 'Loophole Littleton', as he's known in the trade. 'Writers and artists are exempt from tax in the Emerald Isle. Good move, I think, Max.'

The minute I set eyes on this place, I cast England aside. The sheer isolation of the house excited me. The first time I stepped inside, its gloomy interior wrapped its arms around me like a lost relative, reunited after years of painful separation. I adore the wildness of my surroundings, the contradiction of threatening grey skies above and lush greenery below. It's what my books are about, something good flourishing beneath the darkness.

That's bollocks, actually. They're about scaring the hell out of people. Forcing them to look inside themselves. Making them face some of the fears they hide from.

So, I left England, I left my father. I left nothing.

Suffocating? Stifling? No, they're both wrong.

The telephone's ringing. 'Maeve! Eugene! Somebody get that, will you?' I shout. There are none so deaf as those who do not wish to hear. I must get the answering-machine fixed. I snatch up the receiver. 'Hello.'

'Max?'

'Speaking.' I'm not sure if I want to converse with this person yet. I like to keep people out of my life. That way I'm reliant on no one, unless I pay them a wage for their services. I am free from all blackmail of the emotional kind. I have staff to look after my day-to-day well-being: my agent looks after my career, my accountant does the money, my lawyer sorts out the slander, libel and accusations of plagiarism. I sit here in my own world living inside my head. It's what I do best.

You see, I don't *do* life. In fact, I'm crap at it.

'It's Jamie,' says the voice at the other end of the line.

'Jamie! Where've you been? You haven't rung me in ages.'

'Yeah, well, you *can* actually pick up a telephone and call me, you know.'

5

Jamie is my only real friend. I've known him since I was a boy. Now, even this relationship has been reduced to a few phone calls and Christmas cards. He is the one person who has unconditionally stood by me, regardless of my weaknesses. I fear he has had poor return on his investment. 'I know. I'm sorry,' I say guiltily.

'Oh, forget it.' He sounds a little uncomfortable. 'I'm only extricating my pound of flesh.'

'Pound of flesh. Now there's a phrase to excite a purveyor of fictional horror.'

'Been done. Four hundred years ago.'

'Okay. Husband croaks. Boy's mother shags uncle. Makes son vengefully, murderously, bloodily, barking mad?'

'Er ... I have to say I think it rings a bell.'

We used to banter like this at Oxford together. I miss it. Jamie is the only human being who seems to understand my rather warped sense of humour.

'Picky, picky,' I observe. 'All right, final pitch: man adores wife. Suspects her of affair with best friend. Oh, no! He's wrong! Doesn't stop him executing her. Then, lo and behold, she returns to life, having spent the last millennium pretending to be a statue.'

'Been tried, and failed. Doesn't have the required foothold in reality, does it, Mr Patterson? Seriously, what are you working on at the moment?'

'Not much. I'm running out of dead authors whose ideas I can steal. How are Caroline and ... er ...'

'Nigel, Max. They're fine, thank you.'

In the seclusion of the attic I blush with shame. Caroline and Nigel are Jamie's kids. I say 'kids' but they must be teenagers by now. I'm godfather to both of them. My godchildren, and I can't even remember the wretched lad's name.

'Caroline's turning into a real stunner. Boys are beginning to

6

notice her in a big way, and she's milking it to death. She's becoming a bit of a tease, I'm ashamed to say. I'm scared to death every time she goes out the door. I remember what I was after when I was her age.'

'Half the female population of Yorkshire remember what you were after at that age. And that was before you really got into your stride at Oxford.'

'Don't remind me. Anyway, Nigel's doing well at school. He's a bit of a brainbox. Can't guess where he gets it from, can you?' He's fishing for compliments.

'Maybe now's a good time to confess about that affair I had with your wife. Speaking of whom, how is Marcia?'

'She's fine.'

I don't like the pause. 'You sure?'

'I said so, didn't I?'

'Yes but—'

'She's okay, Max. Now, for God's sake, don't press it.'

There's a sudden scent, a taste of something that has never passed between us before, and I don't like it. 'Let's cut the crap, Jamie. What's the problem?'

He sighs heavily. 'Listen, I'm a bit ashamed to ask this but I need a favour.'

'Fire away,' I say uncertainly.

'Things aren't going well. Financially, I mean. My business is in deep shit. Vultures are circling, and the wolves are so close I can feel their breath on my heels.'

'Christ, Jamie. I had no idea.'

'That's okay, mate. It's not your problem. I don't like to ask ... In fact, I've tried everything to avoid it, you know ... not wanting to ponce off a rich and famous friend.' He sounds choked.

'How much do you want?' I'm anxious to save him torturing himself.

'Oh, Max, I dread to think. Look, I don't want charity. I just need a loan. I'll pay you back—'

'What if I send you a cheque for five grand today? Will that keep people off your back?'

'It would be a big help.'

'I'll get it in the post tonight.'

'Thanks. Actually, Max, could you transfer it to my bank account? Only I'm going away and if I have to hold on until I get back and then wait for it to clear—'

'No problem. I'll get old Loophole Littleton on to it. Give us your bank details.' I write them down as he does so. 'Where are you off to then?' I ask, as I finish scribbling.

'Turkey.'

'Business?'

'No. Holiday.'

'What? Tapping me for a loan, then swanning off on a gulet with that gorgeous wife of yours.'

'It's not like that, honest,' he pleads, discomfort causing his voice to sound strained.

'I'm only joking, Jamie.'

'No, please let me explain. You see, Marcia and I . . . well, we've been going through a bad patch. Pressures, you know. I think she thinks I don't love her, and I do. You know how it is.'

Actually, I don't.

'Well, Philip – you remember my brother Philip – he's hired this villa and knows we're struggling, so he's paying for Marcia and me to join him. That's why I can't ask him to help.'

'I'm sure a bit of sun, sea and sex will put you and Marcia to rights. Are you taking the kids?'

'No. We're only going for a week. Sort of second-honeymoon type of thing.'

'Listen, Jamie, you go off and have a nice time, sort yourselves out. I'll get this money transferred. Then, when you get back, I'll

8

arrange a meeting with my accountant. I'll stump up the cash to get you up and running again, and we'll take it from there.'

'I didn't mean—'

'I insist. You stop worrying. Count yourself lucky that, since I moved to Ireland, all my Catholic guilt has come winging back to the surface.'

'Max. I don't know what to say.'

'Just call me the minute you get back. Now sod off and have a good time.'

'Okay, I will,' he says, chuckling with relief. 'Thanks, Max. You're the best.' He puts the phone down.

Except I'm not. I've been a shit friend since I moved to Ireland, and I can't even think of an expression low enough to describe what kind of a godfather I've been. All I can do now is throw cash at Jamie to make up for it all.

Concentrate, Max. Where was I? Stifling? Smothering?

There's a knock at my door. 'I've brought the post. Will you be wanting it?'

'Not now, woman, I'm working.'

'Well, where will I put it? I can't have it littering the hall.'

'Look, Maeve, I'm trying to – Oh come in, why don't you,' I say, as she clatters her way into the room.

Maeve lives in with her husband Eugene, who looks after the house and the garden. She cooks, cleans, washes and generally organises me domestically, while complaining about the 'pitiful salary' I pay her 'for such a wealt'y man'.

'I suppose you'll be throwing these on the floor with the rest of your letters.' She hands me a bundle of mail held together by an elastic band. In her other hand I catch a glimpse of something metal. 'This place is an awful state, Max. One day you're going to have to bite the bullet and let me clean it.'

Maeve is my Girl Friday. Well, I say girl . . . actually, she's in her sixties. She has jet-black hair, streaked with grey stripes in

9

such perfect parallels it's uncanny. She drags this mane back into the severest of buns, which exaggerates the fierce, shining eyes, sharp chin, and red, flushed cheeks that reside beneath it. She is plump and, in complete contrast to her husband, short. Perpetually dressed like a Puritan, she resembles a rather stern matron from a 1930s hospital ward.

She's rude, sarcastic, nosy, interfering and a complete bully. All of which disguise a kind heart. I don't know what I'd do without her. Or Eugene.

'It's all very well writing filth,' she digs at me, 'but living in it is another matter altogether.'

I like Maeve. I suppose that's why I tolerate her rudeness. I pretend I loathe her interfering personality, and she pretends she hates my writing, though I know for a fact she's read every one of my books – all seventeen of them.

'Have you not hired yourself a new secretary yet?' she asks.

'I've spoken to the agency and they're organising me a day of interviews. However, there are problems apparently.'

'Such as?'

'Such as nobody wanting to work for me. I have a reputation for being intolerant.'

Maeve huffs. 'Surely not. You only called the last poor girl a Neanderthal.'

'Yes, yes. Now, if you wouldn't mind?' I gesture at my computer screen, hoping she'll take the hint.

She's looking over my shoulder. 'Jeez, you've only written about two lines since the last time I disturbed you.'

'And small wonder. You've made more appearances than Phil Collins at a benefit gig, Jamie's been on the phone to me for hours, and to top it all I can't think of another word for onerous, or claustrophobic, or—'

'Oppressive,' she says, simply.

She's right. Damn it, she's bloody well right.

'How that failed to come to you working in this rabbit hutch, I can't think. Why don't you move to one of the big airy rooms downstairs?'

'Because I don't want to,' I argue.

A look of concern spreads across her face. 'Ah, Max, it can't be healthy for you stuck up here among the dust. You're knocking forty—'

'I'm thirty-eight,' I correct her.

'You're still far too old to lock yourself away. There's a world out there passing you by, boy.'

'Which is exactly what I want it to do. Stop bullying me.'

'Fine, fine. I'm going,' she says, holding up her hands. 'I know when I'm not wanted.'

I see the metal object in her left hand once more. 'Maeve, what exactly is it you have in your hand there?'

She glances at it. 'Oh, thanks for reminding me.' She holds the object in front of my face. 'What d'you think it is?'

I examine it. 'It's a tap.'

She nods.

'Okay,' I say after a pause. 'Why are you holding a tap in your hands, Maeve?'

'It fell off, Max. In me hand. I was wiping it clean and it just came away. Did you see the state of your bath? There's plaster everywhere. I swear it's coming away from the walls. And what are you going to do about it?'

I shake my head. 'It's coming away from the wall because I'm having a new bath fitted.'

She puts her hand on her hip and stares hard at me. 'Since when?'

'Ages. The plumbers must have come in on your day off. I thought I'd told you.'

'You did not. If you had, would I have spent the last half-hour trying to clean it?'

'I'm sorry.'

'"Sorry", he says. And me an old woman. I drag my legs up the stairs, the varicose veins throbbing, and I work my backside off scrubbing that bath. Then the tap comes off in my hand. I thought I'd broken it. It's enough to give a woman with my blood pressure a feckin' heart-attack!'

Maeve has complained about her failing health for the entire ten years she has worked here, but she still looks to me as if she could tear telephone books in two with her bare hands.

'What do you want with a new bath anyway?' she enquires.

'It's specially adapted. You know, top of the range. It's designed to make bathtime easier for me.' I spin round to face her.

'Ouch!' She shrieks. 'Would you get your wheel off my toe!' I reverse immediately.

'Do you have a licence to drive that thing?' she barks.

'It was an accident, Maeve.'

'And while we're on the subject, your spokes need oiling. I can hear you coming for miles, squeaking your way around the house like a giant mouse.'

'Maeve—'

'Why don't you use that nice electric wheelchair you bought for yourself instead of that old rust bucket?'

'I like this one. It's comfy.'

'Another discarded toy. Electric chairs, new baths. It's people you're needing, Max Patterson. Not toys. People.'

My patience is wearing thin. 'Yes, well, thanks for the lecture, Maeve. Now, if you don't mind, I've work to do.'

'I'm going, I'm going.' She heads for the door. 'If you want to stay locked up in here like some animal that's your affair. It's nearly lunchtime. I presume you'll want your raw meat tossing into the cage in half an hour or so?'

'Maeve!' I shout.

'Only thinking of you, Max,' she says, as she closes the door behind her. 'Same as always. Just thinking of you.'

I hear her shuffling down the corridor, huffing and puffing and grumbling as she goes.

2

So now you know. I'm on wheels.

I can picture the day it happened clearly, almost as if it were a favourite film, or a piece of music associated with a fondly remembered lover.

It was summer. I recall being dazzled, blinded by the light as I followed my mother into the garden, walking in her footsteps, happy to stand in her shadow. The bright, open sky was in stark contrast to the dull, formal décor of the house we lived in, its thick heavy drapes barring entry to the sun's rays.

It's exactly the same here in my house in Ireland. I rarely open the curtains. Maybe I'm comfortable with the familiarity, or maybe it helps me feel the outside world is being kept firmly in its place.

I was eight years old, and would watch my mother's expertise as she tended the garden she loved so much. She smelt of flowers, outside and inside the house, and was always patient with me as I pulled up plants instead of weeds, and decapitated blooms at the neck. If the soil had been dried out enough by the sun, we would gather small lumps of earth and toss them at each other, the two of us laughing as we tried to avoid each other's horticultural arrows.

This was my mother. However, it was not my father's wife. He was a good twenty years older than her – a well-bred, well-educated, well-connected ex-army officer who, upon retirement, ended up as the chief loan manager of a prominent city bank. When asked how he had managed this, he would tap the side of his nose and say, 'Friend of a friend, don't you know?' He would leave home early in the morning and get home late. When I wasn't at school my mother and I would laugh, cuddle and generally fool around, but the minute my father walked through the door, she would change persona. The bonnet of a carefree girl and loving mother swapped instantly for the sharp, angular hat of a dutiful wife.

'You must understand, Daddy needs me,' she would tell me. And I did. At least, I grew to accept it. The minute my father came through the front door I relinquished my claim on her, and the three of us were transformed into one of those old sepia photographs of the stiff, regimented Victorian family. When Daddy came home, I changed from a happy, playful little boy into a child who could be seen and not heard.

On the day I remember so clearly my mother changed my grass-stained clothes and we walked hand in hand the half-mile or so to the nearest shops. Every time I dragged my reluctant feet, or moaned, 'Shopping's boring!', she tickled me. I must have been in top form on the emotional-blackmail front because she felt guilty enough to buy me a present. I was thrilled as she ruffled my hair and told me she loved me. 'I love you too, Mummy,' I chimed back, my legs filled with energy for the return journey.

So, we're about two hundred yards from our front door and I'm carrying this bright, shiny, bouncy new ball. It's luminous orange, the sort you can still see in the dark when you should have been indoors hours before.

I drop it and it bounces out into the road.

Bet you couldn't see that coming.

What happens next? I follow tradition, go bounding out into the road after it, and a bloody great BMW comes roaring around the corner at top speed.

If you're going to step in front of a speeding car, make it a classy one, that's what I say. Should you survive, you don't want the embarrassment of spending the next fifty years telling someone you were run over by a Reliant Robin, do you?

Forgive me if I sound flippant. It's a defence mechanism I've built up over the years, a weapon with which to protect myself against life's crueller sides.

Now, here's the variation on the theme. My mother leaps off the pavement and pushes me out of the way. At least, most of me. Despite the human shield, the car still manages to clip my legs and I do the only perfect forward-roll I have ever managed in my life over its bonnet. My legs hurt like hell and I can't move.

I can see my mother, who is no more than six or seven yards away from me, and I scream at her to help me. I'm angry that she will not come to me and kiss it better. She hears me cry and opens her eyes. I'm stretching my arm out along the surface of the road because I want her to hold my hand. Her eyes narrow in determination and she scrapes her arm along the ground, pointing in my direction. When it is at full stretch she opens her hand, which is balled into a fist, palm facing upwards. When her fingers stop trembling, I know I will never hold her hand again. It does not matter that her eyes remain open and focused upon my own.

Thus began my long association with medical institutions. Two broken legs and a three-week stint in hospital to begin with. My mother was buried while my legs were still raised by a series of wheels and pulleys, my backside raw and glued to the bed.

My father never visited me. Not once. Every day I'd ask if he was coming, at first casually, then pathetically and finally, pitifully.

When the ambulance men took me home my father greeted me at the door, thanked the men politely as if he had just signed for a parcel, delivered registered post, and pushed me into the hall without speaking. The scent of blossoms that reminded me of my mother had been drowned by the sickly smell of stale alcohol. The house was deathly quiet, as if it had decided to rest in peace along with its mistress. My father wheeled me into the sitting room and parked me by the french window. I gazed out over my mother's garden, which had reached a peak of patiently cultivated beauty. A mass of colour, bathed and loved and cosseted by the brightest of warm sunshine. I've hated gardens and light ever since.

I said my father didn't speak, didn't I? Well, that's not quite accurate. On the day I came home from hospital, he said one thing, just before he left the sitting room. 'Because of you,' he whispered, 'because of you, boy, she'll never walk on this earth again.'

And neither have I.

The never-ending cycle of hospital visits dragged on for years: physio after physio, specialist after specialist. The broken bones in my legs knitted back together perfectly well. Good as new – almost. Except they didn't feel that way to me.

'Max, we think we may be dealing with something psycho-somatic,' the doctors told me. 'We have done every conceivable test and we cannot find a physical reason why you're unable to walk. What we have here, Max, is a case of post-traumatic paralysis. What do you think?'

'I think that when I stand up I fall over,' I replied.

To put things more succinctly, my mother ended up *under* the wheels, and I've been rolling around *upon* them ever since. Ain't life ironic?

My father hadn't been that keen on children before, especially his own. Now that he could blame me for Mother's death, he had a perfectly justifiable reason for disliking me intensely.

He wanted a son who would captain the school rugby and cricket teams while spending his leisure time mountaineering, not someone he had to help on and off the lavatory. His obvious disgust motivated me to build up my upper-body strength. I worked hard at being independent, determined never to suffer his shudder of distaste or, worse still, pity. Quickly, I became nothing more to my father than a visual reminder of his dead wife. That I was in a wheelchair became the perfect excuse for him to pack me off to a boarding-school that 'caters for your sort, Maxwell', where ninety per cent of pupils there, whether on four wheels or two legs, were also mentally handicapped. My mother had encouraged me to read from an early age and she had already introduced me to Shakespeare and poetry. I wanted to discuss Kipling's 'If' or *A Midsummer Night's Dream*. The rest just wanted to dribble. I thought I would go insane.

I was also terrified. In the dormitory, the moans and groans from the other unfortunate children would sing through the dark hours of the long nights like an opera of distress. I lay awake shivering, knowing that, whatever might happen, the last thing I could do was run away.

I was eventually rescued by my headmaster. He was a big, jolly man, with a round, reddened face that beamed with a mixture of intelligence and mischief. He was kind and patient with even his most difficult pupils, and adored by them all. Recognising my dilemma, he organised some extra individual lessons for me, sometimes tutoring me himself. We became friendly and, one weekend when other pupils were being visited by their loved ones, or going home to see their families, he invited me to his house in the grounds for Sunday lunch. It was here that I first met Jamie. My headmaster's son, he shone like a beacon of intelligence and normality among the misery from the first moment I met him. In many ways he was dafter than my classmates, his rather off-the-wall sense of humour mirroring his father's. He never pussyfooted around my disability, he just accepted it as part of who I was.

Jamie had also lost his mother, to the ravages of cancer, some two years previously. To this day we have never discussed our respective mothers' deaths or the impact it had upon us both. Yet I suspect we both realise it was a shared experience that helped draw us together.

When I was eleven, the headmaster phoned my father and told him he was no longer able to provide the education I deserved. Reluctantly my father let me return home. A string of private tutors took over responsibility for my education, and I worked three times the hours I had at school. District nurses and home-helps were paid to take care of my other basic needs. I saw less of my father when we lived under the same roof than ever before.

Your heart bleeds for me, doesn't it? Well, stick your finger in it because, on the up-side, I'm now stonking fucking rich.

Being forced to work helped me earn excellent A-level grades. Jamie was already going to Oxford and, heavily backed by his father and my tutor, I too won a place to read English at Balliol.

Jamie and I roomed together. He looked after me, and I have fond memories of sunny days and heady, boozy lunches. But I didn't venture out at night with him. Evenings were the time when the pretty, intelligent girls and handsome, witty men would dance around each other in flirtatious sexual courtship and I knew my limitations. After six p.m., I handed him over to a wealth of soft-faced girls with desire in their eyes, in the same way that I had handed my mother to my father in years gone by.

I shut myself in my room with dark thoughts of my mother's death and the cries of mentally disturbed children from my old school, and I wrote my first novel, *The Inner Scream.*

I was brave enough to show the manuscript to my tutor who told me it was rubbish, then passed it on to an old schoolfriend of his who just happened to be the managing director of a literary agency in London. The agent liked the book, auctioned it, and sold it for what was, in those days, a large sum of money. I was just twenty-one years old. Within weeks of publication, a film deal was on the cards, and I have never looked back. Well, maybe I have occasionally.

The dedication inside the front of that novel read, For my mother, who I will always love.

I have never told anyone else I loved them. And I don't suppose I ever will.

3

We're driving the Range Rover down to the village of Ring. As we do this I feel guilty. It's Friday, it's daytime and I should be working.

I'm with Eugene and he's driving. That's why we're in the Range Rover. I have a specially adapted car, but it's a Ford Mondeo. Not a car bursting with street cred, but altered for Old Rubbery Legs here, it takes on the persona of extreme naff. However, sitting in the back of my Range Rover I can still play the starry author.

It's about a fifteen-minute drive or so to Ring, most of it downhill. Leaving the house, we pass rolling green fields, some decorated with feeding cattle, until we reach the coast. I live quite close to the sea. If I open my bedroom window at night, the wind, which inevitably roars angrily around this neck of the woods, carries to me the sound of the waves buffeting the coastline. We pass the small but beautiful beach at Dunworley, with its anaemic-coloured sand. It is never less than damp, and I am told by those lucky enough to be able to walk upon it that it always feels firm beneath the feet.

The road is narrow, so when you meet a car coming in the

opposite direction, you breathe in and go as far up the grass verge as you dare. Then you crawl past each other, lifting a finger of acknowledgement while keeping the fingers on your other hand firmly crossed.

We're coming into Ring now, and it's a charming sight. Built on a series of bends, it gives the impression that the whole place is curved. The harbour is always full of boats, but not the ritzy, swanky vessels you would normally find in Kinsale, just along the coast. Practical, well-used fishing-boats bob and vie for space with small, tatty vessels used merely for pleasure.

It's June. In the rest of Europe it's summer, but not here. There's been a breakdown in communication somewhere and, in Ireland, Mother Nature has failed to pass down the message. Consequently, it's freezing bloody cold and bucketing down with rain.

I should explain a bit about Eugene. He's turned sixty, tall and whiskery, with a belly that resembles a concertina when he's stripped to the waist. He's been married to Maeve for thirty years or more, and they've no children, a bitter pill to swallow in this part of the world. Here, you're still considered a novice in the breeding stakes until you've got beyond your fourth child.

The key thing about Eugene is that he wants to be a writer, just like me, except his particular interest is crime. He's convinced he's created the Irish equivalent of Hercule Poirot. Somehow Sunny O'Flaherty doesn't quite have the same ring to it. What's interesting is that he's the antithesis of Maeve. She devours my writing while continually putting me down, and Eugene fawns all over me, praising my work as if it were Booker Prize material.

That's why we're on the way to the pub today. Eugene wants some literary advice, plus the chance of a couple of lunchtime drinks. These days, a draught pint is one of the few things that can tempt me from home.

It is impossible to park anywhere near the pub without running the risk of someone colliding with you head-on. Eugene turns the car round, so the passenger door is on the outside, before positioning the Range Rover as close to the harbour wall as he can. He then squeezes his massive frame out under the driver's door, cursing and grunting. It's such a tight fit he almost shaves his stubble off on the doorlock. Mission accomplished, he goes to the back and gets out the wheelchair.

It's my old faithful, not the posh electric job – I try not to use that too often as, with the battery pack, it weighs a ton and Eugene risks a hernia every time we take it out. Ordinarily, I use upper-arm power to propel me. I've spent many years building up these muscles. I even have a fully equipped gym in the house. I may have legs like two boneless chickens, but my arms are like Popeye's. I could have used my crutches, but I've been glued in front of my computer of late. Visits to the gym in my house have dropped off as a consequence, so my arms are feeling a bit feeble. Basically, I can't be fagged to work that hard.

The sheer height of the Range Rover makes it awkward for me to get out, so, huffing and puffing, Eugene opens my door and I swing my legs around to face him. He then prepares himself like an Olympic weightlifter, and sweeps me up into his arms.

'Christ! Do you have to grab me by the knackers when you do that?'

'Sorry there, Max.' He groans as he dumps me in the chair. 'I thought they was your kneecaps.'

'Flatterer,' I mutter, as he steers me across the road.

We get half-way across before a tourist's car comes tearing round the bend. Eugene just manages to lean forward far enough to stop the Toyota separating his left buttock from his right. Suddenly I'm a small child again, clutching an orange ball, repeating, 'Sorry.'

Breathing a sigh of relief, Eugene pushes me and my palpitating heart across the second half of the road and we enter the pub.

It's a small room, at least on the side we're drinking in. The bar fills up most of the space. Round tables cover the floor, spreading into alcoves, with barely enough space to squeeze between them as you carry your pints. Unusually for an Irish pub, the décor is, predominantly, of varnished pine.

It isn't very full, but it goes quiet immediately I enter.

There are reasons for this. First, I'm in a wheelchair. Second, I'm that weird English writer who shuts himself away in that creepy old house in the middle of feckin' nowhere. Third, I write those God-forsaken books full of madness and death and blasphemy. Fourth, apparently I'm not just eccentric, I'm barking mad. Last of all, there's my attire. I always wear black. Today, I'm wearing black jeans, a black open-neck shirt, a long black velvet frock-coat and a black wide-brimmed hat.

I dress this way purposely. It's the perfect costume. When I'm working it helps me get a feel for the sort of material I write. When I go out it perpetrates the myth and reinforces my sense of identity.

Eugene breaks the silence. 'Will you have a drink, now?'

'Please, Eugene. Do they have Beamish Red here?'

'I don't think so, Max. No,' he says, his eyes scanning the pumps and taps.

'No matter. Guinness will be fine.'

Actually, for once, I didn't want a pint. Right now I could do serious damage to a Bloody Mary, but if I'd said that I think half the locals would have begun dusting down the ducking-stool.

'Right, pint o' Guinness for your man and a Murphy's for me, Justine,' Eugene instructs the barmaid, who smiles at me.

I know her. I've flirted with her before.

'Will we sit?' He gestures to a table in the corner.

'I already am, Eugene.'

'I meant, will we move over here?' he says, making his way towards it, lifting his arms and backside to fit through the available gaps. I roll along behind him, scraping the legs of wooden chairs until I'm wedged in a corner between our table and a stool on which resides a gigantic man with elbows that, according to my ribs, should be registered as lethal weapons.

This is another reason why I rarely venture out of the comfort and security of my own four walls. In my house, everything is organised for me to manoeuvre myself around with relative ease, to the extent that there is a ramp running parallel to the flights of stairs. I sometimes even come close to forgetting I'm disabled. But in the big wide world difficulty of mobility is a constant reminder. It's movement usually accompanied by the embarrassed stares of others.

'I've seen your new book all over town, I have so,' he tells me, as he sits down opposite me.

'That's because nobody in town has bought the bloody thing, Eugene.'

'Not at all, not at all,' he repeats, with the stress on 'not'. 'They just don't like to admit to buying it. Anyway, what do you care? A man of your talent and standing with millions of sales world-wide. What's it to you, boy, if a few farmers and shopkeepers are too stupid to know a great work when they see one?'

'Have you read it?' I enquire, a trifle unfairly.

'No, no, no, I must confess I haven't. But I will now. Ah, come on, Max, you know me. The minute I have the time, the minute I have the time. Fair play, it's your fault for overloading me with work.'

Sure, Eugene. He's sprinting off to the bar to collect our settled stout.

'"I will slip into your subconscious mind the way alcohol slides down your throat and into your bloodstream,"' Eugene quotes from one of my previous books as he returns and places our pints on the table. It's the one I know he's read, because he can quote it like Jehovah's Witnesses can quote the Bible. 'Fantastic piece of writing that, Max. Now if only I could evoke such an atmosphere with my pathetic attempts at art, I'd die a happy man, so I would.'

'We're here to discuss your manuscript, remember? How's it coming along?' I proceed to pour half my pint down my throat.

'Ah, well, now, Max,' he begins, and I watch the sparkle come into his eyes. 'I believe I've found the answer to that little problem I was harping on about the last time we spoke. Will I remind you?'

'Do.' I speak with as much enthusiasm as I can muster.

Eugene takes a long pull on his pint before placing it back on the beer mat. He fidgets nervously in the chair and, when he has finally settled, he transfers his tension to his hands, which he washes with an imaginary bar of soap.

'Sunny O'Flaherty, ace detective, has solved the murder in the church. He's about to point the finger of justice at the beautiful but desperate Sorcha Mulligan, who has been having an illicit affair with the local priest.'

As I listen, I take some comfort from the fact that, if this gets published, somebody else's book will offend the locals more than mine.

'The dear departed Father O'Hea has, as we know, been a bit of a lad, shagging the life out of Laura McCarthy, a local girl from the convent. A girl so young, the ink is barely dry on her Leaving Cert. Now, Sunny O'Flaherty knows the murderer was one of them two. He knows one of them drove the knife into Father O'Hea's back. The question is, who? If you remember, I was after having a bit of difficulty working this out.'

'That's right,' I say, finishing my pint.

'Last time we talked this through, I suggested that the dying Father O'Hea managed to write the word *American* on the wall in altar wine before he died.'

'Yes.' I wince slightly at the memory.

'But you quite rightly pointed out that as neither of the two female suspects was American, this wasn't much help.'

'I also pointed out that the altar wine might just have dripped down the wall into a pool of illegibility by the time your detective saw it.'

'Okay, okay, okay,' he repeats, each one a little more excited than the first. 'How's this instead? Father O'Hea still writes the word "American" as he's dying—'

'How does he do this?' I interrupt.

Momentarily dead eyes accompany his pause. 'Forget the wine. Perhaps he writes it in blood.'

'Bit awkward to get at the blood if he was stabbed in the back, isn't it?'

'Bear with me, Max. He writes the word American, but what use is this to the great Sunny O'Flaherty? Yet he knows if he can work this out he can solve the case.'

Eugene thinks he's cracked it. He's sitting back, arms folded, smiling. 'Go on now, Max, have a guess. Take a stab, if you'll forgive the expression.'

'I give up. I do honestly. Tell me.'

He's grinning. 'Tights,' he says.

'Tights? You mean tights, as in an alternative to stockings?' I scratch my head in confusion.

'That's right.'

'I don't get it.'

He smiles at me with patronising sympathy. 'The colour of the tights was American tan. What do you think now, Max? Fierce clever stuff, eh?'

'What tights, Eugene?'

'The ones the altar-boy saw under the curtain, behind which Father O'Hea was murdered.'

'I see,' I say slowly. 'Were these tights just sort of lying on the floor by themselves?'

'Of course not. They were definitely attached to Sorcha Mulligan. From the tips of her toes to the top of her bum. That's the point, don't you see? Sorcha Mulligan, the rich socialite, only wears American tan tights. Laura McCarthy always wears the black, usually thick, woolly tights that go with her convent school uniform. That's how Sunny O'Flaherty knows which one of them did it. Something as simple as the colour of a lover's hosiery gives the game away.'

I'm struggling to keep up with this. I lean forward to question further. 'You say the altar-boy saw them under the curtain, these tights? How come? Wasn't Sorcha wearing shoes?'

He appears irritated by my pickiness. 'You're being difficult now. Maybe she was wearing sandals.'

'With American tan tights? Not much style and taste for a rich socialite.'

He's staring at me. I'm in a no-win situation here. It's not really fair of me to steer him wrong if he wants to get this published. And, believe me, he does. On the other hand, if I tell him the truth, I'm the snobby writer who wants to keep Eugene slaving away for me for the rest of his life.

'What's wrong?' he asks tensely. 'Come on now, Max. This is your ol' friend, Eugene. Talk to me, boy.'

'Well, one thing bothers me,' I confess, 'would the first thing that enters the thoughts of a dying man be the colour of his slayer's tights? I mean, having contorted his hand around his back to dip his fingers in his own blood, couldn't he have thought of something more useful to write with it? Like the killer's name, for example?'

He is frozen in thought, an expression of anguish etched on

28

his face. 'You're right, you're feckin' well right. You've got to help me with this now.'

'Me? You're the crime writer. This is your bag, not mine.'

'Please, Max, that mind of yours has thought up some of the most complicated plots in modern literature. Come on, man, help me out here.'

'Of course I will, Eugene. Just let me order us another pint. Help the creative juices flow, eh?'

'Ah, good man, so you are, Max.'

I make my way to the bar. 'One pint of Guinness and one of Murphy's, please, Justine.'

'Certainly, Mr Patterson, sir,' she replies saucily, her face lighting up with the most beautiful of smiles. I've had this one on the boil for a while. We've flirted every time I've been in.

'Nice to see a good-looking feller in here for a change,' she says, as she begins to pull the stout.

I look over my shoulder.

'Now, don't be modest, Mr Patterson. You know I was talking about you.'

I've been told this before, but I've never believed it. On the rare occasions when I'm upright I'm about six foot tall. I have auburn hair, which is quite long and wavy, and green eyes.

Physical compliments have always sounded hollow. Am *I* good-looking? Or is Max Patterson, well-known horror writer, the handsome man? Put it this way, it's no coincidence that I lost my virginity two days after news of my book deal became common knowledge.

She's nice, Justine. Fresh, pretty features, set beneath long red hair – a soft mouth, and large blue eyes that twinkle mischievously.

'Please, call me Max. Thank you, Justine. It's nice to be here.'

'We're not honoured with a visit from the great writer very often, mind.'

'I don't get out much,' I tell her.

'You should, Max. Don't you get lonely, living in that big old house all by yourself?'

'Sometimes,' I reply.

'I've seen it, just from the road, like. Looks awful spooky to me.' She rolls her blue eyes in a coquettish manner.

'Actually, it's quite nice inside, depending on your taste, I should add.'

'Is it, now? Well, maybe I should be after seeing it for myself one day.'

'Would you like to?' I ask.

'Could I?' she counters.

'What time do you finish here? You could come then, if you want to,' I say loadedly.

'Mr Patterson! That's an awfully forward suggestion to make to a young girl.'

She *is* young. Late teens. All my lovers are young. They're the ones who go for the image. Older women tend to reach for the crucifixes and garlic when they see me approach.

'No, I didn't mean that,' I lie. 'I'll give you a guided tour.'

'Finishing in the bedroom, from what I've heard.'

She probably has. And not only from Maeve.

'You don't have to look at the inside of my bedroom, if you don't want to. I promise.'

She's leaned across the bar. Her breasts are encased in a Lycra top so tight you would not blame them if they leapt free, gasping for air.

'I never said that, now, did I?' she whispers.

Bingo! 'When can you come?'

'Half an hour.' She winks at me. 'I'll bring your drinks over.'

'Thanks.'

I roll back over to Eugene, feeling dreadful about my lack of tact over his novel.

'Was it worth all the work?' he asks, knowing me all too well.

'Half an hour. We'll have to make room for one more,' I say, and he grins, which means he'll help me sneak Justine in past Maeve's radar-like ears.

'Now, come on, let's sort out this plot of yours.' I light a cigarette as an aid to concentration.

We're in the kitchen, Justine and I.

Eugene is somewhere in the grounds, and thankfully this is Maeve's day for food shopping. She'll be gone for hours, gossiping her way around Ballinkilty.

When we get back to the house I pop upstairs to slip into something more comfortable while Justine makes herself a drink. It's a hell of a palaver getting my trousers off, so I slip into my towelling robe, slide into my posh electric wheelchair and make my way calmly downstairs.

I suggest we move to a more comfortable location but she just smiles at me.

We quickly run through the 'Why are you staring at me like that?' and the 'I'm sorry, I just can't help myself' routine, and off comes the Lycra top within seconds. She isn't wearing a bra and, here's an odd one, just tights and no knickers. It's sexy though. Thankfully they're not American tan.

And so the dance begins.

Justine's kneeling in front of me, and I'm leaning over the top of her and looking at her gorgeous bottom. It's tight, firm, and seductive.

'I've heard all about what you get up to in this house, Max Patterson,' she says suddenly, freeing her mouth and replacing it with her hand.

'All true, I'm afraid,' I confess.

You'd think it would put them off, the exaggerated scores of other lovers, but maybe the thought of passion with the famous man in black in the big old house turns them on.

'I bet no one has ever made love to you while you sit in that chair.'

'No,' I lie.

'I'm a bit tired,' she says, winking. 'Would you mind awfully if I sat down?'

Funnily enough, I've no objection at all.

She rips a hole in her tights as she leaps on me. With her back towards me, she allows me to caress her breasts as she rides me. Part of me hates myself for doing this, but I need to feel wanted, if only for a brief time.

When it's all over, she'll make me promise not to tell anyone, and I won't. But she will. There's the sound of a car in the drive and Justine has frozen.

'Shit! Is someone coming?'

'Almost.' I begin to move inside her again. 'It's only Eugene. He's driving off to Ballinkilty to collect Maeve.'

'He won't come in, will he?'

'No.'

'Are you sure?'

'It's okay,' I say, thrusting a little quicker now. I want to get this over with before she changes her mind.

'Oh . . . Max,' she moans. She's squealing, suddenly. I'd like to pretend it's because I've suddenly done something sensationally sexy to her. The truth is her hand has touched the control button on the electric wheelchair and we are whizzing round the kitchen bumping into things.

'Whoa! Ride 'em, cowboy,' She waves her free arm in the air, as if she's trying to break in a stallion.

'Oh, Justine! Is the earth moving for you too?'

We're both in hysterics, as the chair bumps its way around the kitchen like a pissed Dalek with us on board.

'Oh ... oh ... *oh* ... MAX ... yes ... yes ... *yes*!'

'*Oh*, Justine!'

'*Oh, Max, Max!*'

It's over. I feel empty. Hollow, the way I always do.

I stroke Justine's breasts, and gently kiss her back in the hope that she'll tell me she loves me. Except she doesn't. They never do.

4

It's over a week later. I know this, because I've realised Jamie hasn't phoned me. Either he's having a good time and is staying on in Turkey for another week, or his pride is refusing to allow him to take me up on my offer of help.

I'll have to ring him when I've finished working. I've struggled a bit today, only managed ten pages. Not bad, considering. They're crap, mind you, but at least I now have something I can improve. I've printed them up in order to mark corrections. I've decided on a change of atmosphere to do this so I've taken a coffee into the drawing room.

This is the sort of room Dr Jekyll would use to entertain guests while his laboratory remained hidden behind oak-panelled doors. It's a sort of decorative homage to a ground-breaking book. In my opinion, Stevenson's book was the first horror novel to explore the human psyche. Its walls are painted in dark Victorian green, full bookshelves everywhere, blazing log fire, and large, brooding pictures of moorland countryside on the walls.

I've just read through today's offering. For all my outward indifference and bouts of self-deprecation, I am secretly quite proud of my books. They may be given the tag Horror, they may be commercial and sell in lorryloads around the globe, but I would like to think they are well written. Whether I use human psychology or the occult or a mixture of the two, I write about the demons that unite us all: fear of this life, of losing our sanity, of death, or fear of the next life. They may be entertaining, but I'm not convinced that reading my books makes people feel comfortable.

The only criticism my editor repeats every time I send in a new manuscript is that they are always short on romance. But, then, she's a woman. 'Beef up the emotion, Max. Slot in a couple more love scenes. We have to empathise with your hero when he finds his lover crushed under a car.'

I can't do love in life or in fiction, apparently.

The telephone's ringing. Why do I keep forgetting to get the ruddy answering-machine fixed? Why hasn't that useless bloody agency found me a secretary yet?

'Maeve! Can you answer the phone for me?'

No reply.

'Maeve. I'm not in. I'm working!'

It's still ringing. I've got one of those old, thin stick-phones in this room, with the mouthpiece fixed to it and just the earpiece attached by a piece of cord. The sort they were always tapping while they shouted, 'Operator, operator, I seem to have been cut off,' in black-and-white films.

I pick it off the table. 'Hello. This is Max Patterson. I'm afraid I'm not available to take your call. If you would like to leave a message please do so after the tone. On the other hand, you could always try sodding off and ringing back when I'm not working.'

'Max? It's Paul.'

My lawyer. He was at Oxford with Jamie and me. Well, strictly speaking, he was a year or two above us. I hated him. He was an arrogant, obnoxious, argumentative, bloody-minded, conniving bastard, which is exactly why I hired him as my lawyer when I discovered he'd moved into that profession. He's now my agent's lawyer, my accountant's lawyer – and Jamie's lawyer, come to think of it.

It's new-contract time with my publishing house, and they've snuck one or two dodgy clauses into the small print I'm not that happy with. My agent suggested we sent a copy to Paul to examine, just to be on the safe side.

'About time you got back to me.'

'Is it?' he queries.

'Yes. You've had that contract for over a fortnight.'

'Never mind that now, Max. Has anyone contacted you?'

'Contacted me?'

'Yes, been in touch?'

'Contacted me? Been in touch? From the other side, do you mean?'

'Believe me, that's not funny under the circumstances.'

'Excuse me!' I reply, offended.

'It's obvious no one's told you about Jamie. I was rather hoping they had. Looks like it's down to me, then.'

'Jamie? Have you heard from the bugger because he –'

'Max . . .'

' – calls me last week and tells me he's in dire financial straits. So I send him five grand and he sods off to Turkey, and he promises to call when he gets back –'

'Max, listen . . .'

' – and the git hasn't bothered calling me. I've not heard a word. I assume he's still rogering the life out of Marcia on a beach in Tur—'

'*Max, shut up for pity's sake! Jamie's dead!*'

There's an echo in the room. The sort that bawls back at you when you shout into the mouth of a hollow cave. Only this echo isn't in the room, it's inside my head. And I don't like what it's roaring back at me, because I don't want to hear it.

'Max? Are you there? Are you okay?'

I kick-start my breath again. 'Yeah, yeah. I'm fine.'

'Did you hear what I said?'

'Yes. Yes . . . I heard you.'

'I'm sorry to break it to you like this.'

'It's fine . . . that's . . . that's okay.'

'No, it's not, Max. It's a hell of a shock. It stunned me and I didn't know Jamie anywhere near as well as you did.'

Didn't know. Past tense.

'Do you want me to tell you what happened?'

'Ah . . . yes, actually. Tell me.'

He's explaining the events to me, but I'm not sure how much I'm taking in. I feel the same surreal distance from reality I felt when my mother died. I sense the impact inside my body, and fear it will never seep back out.

'. . . and that's about as much as I know,' he concludes.

'Right. I see.' I try to shake myself back to my senses. 'Anything I can do?'

'Not unless you fancy flying off to Turkey and retrieving the bodies.'

Embarrassed silence.

'Sorry, Max. Ignore me. I tend to be a bit abrupt at such times. Professional habit. Forgive me.'

'Well, obviously I can't go and fetch them home. But I can pay for it. You organise it for me, and I'll let you have the money as and when necessary.'

'Are you sure? It could get very expensive.'

'Of course I'm sure!' I snap. 'What about – what's her name? – the sister?'

'Sarah.'

'Yes. What's happening about her medical bills? Are they flying her back to an English hospital? Was she insured?'

'I don't know. I don't act for that branch of the family.'

'If there's a problem, let me know. While we're on the subject,' I feel fleetingly safe behind this veil of practicality, 'Jamie was skint. Who's paying for the funeral?'

'Good point.'

'You must have a copy of his will?'

There's a long and seemingly awkward hiatus.

'Er ... yes. Yes, I do, but we can come to that later.'

'Not later. Now. Find out what Jamie wanted. I'll pay for that too.'

'It's very generous of you, but don't you think you should take a little time to think about this before you decide?'

'That won't be necessary. Do it, Paul.'

'Okay, don't bite my head off. I am *your* lawyer as well, remember. It's my job to advise you.'

'Yes, of course. When do you think the funeral can be held?'

'There may have to be post-mortems first. I'd say the end of next week some time.'

'Call me when you have news.'

'Sure. Are you certain you're okay?'

'Yes. Took the wind out of my sails a bit. I'm fine now.'

'Right. I'll press on, then. Start making some calls. You take care. I'll be in touch shortly.'

He's gone.

I stare into the fire, watching the logs disintegrate.

'Were you after calling me a while back, Max?'

Maeve appears out of nowhere, and I jump a bloody mile. She's dragging the Hoover behind her. She wears wax earplugs while she's vacuuming, which is probably why she didn't answer before.

'Pour me a large whiskey, will you, Maeve?'

'Don't be such an inebriate. It's barely after eleven, so.' She ambles closer and studies me. She looks hot and bothered, and I notice she's taking short, staccato breaths as she approaches.

'You okay?'

She waves a hand dismissively. 'That Hoover weighs a ton. Never mind me, boy, you look as pale as one of them ghosts you write about. What's wrong?'

'I've just had some very bad news.'

She stares at me for a minute. 'I'll get you that whiskey.'

She crosses to the drinks cabinet and comes back with a tumbler three-quarters full. Handing it to me she asks, 'What's happened, Max?'

'You remember Jamie? My friend.'

'The English feller. 'Course I remember him. He's one of the few friends you have. Not as if he can get lost amongst the crowd, is it now?'

'Jamie's dead, Maeve.'

'Holy Mother of God, no!' She puts a hand to her mouth, then crosses herself.

'A boating accident in Turkey. Choppy sea, jagged rocks, and a young, under-qualified captain, or some such combination.'

'I'm so sorry, Max.'

'Yeah.' I sigh. 'His wife, Marcia, was killed too, along with Philip, his brother. Philip's wife, Sarah, was saved, but she's in a coma in a Turkish hospital.'

'May they rest in peace,' Maeve responds, with genuine sadness.

'Anyway, I've got work to do. Thanks for the drink, Maeve.'

'Surely you're not going to be working now, are you?'

'Yes. I must. I have to.' I pick up the pages of my manuscript.

Maeve walks past me towards the door. 'Didn't he have children, your friend?' she asks from somewhere over my shoulder.

39

'Yes, he did.'

'Poor lambs. What's to become of them?'

I hadn't given my godchildren a thought, which is probably just as well. It seems anyone I form an attachment to is destined to die young.

5

I'm flying. In an aeroplane, I mean. My ears are popping. Either
that, or I can hear my brain cells exploding due to the amount of
alcohol I'm knocking back. On the tray in front of me there is a
pile of empty gin bottles, tonic tins, plastic tumblers and swizzle
sticks. They're all lined up like dead soldiers.

It's the end of the following week. Jamie was buried today.
And Marcia. And Philip. No reduction for bulk bookings,
apparently. Sorry. Poor taste. Then again there's nothing
particularly refined or dignified about death.

Actually, they weren't buried, they were cremated. I'm not
sure which is worse. I don't suppose either is a barrel of laughs.

The journey over was a pain. I had to fly to Dublin, then catch
a second flight to Leeds-Bradford airport, where I was collected
and driven towards the Yorkshire village where Jamie spent part
of his youth, not far from where my old school used to be.

During conversation, the taxi driver asked me if I'd ever been
to a cremation before. I confessed I hadn't, so he proceeded to
give me a blow-by-blow account, a sort of sneak preview,
containing graphic detail. I felt my resolve weaken. I asked what
they would do with the ashes afterwards. He informed me if

Jamie hadn't left any special requests they'd probably sprinkle them in the garden. 'Beautiful garden they've got up there,' he said. That was enough. I had suffered the connection between death and a beautiful garden once before in my life. I couldn't face it. I made the driver turn round, and bring me back to the airport. I sat in the bar waiting for my flight, feeling guilty and checking my watch.

I couldn't help thinking what a terrible waste it all was. Not one of them had reached forty. A waste of time, a waste of life, even the waste of putting someone in an oak coffin, only to use it as an oversized piece of kindling. It all seems so pointless. I know I write about death every day, but that's fine, that's fiction. It's all very well Maeve going on about there being a life out there, but if this is the real world she's trying to drag me into, she can forget it. I'll stay where I'm safe, thank you. There's nothing to gain by allowing yourself to feel ... affection for someone, because they just up and die on you. So I'm concentrating on getting sloshed instead.

I reach up and press the call button. The little matchstick-woman symbol lights up, accompanied by a pinging bell.

I feel such an emptiness, a hollowness inside. I should have been there. Of course I should have been there. Jamie wouldn't have let me down. And now he's gone, I can't think of a single way I can make it up to him.

The stewardess has arrived.

'Gin and tonic, please.'

'Another, Mr Patterson? We're going to be landing soon.'

'Please. I have to raise a glass to a very special friend.'

It's very foggy.

The nice man from the airport met me off the plane and wheeled me across the tarmac, which was just as well as otherwise I might have been breathalysed, and found drunk in charge of a wheelchair.

The nice man has now collected my bag and pushed me to my car. 'Will I be putting the bag in the boot, sir?' he's asking.

I nod, to be on the safe side, and press a ten-punt note into his hand.

'Thanking you very much, Mr Patterson. Drive carefully now.'

Here comes the difficult bit. I've got to stand up. Thish is going to be a bit . . . tricky.

Crutches. Yup. Got 'em. Right, here we *go*! No, we don't – Bugger! I'm still in the sodding chair. I think I got my bum about two inches up before it decided it wanted to shit . . . sorry, sssss . . . sit back down again.

Steel yourself, Max. One, two, *three*! I've flung my arms across the roof of the car. I'm still upright – in a beached-whale sort of a way – but I'm stuck. Maybe I should yell for help.

'Excuse me?'

'Arghh!'

'Sorry, sorry. Did I make you jump?'

'You would have if I could. Jump, I mean.' It's a woman. Out of the blue. A woman.

'Only I've got a bit of a problem. You see, my car won't start. The starter-motor's jammed. I was wondering if you could give me a bit of a push?'

Ish she taking the pish? 'Pardon?'

'Well, that usually gets it going. Only I'm by myself, and what with the fog and everything – would you mind?'

'Slight problem there. You see—'

'Oh, no. You're drunk!'

'It's worse than that. I'm legless.'

'Oh, God!'

'I mean, I still fall over whether I'm drunk or sober. 'Cept it

43

hurts more if I'm sober, of course.' I can vaguely see the mist clearing in front of her eyes.

'Oh, I'm so sorry. I didn't realise.'

'I'm rather glad you happened to pop along. You see, I'm a bit stuck.' I've just had a brainwave. 'I can't push your car,' I tell her. 'But why don't you help me get in mine, and I'll give you a lift?'

'I don't think that's a very good idea.'

I think it's brilliant. What's she talking about? 'Look, where do you live?'

'Ballinkilty.'

'So do I! Well, near enough. I'll take you there.'

'That's what worries me.'

'Right, right. Let's get a taxi.'

'No chance. There's hundreds of people waiting for them to arrive, and not one in sight.'

'Okay. You drive, then. Drive my car home, drop me off . . . and bring it back in the morning.'

'But you hardly know me. What's to stop me stealing your car?'

'Don't be silly it's a Ford Mondeo! Who'd want to steal a – I say, could you help me into the car? I think my arms are about to give out on me.'

She's grabbed me by the waist. Not an unpleasant sensation. 'Blimey, you're heavy.'

'Am I? Only I've never tried lifting myself.'

'No. I've got you. I got you . . . There.' She's managed to bundle me into the car.

She's leaning in to talk to me, and our faces are close enough to kiss. I realise that she's very pretty, with a fresh face devoid of makeup, and large blue eyes you just want to drown in.

'Will you drive me home now?'

'No!'

'Please. You can't leave someone like me here all night, can you?'

'I'm not thinking straight. I'm all muddled.' She pauses as she gathers her thoughts. Her eyes are hypnotic, I swear. 'Okay,' she says at last. 'You win. I'll just lock my car.'

She's climbed into the driver's seat and I can smell her perfume. It's flowers. She smells of new blooms, like someone else did once.

'Keys?' I've given them to her and she's adjusting her seat. 'There's no pedals. Where's the clutch, the brake, the—'

'No point in them, really,' I tell her. 'You see, if I reach down to push the pedals, I can't see the bloody road.'

'Oh, God, this isn't happening to me!'

'Don't worry, it's easy. Look, here'sh your gearstick doobrie on the steering column, automatic gears, automatic crutch—'

'Clutch.'

'Sorry. Ff – Ff – Freudian whatsit.'

'Slip.'

'Thank you. That's your brake and this is your accelerator.'

'Right. Let's do it,' she growls. 'Ignition. Gear. Accelera—'

I'm sure we should be going in the opposite direction. Like forwards. And a bit slower.

Ouch!

'I appear to have reversed your car into mine,' she's telling me, and remarkably calmly under the circumstances. '*Ahhh!*'

She can't half scream, I'm telling you.

There's a light shining in my eyes. I think aliens have landed. No. Ish jusht Airport Security doing a bit of checking up.

Oh dear . . .

6

I feel awful. I'm sick, dizzy, and someone has painted my mouth with dried crushed chickpeas.

I keep trying to work, but staring at the computer screen makes me feel worse. Words keep moving, and I feel a sudden empathy with dyslexics.

Eugene has just popped his head around the door. 'What's happened to the car?' he asks.

'What car?' I reply.

He runs the palm of his hand over his face. 'Your car, Max. The Mondeo.'

'Well . . .' I begin slowly, in the hope he'll interrupt and tell me, because I'm not aware that anything has happened to it.

'It's a bloody wreck, man.'

I hope he's exaggerating. 'Ah, yes, that. I had a bit of an accident. 'I . . . er . . . drove it into a tree.'

'A tree?' He sounds aghast.

'I'm ashamed to say I was a little tiddly.'

He shakes his head. 'A little tiddly? You must have been pissed out o' your mind to reverse into a tree, boy!' Imparting that, he leaves.

What did I get up to yesterday? How did I come home from the airport? I cannot remember. I have never had a blackout before, and it scares me.

The telephone is ringing. I'll have to answer it if only to make it stop. 'Hello.'

'*Where the fuck were you yesterday?*' Paul screeches down the line.

'I couldn't face it,' I manage to articulate.

'Well, it didn't look good, I can tell you. Especially as—'

'As what?'

'Nothing. Where did you get to?'

'The bar at Leeds-Bradford airport,' I confess.

'For God's sake, Max, Jamie was your friend.'

'I know. I feel bad enough as it is, but there's nothing I can do to make up for it now, is there?'

'Actually, Max, there is.'

I must be hearing things. 'Is there?'

'I didn't want to tell you this over the phone. I was going to talk to you after the funeral, take you to lunch and break it to you gently.'

'Paul. I'm tired and I'm hung-over. What on earth are you going on about?'

'Are you sitting down?'

'Are you trying to be funny?'

'Sorry.' I hear him take a deep breath. 'How much do you know about Jamie's family – his extended family, I mean?'

I'm trying to think, but I'm not finding it easy. 'Not much. His mother was dead when I met him. His father died several years back. I think there was an aunt and an uncle.'

'Not any more, there isn't. They're dead too, I'm afraid. To make matters worse it's the same on Marcia's side. Not so much as a living cousin twice removed on the planet.' He sighs.

47

'Why are you delving into their family tree, for crying out loud?'

'Brace yourself,' Paul suggests. 'I'm going to read you a section of Jamie's will. Listen closely, and don't let your attention wander.'

I feel myself begin to tense.

'"... In the unlikely event that everyone else here named has died too, then we appoint as legal guardian to our two children, Caroline and Nigel, their godfather, Mr Maxwell Patterson."'

There's a long pause. I feel confused.

'Are you still there, Max?'

'Legal guardian? What does that mean? I pick up the bills, I suppose.'

'Well, yes.'

'Thank goodness for that. You had me worried there for a moment.'

'Hold on, Max, there's a little more to it than that.'

'How do you mean?'

'They're teenagers. They've lost both their parents and there's no family left to take care of them. Jamie has entrusted their care to you. You've inherited them, if you like. The theory is that they will come and live with you.'

'Live with me?'

'For legal guardian, read substitute parent.'

I think I just went into shock. 'Don't be bloody ridiculous!'

'Calm down, Max.'

'I will not calm down. The suggestion is outrageous! What will I do with two teenagers?'

'You'll raise them, I suppose.'

'I wouldn't know where to begin. What about the sister-in-law? Won't she look after them when she gets better?'

'Sarah died the day before yesterday. She never came

out of the coma. That's why I never said anything to you before. I was hoping she'd recover.'

'Paul, do something!' I shout.

'It's no use hollering at me. I'm only the solicitor. I'm just giving you the facts.'

'Facts or no facts, Paul, I'm not having this. I can't. For the kids' sake as much as mine. Get me out of this.'

'Max, for God's sake! You're their godfather!'

I'm panicking now. 'So what? Are you a godfather, Paul?'

'Yes, I am, as it happens.'

'And have you ever done anything for your godchildren other than turn up at the christenings? I bet nine times out of ten you forget to send them a card on their birthdays, let alone buy them a present.'

'I take your point,' he mutters.

'Have you helped raise them in the faith? Have you taken part in their moral upbringing? No. All that went right out of your head when you got pleasantly tipsy back at their parents' house at the post-baptism bash, didn't it?'

'Fair enough,' he replies, anger in his voice. 'But Jamie didn't leave his children to me. He left them to you.'

'And I'm a stranger to them. No, Paul, contest the will.'

'I'm not sure it's something we need to contest as such.'

'You're my solicitor. Just do whatever's necessary, whatever it costs. I can't do this, Paul. I'm just not capable.'

He sighs heavily. 'I realise I'm your solicitor and I have to accept your instructions. However, I'm not going to do anything about this for forty-eight hours. Caroline and Nigel are staying at their boarding-school. It was thought best to leave them there, though the school breaks up for holidays soon. That buys us a bit of time. I want you to have a chance to sleep on this, Max.'

'Sleep? *Sleep?* You don't think that after this bombshell I'm actually going to be able to sleep, do you?' I scream at him as I slam down the phone.

I can't believe I'm saying this, but I need a drink. One way or another, Jamie's death is turning me into an alcoholic.

I'm in the drawing room pouring myself a large tumbler of whiskey from the decanter. I'm physically shaking.

Maeve's just strolled in, duster in hand. She never bothers to knock, needless to say.

'Huh! At the booze again, are we? I'd have thought you'd never want to *look* at another drink, the state you came home in last night.'

'I've had a nasty shock. Anyway, it's my house so I can do what I want.'

'Ah, Max. Will you stop behaving like a big kid?'

'Big kids is the problem, Maeve. If Paul has his way, this place will be crawling with big kids any day now.'

Maeve stops dusting and stares at me. 'What in God's name are you ranting on about?'

'Jamie.'

'The feller that died?'

'He's left me his two teenage children in his will. A girl of about fifteen and a boy of thirteen.' I down my whiskey in one and refill the glass.

She looks astonished. 'Why did he do that?'

'It appears there are no surviving relatives. What was left of his family went down on the boat. And I'm the children's godfather.'

'You – the poor mites' godfather?'

I nod.

Maeve sighs. She looks weary. 'Oh, well, that settles it. You'll have to take them in.'

'Don't tell me what to do! I will not have them here. I've told Paul to contest the will.'

'Feck the will!' she blazes, hands on hips. 'You stood at the altar in church and made a promise. Your contract's with God, and there's nothing your fancy solicitor can do to get you out of that, boy.'

'I don't believe in all that stuff, I'm a pagan.'

'No, you're not! Don't go confusing yourself with one of those characters you put in those devilish books you write. The Man in Black, indeed! And what would your precious readers think when they read in the papers that you threw two young souls, your own godchildren, out into the streets?'

'I won't do that, I'll – I'll buy their parents' house for them. They can carry on living there.' I finish my second drink.

'Well, that's a grand idea. Then the thirteen-year-old lad can park his skateboard in the double garage, and his sister can ask him if he's had a nice day at the office. Are you dreaming, boy? You can't leave them on their own. Who's going to look after them?'

'I'll hire a nanny, or an au pair, or something.'

'And what's an au pair going to do? Sit 'em down in the corner and do a bit o' colouring with them? These are teenagers, Max, young adults. They're going to need attention, and guidance, and—'

'How would you know? You've never had any kids,' I retort, before I can bite my tongue.

Maeve swallows hard. 'No, but I grew up with an awful lot of brothers and sisters. I've had more teenage nephews and nieces staying at my home than you've had harlots in this house.'

'But I can't offer them anything. What do I know about teenagers?'

'For feck's sake, you were one yourself once.'

'I was hardly typical, though, was I?' I fill my glass again. 'I've never even been married. You're supposed to have a wife before you have kids, and then you have babies not teenagers. At least that way maybe you learn as you go along. This isn't *Blue Peter*. You can't just wheel on some you made earlier and expect it to work.'

She folds her arms. 'Maybe they could teach *you* a thing or two.'

'Maeve, I'm thirty-eight. What am I going to do with them? Play ping-pong down the youth club?'

'You're so stubborn.' She's sweating now, which is odd because she looks as if she's cold, not hot.

'Why are you so keen for them to come, anyway? Haven't you enough work on your plate?'

'I have more than enough. Any more and my blood pressure will go off the Richter scale. I don't want them to come for *me*. I want them to come for *you*.'

'Well, I don't!'

'But it'll be good for you to have some youth around the house. No man of your age should have nobody for company apart from two ol' feckers like Eugene and myself. It's not natural. And we won't last for ever, I'm telling you.'

I take another drink. 'Oh, I get it. You think I should take them in and train them up as your replacements.'

Maeve stamps her foot. 'You need some life, Max. This place is like a mausoleum. It needs waking up, like its owner. Jeez, boy, in the ten years I've worked for you, you've hardly ever gone anywhere or seen anyone. You buy this huge fecker of a house, and what do you do? Shut yourself away in the tiniest room, in the furthest place possible from the rest of it. If you won't go out, at least let someone with bit of youth and energy move in here, and see what a difference it could make.'

'But I like it this way,' I argue back. 'If I let the children come, they'll ruin everything. I'll have to take care of them and—'

'You can't go shirking responsibility for the rest of your life. You keep passing the buck, throwing money after everything as if it were always the answer. Heathen or not, you have a duty to God, a duty to Jamie, and above all a duty to those poor children. If you were a half-way decent man, you'd take them in and give them a home.' She's breathing hard as she finishes her lecture.

'Maybe I don't want to be a decent man! Now, if you'll excuse me, I'm going back to work.'

I place the whiskey decanter between my legs, and wheel myself out of the room.

I've been locked in my office for hours. I can't write and I definitely shouldn't have drunk that whiskey on the back of last night. I feel very ill indeed.

Maeve's been up three times to see if I'm all right. I didn't answer the door. She left some food outside for me, which I couldn't face.

Every time she came up, it made me think about her arguments for taking the children which, of course, she knew it would.

I'd better show my face, and explain myself. But there's something I must do first.

It's about six o'clock and I've trolled my way downstairs in search of Maeve.

I've found her drinking tea in the kitchen. Eugene is nowhere to be seen. He's probably trying to weld my car back together.

'Didn't think you'd be after surfacing today,' she observes, as I roll sadly towards her.

'It wasn't easy,' I confirm. 'Can I be brave and try a sip of tea, please?'

She shrugs, then goes to fetch another cup. As she fills it she asks, 'Have you had the decency to give any consideration to what you might do about this whole business?'

I sigh and take a small sip of tea. Instantly I feel nauseous.

'I've been thinking, I've never heard you speak about your godchildren the whole time I've been here. How well do you know them, Max?'

'I haven't seen them for years. The first time I met Caroline was when she was thrust into my arms after her christening. She can only have been a few months old, I suppose. I didn't know what to do with her. I never had any younger brothers or sisters, no nieces or nephews. So I sat there in my wheelchair, frozen. Unable to escape. There we stayed, until she screamed her head off and I handed her back to her parents. I was sort of scared they'd think I'd done something to hurt her.'

I turn away from Maeve. For some reason I can't look at her as I tell her this. 'The next time I had any real physical contact with her was at her brother's christening. Lord knows why they asked me to stand again, if you'll forgive the inaccuracy of the description. I mean, I hadn't been much use to Caroline. Maybe Jamie thought I'd be better with a boy.'

I shake my head. 'I managed to avoid getting Nigel shoved in my arms. But two-and-a-half-year-old Caroline came and sat on my lap and asked why I'd brought my car inside their house. I tapped the side of my wheelchair and said Daddy had given me permission. That's the last real conversation I've ever had with her, except to ask for her father when she answered the phone. I lost touch with them completely when I moved to Ireland. I'm not good with people, Maeve, and I'm certainly not cut out to be a parent.'

'Your friend thought so. Nobody leaves their children to any ol' bugger, rich or not.'

'I suppose not.' My eyes are stinging slightly.

'Tell me, Max. Now you've thought about it, do you honestly

have any choice in this matter?' Maeve's voice is firm yet her expression is warm.

'I've already called Paul and told him Caroline and Nigel can come.'

She smiles at me.

'Help me, Maeve. I can't cope. I don't know anything about being a father. They're teenagers! What am I going to do?'

I'm shocked, because Maeve has just taken my hands and cupped them in her own.

'You'll do what the rest of us lesser mortals have been doing for years, boy. You'll make the best of things.'

Silence reigns while we look into each other's eyes.

'I think I'm going to be sick,' I announce truthfully.

Maeve moves with a speed that belies her years, and before I begin to retch, she has reappeared with a bowl and placed it in front of my mouth.

'Oh, Max! What am I going to do wit' you?' she asks, and as I lean forward and gag again, she places her hand tenderly on my forehead, keeping the hair from falling in my eyes.

Maeve put me to bed.

For some reason, my mind leaps to the biography printed on the jacket covers of my books: 'Max Patterson shot to fame . . . He lives alone in a Gothic mansion in West Cork.'

He lives alone.

NB: Not any fucking more, he won't.

7

It's the last Tuesday in June and I'm tucked away in my attic office trying to work.

It is not happening for me today. Partly because it is now approximately a week till my prepacked family arrives here in West Cork. And also because Maeve has pointed out that it would be unwise to put recently bereaved children in 'rooms that resemble a chapel of feckin' rest'.

So, by trebling their fee, I have managed to hire the noisiest painter and decorators in the western world. Then, just to add to the general disruption, my new bath arrived and for almost forty-eight hours my *en suite* looked like it had been hit by a stray cruise missile.

I can only assume that in order to paint skirting-boards or hang wallpaper, rebuild plumbing or emulsion ceilings, it does not require any real concentration. Otherwise you could not play Radiohead's latest record at full volume on your paint-spattered tape-recorder. Nor could you then try to drown the lead vocal by singing along, always a beat or two behind and an octave or two adrift, with the original still blazing out in the background.

So Caroline and Nigel are still hundreds of miles away and an ocean apart and already they are ballsing up my daily routine.

The woman from the social services department came over from England to do a spot of positive vetting. Paul warned me this would happen. They all look the same, these people. Social workers, health visitors and their ilk. Same hair-do, same clothes, same ability to fucking patronise.

She asked me lots of questions. Some of them were extremely personal, I can tell you. She wanted to know if a person in a wheelchair could cope, for example. Then she asked me directly why I wasn't married, while indirectly trying to find out if I was a shirt-lifter, a paedophile, or had encountered necrophilia while researching my books.

I received a letter today from Paul. Contained within the envelope were two photographs that Paul hoped would be of use. He argued that it was probably a good idea to know what Caroline and Nigel looked like, if only to prevent me picking up the wrong kids from the airport and being accused of kidnapping.

Caroline, if her picture is to be believed, is a disarmingly pretty girl. I'm reminded of Brigitte Bardot. Not the sex kitten of her later films, more of the young nubile that appeared with Dirk Bogarde in *Doctor At Sea*, at a time when Bardot's large, suggestive eyes outweighed other large, suggestive parts of her anatomy. But there's something else: a certain air of determination about the position of her jaw, and the impressive bone structure upon which the soft flesh of her face is set.

Nigel's photo says something quite different. It provokes an instinctive schoolboy response in me: nerd, swot, wazzock. I accept that this is unfair, but the face you present to the world is everything and, man, oh, man, is this boy presenting the wrong face. He has glasses bought second-hand from Woody Allen, a hairdresser shared with Oliver Cromwell, and clothes handed down through generations by Clement Attlee.

The camera never lies, they say. Caroline may turn out to have a soft heart, a frigid personality and a face like the runner-up in a mallet fight. Nigel may prove to be irresistible to the opposite sex, have an insatiable appetite for partying and a personality engraved solely in the depths of frivolity. But I doubt it.

I'll take a break – check that the decorators are actually working and not swapping stories about excessive drinking or latest sexual conquests while sitting on their backsides drinking tea and scoffing Maeve's home-made biscuits.

They weren't drinking tea, they were slurping coffee. Maeve had made it for them, ignoring the fact that the man who pays her wages might be gasping for a drink. I've rolled down the ramp to the kitchen to administer a verbal lashing.

'Coffee smells nice, Maeve. Must taste nice too, judging by the way the workmen were smacking their lips and going "Ah!" instead of soiling their hands with wallpaper paste.'

'They're entitled to a break,' she insists, as she wipes down the work-surfaces with a cloth. 'If you look after these people, show them a bit of courtesy, they'll work twice as hard for you in the long run.'

'And if you show your employer the same courtesy instead of leaving him to dehydrate, he may change his mind about sacking you.'

She raises one eyebrow at me as she puts down the cloth. 'You can't chew me off for disturbing your creative flow one minute then complain I'm ignoring you the next.'

'Two sugars, please, Maeve.'

She pours two cups of coffee from the filter machine and

places them on the kitchen table. Then she sits down and I roll across to join her.

'Well?' She's read the worry on my face.

'I don't know, Maeve. There's more to looking after children than decorating a couple of bedrooms, I'm sure of that.'

'Don't get too down, Max. At least they're not babies. They can hold a conversation, tell you when they're sick, and wipe their own backsides. It could be worse.'

'Maybe I've reached the wrong decision.'

She shakes her head. 'There you go again, running away from your problems.'

'What will I do with them?'

'What everyone with adolescents does, you dozy devil. Help them with their homework, sort out any problems with boyfriends or girlfriends, teach them the difference between right and wrong, discipline them, make them feel . . . loved. They're bereaved, Max. They'll be looking to you to heal their pain.'

Sometimes the most obvious way to show fear is through silence.

'You'll manage,' she says.

'You'll chip in, though, won't you, Maeve?'

'I'm dead on my feet already. Listen, I'll do a bit of extra cooking and cleaning and washing, but that's my limit, now. I'm not their granny. Anyway, 'twould defeat the object of the exercise.' She smiles at me. 'Have you thought about what you're going to feed them?'

'Food?' I say glibly.

'Teenagers don't eat food. They eat rubbish for the most part, which is healthier than them not eating at all. Seeing as you're sat there looking sorry for yourself, I'll do a special shop for you. Get a few things in they might like.'

'Thanks.' Even I can hear I'm depressed from my tone of

voice. 'When am I going to get a chance to work, with all this godfathering? I've got to have a life as well.'

'Max,' Maeve says, a wicked grin on her face now. 'To all intents and purposes, you're a parent. I've news for you. Parents don't have lives, their children do.'

'Thanks for the coffee. I'd better go and write a good murder. Cheer myself up,' I tell her, as I slink out of the kitchen and head for the sanctity of my office.

Just three days until Caroline and Nigel arrive, and panic is setting in.

I can't help dwelling on Maeve's lecture. I know I'm the last person to help anyone else deal with bereavement. My own has left me bitter, and all too literally twisted. So don't ask me to turn it into a 'positive experience' for Caroline and Nigel. I admit I'm frightened that having to cope with their grief will send me spiralling back towards my own.

Maeve's gone off to get food before they arrive. Eugene and I have been hardware shopping. I've bought portable CD players for both children, plus a selection of CDs they can listen to. I had a bit of a problem there, so I took the advice of the salesman on what was hip and trendy.

I've also purchased them a portable television each, and had aerials installed so they can get a decent picture. I've sourced a PlayStation for young Nigel, along with a few tame games for him to play. And, for Caroline, I've bought a VCR plus a few suitable films for her to watch. This way I figure that, with a bit of luck, they'll spend most of their time in their rooms and I'll rarely see them.

Eugene has just carried one of the televisions into Caroline's bedroom and placed it on the dressing-table in the corner. God, I must get a mirror for that. Don't young girls like a mirror in their room?

I'm looking around at the transformation the decorators have carried out and I must admit I'm quite pleased with the result. I hate it. However, it's much more feminine, I suppose.

Maeve changed the duvet and sheets, like I asked her to. I didn't think black silk was quite right so I bought new ones to match the décor.

I handed Maeve the matching duvets, and she just laughed at me. Every time I repeated I wanted them put on the beds today, she just doubled the level of her hysteria and waved me away with her hands.

Oh, and while I was in the electrical shop, I treated myself to a new answering-machine. I'll just finish showing Eugene where to put the children's gifts, then I'll get him to attach it to the phone in my office.

One day more. Tomorrow, Caroline and Nigel arrive, a matter of weeks after their parents sank to their watery ends off the Mediterranean coast of Turkey. They'll arrive with broken hearts and broken minds to live with a man with a broken body. What can I do for them, apart from put a roof over their heads? Maeve was wrong: they would have been better off going into care.

I need to calm my nerves so I'm going to christen my new bath. Then I shall work out in my gym, and later I shall go into the drawing room and have a large drink while listening to my favourite piece of soothing music, 'Scheherazade'. That should help sort me out.

I am seething. I don't care if I am still dripping wet. I throw on a towelling robe and descend to the drawing room. Time to give the decanter a serious hammering.

I have a large whiskey in one hand, and the telephone receiver in the other. I'm calling the people who installed the instrument of torture in my *en suite*.

'Hello. Baronial Baths Limited, Daniel speaking. How can I help you?'

'You can start by ordering me an ambulance. Then I suggest you hire yourself a decent lawyer because I'm going to sue you for damages.'

'Are you sure you've dialled the right number?'

'This is Max Patterson. I have just nearly died using the bath you made for me, and I am not happy.'

I hear his characteristic sigh. 'Surely you're exaggerating, Mr Patterson.'

'Am I? Let me tell you about my experience, shall I?'

Another sigh. 'If it helps, Mr Patterson, if it helps.'

'First of all, when I opened the built-in door on the side of the bath in order to get in, it came off in my hand.'

'That shouldn't have happened.'

'I didn't think it was *supposed* to fall off,' I inform him, through gritted teeth. 'Twenty minutes later, naked and freezing, I managed to get the door back on its hinges. I slid from my wheelchair on to the specially designed seat and proceeded to run the bath.'

I'm momentarily distracted by the sound of a car pulling in to my drive. It's probably the postman. I've no letter-box, so I leave the door open for him to chuck the post into the hall, which he does, regardless of whether it's marked Fragile or not.

'Where was I?'

'You'd run the bath,' he reminds me.

'Yes, I had. So naturally I pressed the button that is supposed to lower the seat, with my bottom on it, down into the water. And do you know what happened next?'

'No, Mr Patterson.'

'Nothing happened. Nothing at all. I stayed exactly where I

was with the water barely covering my shins, realising I had just paid a ruddy fortune for a very large foot-spa.'

'I'll send someone round.'

'Hang on, I haven't finished yet.' Was that the front door? 'I decided to press the descend button again, and this time something did happen. The bloody chair collapsed. It came right off its mountings like an ejector seat in a Harrier jet. My head hit the bottom of the bath and my mouth and nostrils filled with water.'

'I can only apologise, Mr Patterson.'

'Only apologise! Look, my legs don't work. That's why I bought the bloody thing from you. I had to haul my way out of the bath with slippery hands and bits of broken seat stuck up my backside, and it was almost impossible. The point is, Dan, the point is that I could have *fucking drowned*!'

I turn my head as I scream at him, and now I genuinely wish I had died ten minutes ago.

Standing in the drawing-room doorway are two people: a young girl, who looks more like Bardot than in her photograph, and a boy who makes Joe 90 look cool.

Caroline and Nigel have arrived.

8

Their parents die in a boating accident and the first word they hear me utter is 'drowned'. I'm so horrified I'm stunned into silence.

'Are you Max?' the boy asks quietly.

'Of course he is, stupid,' the girl snaps. She looks much thinner than in her photograph. Skinny, in fact. Both look pale and drawn.

'And you're obviously Caroline and Nigel,' I say.

'Obviously,' Caroline replies, with a hint of aggression.

'Look I'm terribly embarrassed. I – I didn't think you were arriving until tomorrow. I was coming to the airport to meet you and take you somewhere for a meal. I had it all arranged.'

'We took a taxi,' Caroline interrupts.

'Did you any have Irish money?'

'Paul gave us some.'

'That was nice of him.'

They don't speak. They just stare at me, she with anger and suspicion, he with hollowed eyes.

'How was your journey?'

'Long,' Caroline replies.

'Really? Listen, do you two want to hit the water and freshen up?' I can't believe I said that.

A drop of water falls from somewhere on my upper body and lands on my lap and I realise I'm still in my towelling robe. 'Look, sorry,' I say feebly, 'I was taking a bath—'

'We know. We heard,' Caroline interrupts pointedly.

'Yeah, right. Help yourself to some tea or something. I'll just go and get dry . . . I mean dressed. I shan't be long.' I steer the chair out of the kitchen.

It takes an eternity to climb the ramp alongside the stairs, and with every inch it painfully covers, I wish the ground would open up and devour me whole.

I have opened my bedroom door, entered, slammed it shut behind me and tipped myself on to my bed. All those plans to make a good early impression, and the first thing they notice about their godfather is that he can't open his mouth without making some tactless reference to bloody water or drowning.

Oh, Max you . . . cunt! What on earth do I do now?

I've dried myself, thrown on a black shirt, matching jeans and some socks, and freewheeled back down the ramp by the stairs.

Entering the kitchen, I find them standing with their backs to the sink, whispering to one another.

'Sorry.' They jump. 'I really thought you weren't coming until tomorrow. Are you hungry? It's Maeve's day off, but I'm sure I could drop an egg in some boiling water.'

Pick up a shovel, somebody. Help me finish digging this hole I've made for myself.

'We've eaten,' Caroline informs me. 'We're tired, can we rest?'

Nigel looks briefly at his older sister and she glares at him. 'We're tired,' he echoes. It's the second time he's opened his mouth since his arrival.

'Right, I'll show you to your rooms, then,' I suddenly feel like a B and B landlord. 'Where are your suitcases?'

'Don't know.' Caroline shrugs.

'Don't know?'

'They didn't arrive at Cork airport.' She tells me this in a tone that suggests she believes somebody lost their luggage on purpose. 'They said they'd ring us later.' There's an even bigger shrug of her shoulders.

'I'll check the answering-machine in a minute, then. Okay, follow me.'

I lead them back into the hall, and we ascend the staircase as if performing a funeral march, the kids on the steps behind me. I've gone for 'eerie, stately manor' on the stairs, lots of dark portraits of evil-looking bastards down through the centuries. There's not a genuine ancestor among them, but it has the desired effect.

'They say this place is haunted. There's a story – something about a young fallen girl led to ruin by the wicked lord-of-the-manor. She's supposed to walk the corridors, cloaked and pale-faced, begging her seducer to save her . . .'

Caroline's face tells me that another brick has just toppled off her virtually non-existent wall of security.

'Look it's all bol – I mean, it's a pile of shi – There's not a word of truth in any of it. This is Ireland! It's full of stories. The telling of them is a national art-form.'

Caroline evidently doesn't believe me.

'I've had your rooms redecorated,' I continue, hoping this will reassure them a little. 'I hope you like them.'

Silence.

I lead them along to the bedrooms at the end of the corridor in the wing furthest away from the one in which I sleep.

Their rooms are opposite each other and I open the door to Nigel's first. He enters, followed by his sister. I retrieve my

66

crutches from the back of the chair and swing my legs into the room behind them. Still not a word.

'Is this okay, Nigel?'

The boy nods slowly. 'Who are those men in shiny suits with crash-helmets all over the walls?'

'Well . . .' I say, trying to fire my memory. 'Wait a minute . . . They're Mighty . . . Morphin . . . Power Rangers.'

'Oh.'

'They're very popular. Very cool, so I'm told.'

'They were. About seven years ago.' I feel Caroline appraising me witheringly.

'They're on the duvet, too,' Nigel observes quietly.

'And the curtains. It's a matching set.'

'Yes,' is all he says.

'Don't you like them?' I ask.

'Yes. Thank you.'

More silence.

'Your room is just over there, Caroline.' I gesture with my eyes across the corridor, and then move back, allowing them to pass in front of me.

She looks around the room without speaking.

'You've got a video,' Nigel whispers. 'I haven't.'

'No,' I say, my patience strained to its limits. 'No, Nigel, but you did get a PlayStation.'

He nods, sheepishly.

'Who's this on my wallpaper?' Caroline asks.

'I think they're Flopsy, Mopsy and Tom Kitten. That's Peter Rabbit down there, and over there is Jemima Puddle—'

'Another matching set,' Nigel breathes.

'Look, I tried my bloody best.' My patience snaps at last. 'If you don't like it, we can rip it off and start again.'

They both look frightened. Caroline is trembling and Nigel

bites his bottom lip. Behind those glasses, I detect signs of watering eyes.

'It's fine. Thanks.' Caroline's voice breaks a little.

I shouldn't have shouted. I feel a complete heel.

'Settle yourselves in. I'll check the answering-machine and see if there's any news on your suitcases. Then I'll put the kettle on. Join me whenever you're ready.'

Angry with myself for losing my temper, I swing myself up to the office. They both looked so terrified. Nigel seems to be in shock. He's withdrawing, disappearing into himself, and if he's not careful, he'll stay inside there for ever. I know about this. And Caroline is angry and hurt, resentful and confused.

I'll check my answering-machine. Missing suitcases chock-full of favourite comforting possessions is what we need at the moment. Before I can play back the messages, the telephone rings.

'Hello?'

'Well, if it isn't Lord Lucan himself. Back from your trip around the Bermuda Triangle on the *Mary Celeste*, are we? Or have we been circumnavigating the world with Amy Johnson?'

'Hello, Paul.'

'Where the fuck have you been?'

'Indulging in the privacy of my own nervous breakdown.'

'I take it they've arrived, then. You weren't really expecting them to be Mr and Miss Cheerful, were you?'

'Of course not.' I check myself.

'Has everything gone smoothly? You got my message about their change of arrival date?'

'No.'

'Why not?'

'Malfunctioning answering-machine.' I bend the truth slightly. Sounds better than confessing that, having purchased a new one, I hadn't bothered to listen to it.

'Haven't you found yourself a new secretary yet?'

'No. I've placed adverts and phoned a few agencies.'

Paul is sighing heavily. 'Make sure you hire one with an abundance of patience, won't you, Max?' He's very square is Paul. Square body, square head, square personality. 'So you weren't at the airport with flowers and chocolates to greet Caroline and Nigel?'

'Obviously not. They took a taxi with the money you gave them.'

'Just as well I did. Anyway, are they settling down?'

'No.'

'Do they like the house?'

'No.'

'Do they like the rooms you decorated for them?'

'No.'

'Oh, well, glad to hear it's all going well.'

'Thanks.'

'Give it time, Max. They're both heavily traumatised.'

'I noticed. I'll do my best. Anyway, must dash,' I tell him. 'I have to track down some missing suitcases.'

'Don't tell me their luggage has taken a vacation of its own.' He groans. 'You'll have to take them shopping later if it doesn't show.'

'Will I?'

'Yes, Max, you will. Unless you want them to walk around stark naked for goodness knows how long.'

'Okay. Now sod off and let me see if I can trace their stuff. You never know, Aer Lingus baggage department might have found them already.'

'Dream on, son. I'll call you soon. Give you a shoulder to cry on.'

'You're all heart, Paul. 'Bye.'

I put down the phone and play the six messages indicated on

the screen. The first is from Paul, telling me of the change of plans. The next four are from Justine. The last runs like this: 'Mr Patterson. This is Kate Mayle. You won't believe how difficult it was to get hold of your telephone number. I wouldn't have bothered ringing you had you replied to my letters. I have sorted out my half of our "little problem", at the cost of a significantly large overdraft. You promised me faithfully you would pay for what had to be done! If I do not receive a cheque for the cost of the . . . the repairs, as you *swore* you would send me, I will have to inform the gardai (sobs), or the newspapers (more sobs), or your mother! If they won't help, I shall come around and personally let down the tyres on your wheelchair, then take your crutches and use them as tinder for my fire. Sorry to be cruel, *Mr* Patterson, but I'm very angry, and if necessary I will make your life hell. It will be like *Fatal Attraction* without the sex. You may have stacks of money with which . . .' Beep!

Who the hell was that? Kate? I don't remember a Kate. Why is she trying to extort money from me? And why does she keep calling me *Mr* Patterson? It's as though she's used to calling me Max, and is only using my surname because she's pissed off. I'd better play that message again.

I've done so and I'm still none the wiser. Am I losing my sanity? What can she mean by 'my half of *our* little problem'? You don't think . . . Oh, come on, be serious. I couldn't have got her . . . and she's gone and . . . and I've offered to pay for it? Surely that's not the sort of thing that just slips your mind.

Right. Calm down. One problem at a time, Max.

I search through the phone-book in the hope that I fall over a contact number for lost luggage.

Success. The luggage has been located. In Tenerife.

It will, I am assured, be arriving back in Cork 'in a couple of days or so now, Mr Patterson'. In the meantime, where the hell do I buy clothes for two teenagers in Ballinkilty? I'll have to busk it.

I've moved myself back down the stairs, swinging my legs between my crutches in an oscillatory fashion, then along the corridor towards the kids' bedrooms.

I can hear them talking to each other.

'Kylie Minogue?' Caroline says. 'He bought you Kylie Minogue? I didn't even know she was still alive. Who else?'

'Ant and Dec, and someone called Clannad,' Nigel tells her. 'They sing like they've got asthma or something.'

I swear I'm going to kill that record-dealer. Right after I finish decapitating the decorators.

'Shall I tell you what videos he's given me?' Caroline asks, and I hear the duvet rustle as she gets off the bed.

I presume he nodded.

'I got *ET*, *Remains of the Day* and *La Cage aux Folles*.'

'What's that?' Nigel asks.

'It's a foreign film, stupid. I've just watched a bit of it on fast-forward. It's a film about French poofs. It's sick! I mean, why did he give me that?'

'He's okay, though, isn't he, Caroline? Max, I mean?'

My heart is in my mouth.

'He's weird,' she answers, and I hear the bedsprings creak as she flops back on the bed.

'Mum and Dad get killed. Then they make me come to this God-awful country, take me away from all my friends and dump me here in the middle of nowhere, out in the sticks, in this depressing house, with that horrible, horrible man. Why have they done this to me, Nigel? Why do they want to make me even more unhappy? It's not fair, it's not fair, *it's not fair*!'

I wince at her opinion of me.

Nigel begins to sob.

'Don't cry, Nigel. Please don't cry. I'm sorry. He's probably

71

all right, and we'll be okay. I didn't mean it. Since we heard about the accident, I don't know what I'm saying. Honest, everything's going to be fine, I promise.'

There's a long pause.

'I wish Mum and Dad were here,' Nigel says eventually, between gasps.

So do I, Nigel, I answer from inside my head. I promise you, so do I. Leaving them alone, I turn and make my way back down the corridor as quietly as I can.

9

I'm in the kitchen where there is an oil-fired Aga and an electric oven and hob. I opt for the latter. The hob is easy enough to reach from my chair, and the pots and pans are kept in a low cupboard. This is in case Maeve is out and I want to cook myself something. I never do, of course, but that's beside the point.

I've started simply. I've opened a can of baked beans. They go with anything, don't they? I've put them in a saucepan and bunged them on the hob. As I finish this complicated manoeuvre, Caroline and Nigel appear in the kitchen. Nigel's face is puffy and he's been crying. I don't want to embarrass him so I say nothing.

'Mr Patterson,' Caroline begins, 'did you find out what happened to our suitcases?'

'I'm afraid they're sunbathing on a beach somewhere in the Canary Islands.'

'Oh.' She looks even more dejected.

'Not to worry,' I tell her. 'Apparently, they'll get here in a couple of days. In the meantime, I'll take you into town after lunch and buy you something to wear just to see you through.

Right. what can I get you for lunch? I've thrown on some baked beans.'

'I've told you, we're not hungry, Mr Patterson.'

'Call me Max, please, Caroline. Are you sure? I've got heaps of food in. There's fish fingers, chicken nuggets . . .'

'We're fine, honest.' I notice she looks a little green around the gills.

'It's no trouble,' I say, turning back to the hob. As I do this I notice the baked beans staring up at me, as cold and unwelcoming as when they left the tin. Then I see that the ring *behind* the saucepan is glowing red. 'On second thoughts, we'll pick up some chips in town or something, eh?'

No reply.

The doorbell's ringing. I busy myself by putting the beans on the correct hob.

'Aren't you going to answer it?' Caroline asks.

'They'll probably go if we ignore it.'

She shrugs limply. Actually, I never answer the door unless I have to, but they don't know this. It just makes me look even odder.

The bell stops ringing.

'There you are, you see,' I say, triumphantly.

The two of them glance at each other, looking somewhat uncomfortable.

Before I can say anything further, I'm distracted by the sound of footsteps coming up the hall. 'Maeve's back. Great! She can give the kiss of life to those baked beans.' I notice a skin forming over them in the saucepan.

'You want to lock that door, Max. Sure anyone could just stroll in and murder you in your sleep.'

It's not Maeve. It's Justine. I really don't need this now.

'Why haven't you returned my calls, you miserable swine? Now you've had your way with me, you're just gonna toss me aside now, is that . . .' Her voice trails off as she notices Caroline, looking pale, but still very pretty.

'So that's why you didn't call me! Well, you don't let the grass grow under your feet, do you, boy? For feck's sake, Max! She's a bit young, even for you, isn't she? What were you going to do? Put her in a nappy and smother her in talcum powder?'

'What is she saying?' Caroline asks, clearly feeling threatened.

'And scrawny too! She's a bag of bones.'

'Justine . . .'

'And who the feck is he?' she asks, pointing at Nigel.

'It's her brother.'

'Jeez! Is she supposed to be minding this feller? What are you going to do with him? Stick him in front of the video with a Coke and packet of crisps or what?' She turns to Caroline. 'Don't you be kidding yourself you're something special. The man has a reputation. Two minutes after you've given your all you'll be no more than another notch on his crutch!'

'You think I'm his girlfriend?' Caroline squeaks, finally catching on.

'Girlfriend?' hisses Justine. 'That's a polite way of putting it. Listen, you're just one of hundreds.'

'I'm not his girlfriend,' Caroline repeats, looking me up and down. 'That's – that's disgusting.'

'You said it, girl,' Justine agrees. 'Far as I'm concerned, he's all yours – well, for the next ten minutes or so, anyway. You,' she hollers, pointing a finger accusingly in my direction, 'you are a bastard and I never want to clap eyes on you again!' And she sweeps out of the kitchen.

Nigel is looking at the floor. Not one for confrontation, I suspect.

'She thought,' Caroline is red with embarrassment and anger, 'she thought I was your girlfriend, or worse, and you let her think it.'

75

'She never let me get a word in edgeways.'

'How dare you!' she shouts at me.

'Caroline!'

'I'm not like her. And don't you dare think I am.'

'I don't. It's just a misunderstanding,' I plead.

'What did she mean, one of hundreds?' she asks, suspicion now mixed with anger.

'Oh, *for feck's sake!*' Justine's voice comes booming down the hall. 'Not another one. You'll find him in the kitchen, love. Though you must be a bit early 'cos he hasn't finished ravishing the last poor girl yet!'

Before I've had a chance to recover from the shock, someone else arrives in the kitchen. A woman. She's tall, with ruffles of long blonde hair, wearing a two-piece suit in dark blue. Her jacket is unbuttoned to reveal an ivory-coloured camisole with a laced neckline, and the heels on her shoes are high enough to tilt her forward slightly.

'Mr Patterson?' She strides towards me, offering me a hand to shake.

'Yes.'

'Elaine Greenstreet. I've come to see you about the position you advertised.'

I glance across at Caroline, whose lips are pursed in disapproval. Damn! This is turning into a calamitous farce. The secretarial agency had set up an afternoon of interviews for me, and I'd forgotten it was today.

'I see. Yes, of course. Well, you'd better follow me upstairs, then,' I suggest, immediately wanting to bite off my tongue. 'To my – er . . . office, I mean.'

'I'd be happy to,' she replies, smiling.

I know she's being friendly because, naturally enough, she wants to impress me. She's dressed like a woman who knows she's going to be interviewed by a man, and you can't really blame her for that either. But Caroline is probably convinced the poor girl is one jump from a prostitute.

'I don't wish to be personal, Mr Patterson, but is there anything I can do for you? Anything at all?' Ms Greenstreet stares at me.

This conversation is going from bad to worse.

'I mean,' she clarifies, gesturing gently towards me, 'is there anything you want me to hold for you, for example?'

Caroline's narrowed her eyes, and is puffing out her cheeks in an I-think-I'm-going-to-be-sick kind of way.

I've twigged. Ms Greenstreet's noticed the wheelchair.

'No, no. I can manage.' I spin the wheels in the direction of the kitchen door. 'Sorry about this, folks,' I say, as I pass the children. 'I forgot I was interviewing today.'

'You forgot?' Nigel repeats.

'Yes,' I snap. 'I was busy planning for your arrival, which wasn't supposed to be until tomorrow, remember?'

His bottom lip quivers, and I feel dreadful all over again.

'Should I come another time? I can always come again,' Miss Greenstreet assures me.

'No, no. I can see you now,' I say firmly. 'The fridge is full. Make yourselves a sandwich, eh? I'll be as quick as I can.' I exit the kitchen, with the would-be secretary tottering behind me on her high heels.

My day of descent into purgatory continues. Three applicants and all of them were flawed.

Ms Greenstreet typed as though she had trotters on the ends of her arms. Number two was a Dubliner – a class act. Her opening line was 'Would you mind if I took off me shoes, Max? Only me feet are red and swollen like a baboon with piles.' The last was from Cork. She wasn't a secretary at all but a fully trained dermatologist. She was, however, a lifelong fan of mine, and a friend of hers working at the agency had tipped her off. All she wanted was somebody to take a photograph of us together, with her sitting on my knee wearing my hat.

I've come downstairs and escaped into the drawing room. I've put 'Scheherazade' on the CD player because if ever there was a day when I needed to calm down this is it. I lift the decanter from the top of the drinks cabinet and splash a large quantity of malt into my Waterford crystal tumbler.

There's a knock on the door.

'Come in,' I say reluctantly.

It's Caroline, her arms folded, and Nigel standing close, apparently afraid to let her out of his sight.

'We're going to our rooms,' she says.

'Look, before you go, please let me explain.'

'No need,' she fires back, a little too quickly.

The doorbell is ringing again.

'I'll go.' Caroline retreats hastily from the room. I don't think she wants to be in the same room as me.

Nigel, unsure whether to follow his sister or not, looks panic-stricken. We stare at each other in some discomfort.

'So, Nigel,' I begin awkwardly, 'what sort of things do you like, then?'

He shrugs.

'Well, do you like football for instance?'

He stares.

'Skateboarding?'

Not so much as a blink.

'Arson? Larceny? Gratuitous violence?'

Nothing I say provokes a response.

Caroline's back. 'There's another one,' she informs me, testily.

I'm sure the agency was only sending three. I only received three CVs.

'Is there? I don't think there should be. Sorry about this, Caroline. Look, I'll take this one in here.'

'Take her where you fancy, I don't care.' Her voice catches and she looks perturbed. She slams the door, and I hear her stomping up the stairs, Nigel behind her.

I reach for a top-up from the decanter and I realise number four has entered the room behind me.

'Please, take a seat. I'll be with you in a minute.' I'm aware I sound a trifle tetchy.

'No, thank you, Mr Patterson. Hopefully I shan't be staying long.'

I wheel around, and there before me is a vision.

This girl – no, woman – is beautiful. She's about five foot four, yet something about the way she carries herself makes you think she's taller. Her blue eyes, soft face and full mouth are all framed by thick ringlets of curly copper hair, tumbling down around her shoulders.

'I need that money, Mr Patterson.' She appears to be trying to contain her anger.

I don't reply. I just keep gazing at her.

'Please do me the courtesy of replying, Mr Patterson.'

Mr Patterson, with the stress on the 'Mr'. Of course! This is Miss My-half-of-our-little-problem. Surely . . . I didn't. No. If I had, I certainly would have remembered. Besides which I'd never have had the confidence to believe a woman like this would be interested in a man like me.

'You don't know who I am, do you?' she accuses. 'Well, isn't that typical of men? Their brains positively floating in booze and when it comes to paying their dues, they either disappear or plead ignorance. Well, it's not good enough. I want my money and I want it now!'

'Now just a minute, Miss . . .?'

'Mayle. Kate Mayle.'

'Miss Mayle, you're right about one thing. I don't have a clue who you are. I'd like to know exactly why you're telephoning, and how come you're in my house trying to extort money from me.'

She stares at me. The anger has gone from her eyes. It's replaced first by confusion, then hurt.

'You *bastard*,' she breathes, and looks away from me, turning her head to one side in an effort to hide that she's crying.

I feel dreadful. This is the third person I've made cry today. Am I that bad?

'Look, Miss Mayle . . . Kate. Why don't you take a seat by the fire, allow me to pour you a glass of whiskey, and explain to me exactly what crime I've committed? It's obviously something dreadful, and I can't apologise properly until you put me in the picture. Please?'

She nods, but keeps her face turned away.

I watch her as she walks across to the large chair next to the fire. It's always cold in this room, so the fire burns regardless of the season. I said 'walks', but I'm wrong. She glides – no, floats. Her movement is instinctively measured, graceful and elegant. When you're a wheelie, you notice how people move. You're drawn to it. It would surprise you how much you can tell about a person from the way they walk.

She places herself on the chair and crosses her legs. Yet, unlike Ms Greenstreet earlier, I don't feel this is contrived, or that she is aware of its effect. I pour her a whiskey, then take a sneaky gulp out of mine before topping it up once more. I ferry her drink across to her.

'Thanks,' she says, and finally looks at me.

I wheel myself to a respectful distance. 'Fire away, but be gentle. After a day like today, I bruise easily.'

'You really don't remember, do you?' she asks again. 'We met one evening at Cork airport. You were . . .'

'Seriously sloshed, I know. I'm not usually drunk. Tipsy, occasionally, but I hate being plastered. The only reason I was that day was – Oh, it doesn't matter. Go on.'

She drinks, then shrugs her shoulders. Even that simple movement is poised.

'Well, you were too plastered to get into your car, let alone drive it. Mine had broken down and I came to ask you to help me start it. Then you suggested I drive yours.'

'And you reversed my car into yours. Of course!' The alcohol-induced mist clears from my memory.

'So you recall what happened?' Kate swallows most of what's left of her whiskey.

'Yes. Well, bits of it . . .' Actually, what I remember most is how pretty I thought Kate was. And those lovely, compelling eyes that I cannot turn away from. 'How did we get home?'

'Airport Security. They recognised the famous author Max Patterson,' she says, in a way that tells me *she* is not impressed. 'So, they got my car started, organised a garage to tow your car home, and poured you into a taxi. I mean, haven't you had bills from any of those people?'

'I might have done. I'm a bit behind on the administration front at the minute. Top-up?' I ask, referring to her drink.

'Go on, then.'

I replenish both our glasses. 'Correct me if I'm wrong,' I hand her glass back, 'I promised to pay for the repairs to your car, and I haven't. That's the nub of the matter.'

'Yes.'

'Okay. How much did it cost to fix?'

'A hundred and fifty pounds.'

'Is that all?' I remark. 'Blimey! All this fuss over a hundred and fifty pounds? Not exactly a fortune, is it?'

'It is to some of us, Mr Patterson.' She smooths her hair from her face and straightens her back. 'I'd like you to pay it immediately. You see, I can't, and the garage are getting very cross. We're not all as privileged as you. So, if it wouldn't be too much trouble . . .'

'Hold on, hold on. Let's just remember it was *you* who crashed my car, into yours.'

She tenses. 'But it wasn't my fault. I'd never driven a car like yours before.'

'Even so, the car-park was huge. Yours was the only other car in it at the time, and yet you managed to hit it going backwards. Now, that takes real skill.'

'You can't think I did it on purpose?'

The way she just straightened her back again – that's what it is. That's what I've been missing. 'You're a dancer!' I announce, my sudden change of subject startling her. 'I knew there was something different about you. You're a dancer.'

'No, I'm not,' she snaps.

'Yes, you are,' I bark back at her, completely irrationally.

There's a pause while she stares at me. 'I was a dancer, okay? Satisfied? But I will never dance again, understand?' She turns her head from me again, and sighs. 'I was a dancer. I trained at the Royal Ballet, and then I joined the *corps de ballet* when I was eighteen. Three years later I was a soloist. I was about to dance my first lead in a new ballet when my left knee gave way during a class. I had an operation, then intensive physiotherapy for ages. The company kept me on for a year. Then they decided my knee wouldn't be strong enough to stand up to the demands required of it. That's why I'll never dance again. Touchy subject, I'm afraid. You just surprised me when you noticed.' She looks down at her drink, then slowly back at me. 'Sorry. I don't know why I'm telling you this. Must be the whiskey.'

I sit here, a man who would love to be able to dance just once. 'It's okay. When did you stop?'

'Three or four years ago now.'

'What have you been doing since?'

She pauses again, reflecting. 'I moped for a while. Signed on. Then the Job Centre said I had to do some career-orientated training. I had the choice of taking a course in computers or studying to become a train-driver.'

'Must have been tough for you,' I sympathise, a surprising emotion for me. 'I mean, not much work for qualified train-drivers in this neck of the woods.'

She almost smiles, and I realise I want her to very much.

'I took the computer course.'

'Pity. You'd look dead dinky in one of those little hats, with your delicate hand grasping the dead man's handle.'

'Do I have delicate hands?' She smiles finally, and when she does she looks like a child – innocent.

I choose not to answer her question. For some reason I feel shy, like a teenager complimenting a girl for the first time.

'Anyway,' she says, breaking the silence, 'I did the course, became a secretary and worked hard. Then just before I left London for Ireland, I was offered promotion to the dizzy heights of PA to the MD.'

I'm happy for her to go on talking. For the first time today, or longer maybe, I feel relaxed.

'So what made you come to Ireland?'

'A man! What else?' She clinks the edge of the glass against her teeth as she drinks from it. 'I met an Irishman in a bar in Camden Town. He swept me off my feet and brought me over here. I left my promising career and sold my flat in order to buy a smallholding for Séan and me to work together. We rented a cottage while we searched for affordable land. He lived off my savings, then ran up a small mountain of debts in my name.'

'Really?'

This woman would be a catch for any man. Why had she allowed this to happen? Is that what love does to you?

'The problem is no one seems keen to give a blow-in a job around here. I have no money, and I have to leave the cottage in a week's time. That's why I was at the airport that night. I'd flown over to Yorkshire to throw myself on the mercy of my parents.'

'How did it go?'

'My father is an extremely successful accountant, who cannot understand anyone who does not have financial security at the top of their agenda. My mother is a serial housewife who married at eighteen and has never had a serious problem, emotional or otherwise, in her life. How do you think it went?'

I screw my face up. 'They wouldn't help, then?'

Kate tosses her head. 'Oh, yes, I can go and live back home. But I've had the I-told-you-so speech, and the things-will-have-to-change-young-lady diatribe, and I just can't face it. So I came back here to face the music.'

I finish the remains of my drink. 'What will you do now?'

'I don't know. I just don't know.'

A tear slides down her cheek and she shrugs in despair. 'All this grief for a man. I fell for such a bastard.'

Grief. I seem to be surrounded by it, though everyone else's seems to be greater than my own. Unless I'm just hiding from mine. Maybe I've simply not had time. Today I seem to have added to the children's, much as I've tried not to.

I'd actually like to help Kate. Forget it, I'll probably only make things worse. 'I'll write you a cheque for the car repairs. At least that's a start,' I say weakly.

'Thanks.' She wipes her face with the back of her hand.

I go to the writing desk situated a few feet to the right of the drinks cabinet, open a drawer, take out a cheque-book and fill in one of the leaves. As I tear it free, a thought strikes me. I dismiss it as ridiculous, then recognise it as being so blindingly obvious I can't think why it didn't occur to me sooner. I wheel myself over to Kate and hand her the cheque. 'Computer course?' I say to her.

'Pardon?'

'Secretary, and then PA?'

'Almost PA. Yes.'

'So you can type?'

'Yes.'

'Spell?'

'Yes.'

'Punctuate?'

'Yes.'

'Good telephone manner?'

Kate holds up her hands. 'Listen, Mr Patterson—'

'Max.'

'Max. I've talked too much. Thanks for listening, but I really think I should go.' She brandishes the cheque.

'No, no, no! I think I may be able to help. Prove to you that not all men are bastards.' I smile. 'Would you like a job?'

Her eyes narrow in suspicion. 'What kind of a job?'

'Secretary, PA, Girl Friday kind of thing. You're never going to believe this, but I've spent the afternoon unsuccessfully interviewing for a secretary.'

'What would I have to do?'

'Deal with the fan-mail, type correspondence to my lawyer, my accountant, my agent and my publisher. Answer the phone, take messages, the usual sort of stuff. A bit of everything, really. Basically, I'm completely disorganised. I need sorting out. Let's say you'd have to be flexible in your work remit.'

Kate sighs. 'It's no use. I have to go back to England. I've nowhere to live in a week's time. Thanks for the offer, but I'm afraid it's come a bit too late.'

'Nonsense,' I declare, throwing my arms in the air as I get carried away with the idea. 'Move in here.'

85

'What?'

'Seriously. At the risk of sounding a flash git, I've dozens of spare rooms. I'll pay you, say, fifteen thousand a year, and I'll throw in free board and lodging. What do you think?'

'"Flexible" in my work? Move in "here"? Wait a minute, Mr Patterson, if you think just because I'm vulnerable and bankrupt, you can regard me as some kind of guaranteed shag, you can—'

'Oh, give me a break, Miss Mayle. I may have acquired a bad reputation round these parts, but when I said flexible in your work, I meant you may have to type when you expect to be doing research, or drive into town to collect something instead of sorting the mail. I may even really take the piss by occasionally asking you to make me a coffee. I do not expect you to massage me in baby oil while dressed like a Norland nanny, okay?'

'Yeah, sure,' she says sarcastically.

'Okay. Stay in your cottage, and drive in to work every day.'

'I can't, the landlord has already let it to somebody else.'

'Then move in here until you find somewhere else to live.' My Good Samaritan act is beginning to wear thin.

'I'm not sure,' she says.

'Look, Kate, I'll come clean with you. There's another reason the house is in chaos. Remember the girl who showed you in?'

She nods.

'She's my goddaughter. There should be a young boy out there somewhere as well.'

'Yes, I passed him on the way in,' she confirms.

'He's my godson. The reason I was drunk the night we met at Cork airport was because I had just flown back from their father's funeral. Actually, to be truthful, I never made it past the airport bar. Jamie was my best friend. There isn't any surviving family so I've just inherited two teenagers. They've come to live with me as from today.'

Her eyes have just widened, considerably. 'And you're not

married? Or divorced?' she asks. 'You've no children of your own?'

'No.'

'My God, that's awful!' and her expression changes to one of concern. 'Here I am rattling on about my problems and you're facing an incredibly difficult situation.' She tilts her head to one side as she thinks, her quizzical eyes assessing me.

'So we were both returning to Cork airport at a time of crisis,' she says finally.

'I suppose we were,' I agree.

'Another coincidence,' she observes. She shakes her head, as if clearing a thought from her mind. 'I'll have to consider it,' she tells me as she stands up. 'When do you need to know by?'

'Tomorrow, really. I'm not trying to pressurise you, I've just got to get someone as quickly as possible.' She drifts towards the door and I roll along behind her. 'I'll see you out.'

'No, it's okay,' she says, spinning round to face me. 'I can find my own way.' She pauses again. 'This music?'

'Rimsky-Korsakov. It's "Scheherazade".'

'I know.' She nods slowly. 'Why are you playing it?'

'It helps me relax,' I tell her. 'I mean, what a woman she was! A thousand and one tales to invent, a different story every night to stay alive. It stops me getting wound up about having to create just one new story a year.'

'The ballet I was going to star in before I injured my knee was a new version of "Scheherazade". It was commissioned especially for me.'

'A hat-trick of coincidences,' I declare.

She's looking at me again. I wish I could read her mind.

'Something like that,' she replies. 'Thanks for the job offer. I'll ring you with my decision in the morning.'

'No problem,' I say, opening my palms.

87

'Goodbye, Max.' She smiles from the doorway, and exits in as lithe and nimble a fashion as she entered.

10

It's eleven o'clock at night and I'm in my office at the top of the house.

Eugene, hot-foot from Cork City, has just knocked on the office door. 'Not disturbing you, am I, Max?' The smell of his breath tells me Maeve has driven home.

'No, you're okay. Have a good day?'

'Feckin' awful, Max. Shopping for new shoes for the missus. She tries on a pair at the start of the day, and I'm after making the mistake of telling her they look nice. Soon as I says that, off the feckin' feet they come. We then have to drag our carcasses round every other shoe-shop in Cork, before coming back to the first and buying the very pair she tried on at the beginning. She only bought them because this time I was smart enough to say I didn't like 'em.'

'It's a cruel world, Eugene.'

'Still, we had good *craíc*, and a few Murphy's at the pub after.'

'Good.' I nod, glad someone has had a good time today. 'Is Maeve okay, by the way? I think she looks a bit peaky, and she keeps wittering on about her ailments.'

'Ah, she's always been pale as a church candle, and you know how she loves to complain. You should o' heard her today.'

He's still hovering.

'Is there anything you need before I crawl to my bed?'

'Nothing. But you could give Maeve a message.'

'Fire away.'

'Tell her the kids have arrived a day early.'

Eugene stops in his teetering tracks. 'You're joking me.'

'I wish I was, Eugene.'

He puts the back of his hand to his forehead, like an amateur tragedian. 'An' us not here in your hour of need.'

'Never mind that. Just tell her they've refused to eat a single thing since they arrived, so a big, cooked breakfast is on the cards for tomorrow morning.'

'Leave it with me better half. Oh, Max,' he lowers his voice and looks conspiratorially over his shoulder, 'one last thing. The book.'

Maeve doesn't like him writing: she believes it gives him ideas above his station.

'I've had a thought,' Eugene continues. 'What about if the tights are "barely black", and I make the murderer a half-caste? Think on it, boy. Night, Max.' With that, he is gone.

I check the time. It's twenty past eleven. Kids should be safely asleep by now. They put in one final appearance at about nine, when they informed me they didn't have anything to sleep in, so I gave them a couple of my T-shirts. Black, of course. Caroline's barely covered her bum and she looked like she'd slipped on a little black number to go to a happening party in Chelsea, and Nigel's, of course, reached his ankles.

Other than that, they've just stayed away.

I went down for a coffee earlier and deliberately passed their rooms. I could hear them playing music, and I didn't know whether to go and say goodnight or not. I still don't. I mean, what am I supposed to do? Tuck them in and tell them a bedtime story? I'm not their father, just their godfather, for fuck's sake.

Oh, sod it! I've rolled down the ramp and pushed myself along the corridor towards their bedrooms. Both their doors are shut.

I glide towards Nigel's room and position my left ear furtively against the door. I can't hear anything. I fumble around trying to find the handle in the half-dark, and it swings open suddenly. Shielding my eyes from the sudden glare of light in the room, I look between my fingers at the bed. He isn't there – in fact, he's nowhere to be seen.

Shit! I thought he was the one who had settled in best out of the two. Now the little swot has gone and done a bunk on me. His bed's not even been slept in.

Well, the media are going to have a field day with this. We'll have police, social workers, scuba divers combing the beaches, posters all over West Cork ... I'd better get on the phone.

Hold on, Max. Stop panicking. He's probably just gone to the loo. I'll wait.

Ten minutes later and no sign of Nigel. Either he's having the longest pee in the history of the universe, or I was right the first time. I'd better tell his sister. That's the best thing to do. Caroline may have some idea of where he's gone.

I pause at Caroline's door, and I put my ear to it to see if I can detect signs of life. But it's too thick so I decide to creep inside as quietly as I can. This is not the house in which to hear strange bumps in the night, and she already thinks it's haunted. I turn the handle and the door opens silently. I roll softly into the doorway and peer in.

The bedside light is still on, but it's a low wattage light-bulb, and it's all a bit blurry. As my eyesight adjusts I see the two figures on the other side of the room. Nigel has crept into his sister's bed. He's sobbing gently and Caroline, whose back is towards me, is rocking him in her arms.

I feel a complete bastard.

They look so young, so vulnerable. They're missing their parents and probably need a bit of . . . yeah, love, I suppose. And I'm no use to them at all.

'It's all right, Nigel,' Caroline is whispering. 'Everything's going to be all right. I'll take care of things, I promise.' The breaks in her voice tell me she's crying too.

I should go to them, offer them both some comfort, but I can't. I wouldn't know where to begin. You see, you can't put anyone else back together when you're less than whole yourself.

11

It's nine o'clock the following morning and I haven't slept a wink all night for worrying about my charges. So I've given up on getting any sleep and have been trying to work. Thirty-seven cups of coffee and six deletions later, I was just starting to get somewhere and now this! My ears are being assaulted by the most obnoxiously tuneless shite that has ever had the audacity to regard itself as music.

I hurtle down the ramp and speed along the corridor. The electrified sounds of several fox cubs caught in a snare appear to be coming from Caroline's room.

'What the bloody hell is this row?' I shout, as I plough through the door like the driver on a smash-and-grab raid.

Nigel turns the music off.

'It's the Cure,' Caroline informs me.

'Sounds more like the bloody disease to me.'

She blinks rapidly. 'The Cure. They're a band. Dad used to like them,' she says, quietly.

I hold up my hands in surrender. 'I'm sorry. I shouldn't have burst into your room like this, Caroline. I should have knocked.'

She doesn't reply, just stands there, nervously tugging at her T-shirt, glaring at me.

'I was frustrated. I'm a writer. Well, you know that. I was trying to work.'

'We didn't know,' Nigel interjects, fumbling with his glasses.

'No, of course you didn't. It's just that I'm not used to the noise. Well, I guess we'll all have to make some adjustments.'

They're staring at me again. Are they angry? Or frightened?

'Anyhow, Maeve will be up and about in a minute. You'll like Maeve. She's horrible to me. You'll enjoy that. I'll get her to cook us some breakfast. You two must be starving.'

'I don't have to stay, you know.' Caroline. 'I don't have to stay. I'm nearly sixteen. I can go if I want to.' Her arms are folded.

'What about me?' Nigel whimpers from his slumped pose on the bed.

'I'm not talking about you, stupid,' she sneers.

'You wouldn't just leave me here, would you?' Nigel looks up, desperate.

'Look, nobody has to go anywhere,' I assure them both.

'Just remember. I can go. Any time I like,' Caroline sulks, sounding like a stuck record.

'Caroline, this isn't easy for any of us. But it's what – it's what your father wanted.'

'Only because there was no one else left. That's all. There isn't anybody else.'

We're eyeing each other intensely. For a minute, it's difficult to tell which of us is the most angry.

Her father. Jamie had a stubborn streak in him, and as Caroline stands before me, pouting, she reminds me of him. A painful reminder.

'You can play your ... music. I'd be grateful if you kept it down a bit, though. I'll call you when breakfast is ready.'

I close the door gently behind me as I leave.

*

We're in the kitchen, and Caroline and Nigel are sitting at the table.

I've introduced Maeve, who smiled at them as though she had recently been awarded a second-class degree with honours on bereavement. We had a chat before the kids came down. I told her about my row with Caroline. She gave me this big lecture on long-term patience and forgiveness. I couldn't believe it was Maeve I was talking to.

'Now, then,' she says, as she places a breakfast in front of each of them, 'get your teeth into this. We all feel better if we start the day with a good meal inside us.'

Nigel picks up his knife and fork, and tucks in with relish. Caroline is staring at her plate as though she had just discovered the chef was Sweeney Todd.

Maeve looks at me quizzically and I shrug my shoulders.

'Is something the matter, Caroline?' she asks.

'I can't eat this,' she replies flatly.

'Ah, come on now, love. A young girl like yourself needs her energy.'

'I can't eat it,' Caroline repeats firmly.

Maeve clasps her bosom dramatically. 'You must, petal. I understand it's difficult. Dear God, I know you've been through enough to put a starving rhinoceros off its food. But you have to eat, my love.'

'I can't eat this.' Caroline underlines her point by pushing her plate away.

I see Nigel, who is already half-way through his breakfast, eye Caroline's plate with hungry optimism.

Maeve's smile is fraying at the edges. 'Listen, I may not give Marco Pierre White sleepless nights, even if I am better-looking. But what I serve is honest, wholesome, plain food.'

'I can't eat it because it's meat,' Caroline says, fixing Maeve, unwisely in my opinion, with an icy stare. 'It's murder,' she explains for everyone's benefit.

'Now be sensible, Caroline,' I chip in. 'You've not eaten a thing since you arrived, and you're extremely thin. Besides, these are animals raised for the dinner table. God made us carnivores. He made us hunters. He blessed us with superior intelligence and placed us at the top of the food chain.'

Caroline remains unmoved.

'Sure the disciples themselves were fishermen!' Maeve argues, the first signs of desperation in her voice.

'That's just an excuse so we can massage our consciences while we satisfy our appetites with some poor creature's flesh,' Caroline recites, as if she is quoting directly from a book, which she probably is.

The colour of Maeve's skin changes from pinkish to dark red as the blood boils and bubbles upwards through her veins. 'Caroline, some poor farmer has broken his back to bring that meal to your table, girl. Worked long hours scratching a living, only to have a few pen-pushing bureaucrats in Brussels tell them their stock is worth half what they raised or bought it for. So, the least you can do is show your appreciation and support by eating a mouthful or two.' Farmer's daughter, is Maeve.

I watch Caroline as she dusts down her soapbox and chains herself to the railings.

'I will not! You don't understand. Cows, pigs, chickens, whatever. They all feel pain. They have feelings, emotions, you know.'

'Emotions?' I can't believe she said that. 'Since when did you see a pig paying a fortune to sit in a psychiatrist's chair? Are there many chickens gulping anti-depressants? Do you person-ally know any cow that has gone in for a bit of regression and woke up screaming because she discovered her father interfered with her udders when she was a calf? Emotions? Crap! It's only those of us who walk on two legs who are stupid enough to go in for all that garbage. Now stop talking drivel and eat your bacon,' I order her.

'No, no, no!'

'It's a phase,' Nigel chips in, trying to sneak Caroline's plate away and replace it with his empty one.

'It is not, stupid.' Caroline raps his knuckles with her fork.

'Ouch!' he whimpers, looking more hurt that she struck him than by the pain of the blow.

'Look,' I say, trying to smile, 'if we hadn't told you it was bacon, you'd never have guessed. Not the way Maeve cooks it. It's full of grease, it'll slip over your tongue and down your throat before you've even had chance to taste it.' I shoot Maeve a quick, knowing wink.

'I beg your pardon!'

I guess she missed the wink.

'Right, that's it! Suit your feckin' self, girl,' Maeve roars, untying her pinny. 'If you're going to be stupid now,' she continues, pulling it over her head, 'I've no sympathy for you,' she spits, as she throws it on the floor. 'You can feckin' starve for all I care!' She folds her arms aggressively. 'And that goes double for you, Max Patterson. If my food isn't good enough, you can find yourself another mug to cook. I resign.'

'What?' I round on Caroline. 'You're unbelievable, girl. You've deliberately been bloody awkward since the minute you arrived, and now your stubbornness has cost me a member of staff.'

'It's not my fault,' Caroline snaps back. 'You insulted her cooking.'

'Only because I was trying – Look, just eat your bloody breakfast, will you? You're a gnat's cock from being anorexic as it is.'

'I am not anorexic!' Caroline shrieks, hysterically.

'Yes, you are!' Maeve puts in.

'Stop ganging up on me!'

'We're not. Back off, Maeve!'

'Feck you!' Maeve retorts, pointing at me.

'Leave me alone, *leave me alone*, LEAVE ME ALONE!' Caroline howls. 'I'm not anorexic. I didn't want to come to this horrible house, full of horrible bullies, and I will not eat dead animals!' She throws her plate against the wall, and runs sobbing from the kitchen.

The wall is streaked with bacon and scrambled eggs, and mushrooms. It looks like a piece of modern art, which changes shape as the different elements slither towards the floor.

'That went well, didn't it? Thanks, Maeve. I can see you're going to be a big help. Patience, that's the answer, am I right? Be prepared to forgive them anything, isn't that what you said?'

'Listen now,' she says, holding up her arms, 'I said you were the one that had to make the effort. I said nothing about me. I'm just the hired help.'

'That's the first time I've ever heard you admit to that. And on the day you resigned. How ironical.'

'Oh, stop! I was fierce mad with that stupid little English madam.'

'I thought you were quite restrained, by your own high standards.'

'It's a fad,' Nigel says, out of the blue, reminding us of his presence.

Maeve and I exchange a look of guilt.

'She gets them. Fads. She's had worse.'

'Really?' I say, too embarrassed to apologise to him.

'Yeah. She talked to plants once.'

I give a polite sort of chuckle.

'It was embarrassing. You bring your friend home and your

sister is asking a cactus for help with her maths homework.' His expression is deadpan beneath his bushy eyebrows.

'I can imagine,' I sympathise.

'Dad used to call her . . .' Nigel falls silent and looks at the floor. 'May I be excused now?'

'Yes, of course you can.'

Before he can stand Maeve catches his arm, and he freezes. I watch as she lowers her craggy face until it is breath-sharingly parallel to Nigel's.

'Now, Nigel, just between ourselves,' she whispers grinning, 'would I be right in thinking you've no objection to a bit of meat yourself?'

His eyes flash quickly from Maeve, to me and back again.

'Are you still a mite peckish?' she asks.

The slightest of nods.

'You know, I can see into the future. It's a gift I have. And I reckon if you were to sneak down to the kitchen in half an hour, there may just be a bacon sandwich sat on the table that some fool forgot to eat.' She winks as she finishes. At least I saw that one.

He looks again from Maeve to me.

'I never heard a word,' I say, looking at the ceiling and whistling badly.

He stands up and slopes quietly out of the kitchen.

'I'd forgotten he was there,' Maeve confesses.

'Me too.'

'The lad's all right,' Maeve opines, as she begins loading the breakfast plates into the dishwasher. 'But the girl? You've got your hands full with that one, and that's no lie. She's unstable, and she's a fierce temper on her. Almost as bad as mine. She's an opinionated little vixen, make no mistake. I don't know what you're going to do with her.'

'Thanks. I don't know either. I'm praying this is not the way she behaves normally.'

Maeve takes the last of the cutlery from the table. 'Listen, I have a niece –'

'You have a small army of nieces.'

'– called Julie. She's seventeen or so. She's a little car she drives. I had a word, and she's promised to pop up and take your girl out for a spin. Introduce her to a few young ones.'

I'm a bit taken aback. 'Thanks, Maeve, that's very good of you.'

'Couldn't leave it to you to sort out now, could I?'

'Look, I'll go up and have a word with her. See if I can sort a few things out. I'm sure it'll get better in time.' I wheel myself towards the kitchen door, then stop and turn as I reach it. 'Are you really resigning?'

'Ah, behave yourself,' she replies, as she slams the dishwasher door shut, and switches it on.

I'm knocking on Caroline's bedroom door.

'Go away,' she calls from within.

'Caroline, it's Max.'

'I don't care. Leave me alone.'

'It's all right. I'm not coming in to beat you round the head with a large piece of sirloin or anything.'

'It's all a joke to you, isn't it?'

'No, it's not. I didn't know you were a vegetarian.'

'I'm a vegan, actually.'

'I thought they were only in *Star Trek*. Does that mean you've got pointy ears?'

'Just go away!'

'Come on, Caroline. Give me a break. I'm beginning to feel a bit of a nelly talking to a door. Can I come in for two minutes? I won't disturb you for long, I promise.'

She doesn't answer so I open the door and wheel my way gingerly into the room. Caroline's sitting on her bed, her legs stretched out in front of her.

'Nigel not here?' I ask, though it's blindingly obvious he isn't.

She shakes her head.

'In his room?'

She nods.

'Probably getting on down to Clannad,' I say. I notice her eyes are blotchy, and her teenage-style makeup is smudged. She would look a perfect match for this Gothic house, were it not for Squirrel Nutkin smiling down from the walls.

'Congratulations.'

'What for?' she mutters.

'I thought it was only me who could wind Maeve up like that.'

'Why do you allow her to be rude to you? I mean, you pay her.'

'I do. But I suppose I've sort of got used to it, even learned to enjoy the daily battle in a funny sort of way. She looks after me very well.'

'She was horrible to me.' The tears are now running down her cheeks and she has given up any pretence of not crying.

I sigh. 'She's had a tough life, has Maeve. She has two brothers and nine sisters. Can you imagine? You have to learn to fight your corner when you've got that level of competition. Farming family. Not a lot of money to spare. And Maeve's been unable to have kids of her own. She worked her backside off for peanuts until she came here. Cleaning, farming, a spell in a black-pudding factory—'

'You want me to feel sorry for her now? Is that it?' Caroline punches a pillow angrily. 'You're just sticking together because you're as bad as her. You're just a – a dirty old man in a wheelchair.'

'Now, just a minute, you don't know me and you don't know

Maeve. And quite frankly, young lady, you've not exactly been the end of a perfect bloody day since you arrived, I can tell you.'

'It's not my fault!' she shouts at me.

'I never said it was!' I yell back. 'But at least we're trying. We're bloody well trying! It has to be give and take, you know. You're rude, you won't eat, and you never open your mouth except to be nasty. I know what's happened to you and Nigel, but you can't keep taking it out on everybody else.'

'What do you know?' she shrieks. 'How would you know what it feels like to have your parents killed – and then – and then be sent away to the middle of nowhere to live in some *nut-house*!'

I pause. 'How could I?'

I've been sitting outside Caroline's door for a bit, trying to gather myself together.

Nigel has just opened the door to his room. Oh, for crying out loud! His eyes are cracked with red as well, only they look ten times worse, magnified behind those Elvis Costello-style glasses he wears.

'Is she all right?' he asks.

'So-so,' I inform him. 'It'll blow over. These things generally do.'

'She's cross with me,' he says, unhappily.

'I think she's cross with everyone at the moment.'

He nods.

'It wasn't your fault, you know.'

He nods again, and I'm reminded of the way he looked before he left the kitchen table when he mentioned his father.

'Your mother was the same,' I tell him, in a stage whisper, and I see the sadness in his eyes at my use of the past tense. 'She was always one for fads and phases when she was younger too. Your father told me that when he first met your mother he used to call her Mania Marcia.'

102

'Really?' he asks, his mouth turning up in the faintest of smiles.

'Yep. And she didn't turn out too badly, did she?'

'No.'

'Why don't you pop down to the kitchen? See if Maeve's forgotten to clear anything away. She's getting very absent-minded in her old age.'

'Okay.' And he walks down the corridor towards the stairs.

'And don't tell her I told you that,' I call after him.

Sod the coffee, I could use a tot of whiskey.

Mania Marcia. One white lie is okay, if it makes the little nerd feel a bit better. Isn't it?

I'm in the gym in the basement of my house pumping iron, working out, feeling the burn. No, I'm not. I'm grunting and groaning and pulling muscles I never knew existed.

Actually, it's the only other way I can deal with tension, apart from listening to 'Scheherazade'. I must be screwed up today, though, because I have that playing on the portable CD in the corner, accompanying my twanging ligaments.

I am lying on a bench, behind which is a machine containing weights. When I'm feeling brave, Eugene occasionally adds another to these. There's a bar I grasp with my hands, situated behind my shoulders, which you use to pull the weights up and down. Builds up the muscles in my arms and shoulders.

Damn. The telephone's ringing. What a pity. I'll have to stop disintegrating my arms and answer it. I have a portable phone on my lap. 'Hello,' I grunt.

'You sound healthy.' A soft warm voice slides down the line. 'And you're playing "Scheherazade". I take it you're having another bad day, then?'

'Don't ask. Now you're going to depress me further by telling me you're not going to take the job, aren't you?'

There's a pause.

'Well, no. Originally I intended to turn it down. But I've thought about it very carefully, and I've decided I've nothing to lose by giving it a try. So, if it's all right with you, I'd like to accept.'

'Kate,' I'm trying not to sound as overjoyed as I feel, 'I'm delighted. I swear my correspondence is breeding behind my back. Maeve beat me about the head with another pile she picked off the mat this morning.'

There's a pause. 'Maeve? Who's she?'

'My woman who does. She cooks, she cleans, she washes. Her husband is my handyman, DIY expert and mechanic. And now I have you to answer my fan-mail, type my letters and deal with the phone calls. All the things I'm crap at sorted.'

She's laughing. It's a lovely sound. 'So. What happens next?' she enquires.

'Would you mind popping round this afternoon? About three o'clock? Then we can pin down a few details, make it more official and a bit less airy-fairy.'

'I look forward to seeing you later, then,' she says, and I find myself hoping that it's true. ''Bye.'

I can't see the sky from down here in the basement, but I suspect the sun has just come out.

12

Caroline, Nigel and I are taking a drive into Ballinkilty. I've brought them down in the Mondeo, rather than drag Eugene along. It's the first run I've given it since it came back from the garage.

I started the journey off by giving them a running commentary of the area. They sat in the back like carved bookends, but I've been trying to engage them in a bit of conversation. There's not been so much as a grunted syllable in response, so eventually I give up.

We've driven down the coast road, separated from the water by the lowest of stone walls, through Ring and out along the narrow road that leads to Ballinkilty. The sun is out today and its rays are playing on the water, magically changing its colour from muddy grey to turquoise blue. On sunny days in Ireland, Mother Nature waves a wand and transports the country deeper into Europe. Today I expect to turn a corner and find a Greek taverna, instead of a pub, or see a French château nestling in the hills, instead of a dormer bungalow.

The journey completed I park the car opposite the small

village of holiday homes known locally as Tutti-frutti Land because of the brightly coloured paint used on their exteriors.

'Nigel, do us a favour. Can you haul my wheelchair out of the boot and wheel it round for me? It's not that heavy.'

He does as he is asked.

'Come on, then.' I struggle to climb out of the Mondeo. 'Unfold the thing for me, could you?' He does so again without complaint.

I emerge through the driver's door on to the road, using my crutches. After the usual huffing and puffing and cursing, I manage to dump myself into the chair.

Caroline has slunk out of the back seat and is standing on the pavement. Nigel has joined her there.

'This way.' I take my life in my hands, and wheel myself a few yards up the road before I find a convenient ramp, and slip up on to the pavement to join them.

'Do you need help?' Caroline asks, leaving me feeling a little disconcerted.

'Thanks. I can manage.'

I'm leading the way like an Indian scout, and they are trotting behind me, noses in the air, like the most imperious of cavalry horsemen.

Ballinkilty is not blessed with oodles of clothes shops. There is an ale-house every other step, increasing numbers of places to have tea and cakes and three-course meals, and hotels currently being erected in every bit of available space. But teenage retail outlets?

Ah! I emergency-stop outside a sports shop, and Caroline and Nigel collide into the back of me. This'll do, at least until I can find out where someone like, say, Justine buys her clothes. If she ever speaks to me again.

'We'll just get something comfortable for now until your own clothes arrive,' I tell them, ushering them inside.

As Caroline and Nigel try on an outfit each in the changing rooms, I'm shifting uncomfortably in my chair. Nothing on the racks seemed to generate much excitement, with the possible exception of the Nike trainers, which cost as much as everything else put together.

I notice the pimply young sales assistant lean back on his heels and try to peek behind the curtain where Caroline is changing. I should rollock him, shouldn't I? But at the same time I can't really blame him. He's young and Caroline's pretty. The attention she's bound to receive might turn out to be a major problem, though, and I'm not really sure what my jurisdiction is on all that.

Caroline emerges from the changing room, looking lean and athletic. She is wearing a tight-fitting pair of grey leggings, a white armless top with halter-neck, and a fleecy sports jacket. Her figure suits this type of clothing. The Sporty Spice image. The Nike trainers are the only things that spoil the ensemble for me. It's as though she were wearing small kayaks on her feet.

'You look very fit, Caroline,' I say, and immediately wish I hadn't.

'Yeah, right. Thanks,' she replies, taking the compliment as mistakenly as I feared.

Nigel has emerged from the next cubicle.

I sent him to try on the most expensive designer-labelled quality gear the shop had to offer. I figured he needed the most help. But Nigel doesn't look fit. I suspect he wouldn't look athletic if you sprayed him black, pumped him full of steroids and transplanted Linford Christie's lunch-box on to him. He is not so much a wolf in sheep's clothing as a nerd in dudes.

'Very cool, Nigel.'

'You think so?' he asks, hoping he's wrong and that I'm not lying to him.

'Yes. Caroline, doesn't your brother look good?'

I look directly at her as I ask her this.

There's a pause. 'Yeah. You look fine, Nigel.'

'Why don't you keep those things on? Shove your other clothes in a bag and I'll pay,' I say, handing over my credit card.

'Thanks, Max,' Nigel states, almost genuinely from what I can tell.

'Yeah, thanks.' There's an air of suspicious distance in Caroline's voice. And something else.

'Shall we go?' I ask, straightening my hat as I speak. Behind my back, I can hear the whispers of gossip begin.

'Max.' Caroline stops me while shuffling awkwardly in her kayaks. 'I ... er ...'

'Yes?'

'I need ...' she continues, but it's muffled.

'Speak up. I can't hear you.'

'I can't shout it out.' She blushes and looks surprisingly awkward.

'Look, Caroline, part your teeth, open your mouth and just tell me, otherwise we're going to be here all day.'

'I need a bra, we both need knickers, and I need some Tampax!' she shouts.

I'd never noticed there was an echo in the high street before. I cringe with embarrassment as passers-by stare.

'Satisfied?' she asks, with a false smile.

'Oh, right, okay. Er ... this way,' I say, heading off in panic. I've no idea where one would buy a bra in Ballinkilty. Never mind those other things. I'll have to ask someone.

I've wheeled into the paper shop on the corner. Caroline and Nigel follow me in. I go to the counter and the two middle-aged women behind it recoil visibly. I know instantly that they are among those who believe I eat the first-born from every house in Ballinkilty.

'What can I do for you, now?' one hisses at me.

I am suddenly aware that Caroline, looking like Jane Fonda's under-the-age-of-consent daughter, is standing right next to me.

'I'm looking for some ladies' underwear.'

The women's eyes are like saucers.

'It's not for me. It's for this one here,' I say, pointing to my left.

They look at each other slowly, a mixture of shock and disgust on their face. I turn round and realise I am pointing at Nigel. Caroline is on my right.

'Sorry, I meant the girl, this young – I mean, my friend's daughter here.'

The ladies exchange glances of disbelief. 'Try Cash's around the corner.'

I'm about to get the children out of here as fast as possible, when I notice Nigel has picked up a Mars bar.

'Do you want a sweetie?' I cannot believe I said that.

As I slope out of the shop, I can hear the words 'little boy' beam into my brain.

Caroline has her underwear, Nigel his Jockey shorts, and we went to the chemist where they bought toothbrushes. Caroline also stocked up on face creams, essential makeup, and those things that are supposed to keep girls fresh and dry. It cost a bloody fortune. My wallet is still smoking from the hole that little lot burnt in it.

So far, so disastrous. But I've had a redeeming idea. I'm parked outside Ballinkilty's only record shop, which always seems on the point of closing down. The two orphans stand in front of me.

'Here,' I say, handing them each a twenty-punt note. 'Go inside and choose some decent sounds.'

Nigel takes his money, but Caroline's hands remain firmly by her side.

'It's okay, go on,' I urge. 'I overheard you talking about my choice of music. What can I say? When I hear the word hip, I don't so much think "cool" as "replacement". So get what you like.'

'You can't buy us, you know.' Caroline's eyes turn cold beneath my astonished gaze.

I'm staggered. 'I never said I wanted to. Look, money's not a big thing for me. I'm lucky, that's all.'

'You think just 'cause you're rich and my father wasn't you can buy everything. Well, you can't buy us.'

'Is that what you think I'm doing?'

'Isn't it? Videos, PlayStations, clothes. You're bribing us. Trying to make us like you.' Her eyes are fixed hard upon mine.

I cannot believe how uncomfortable this girl is making me feel. My patience snaps. 'Look, just bloody well go in there. I don't care whether you buy anything or not. I want you out of my face for two minutes. I need some peace.'

Caroline snatches the money from my hand and the two of them disappear inside the record shop.

I am stunned. Cut. Fucking wounded. Perhaps because she's hit upon an unkind truth. I told Paul, I told Maeve, I told anyone who'd listen. I would have told Jamie too, if he'd ever damn well asked. This wasn't my idea. I never wanted kids, and I never wanted these two to come to Ireland. And now they're here we're just screwing up each other's lives.

I feel like a man who's never had a flying lesson trying to land a jumbo jet because the pilot's had a heart-attack.

Feeling sorry for myself, I wheel myself slowly back to the car.

13

I'm still bloody furious with Caroline over that you-can't-buy-us routine. Buy them? Give me a half-way decent offer, throw in a free sunroof, and I'll sell the little swines to you.

However, I'm beginning to calm down now. That's because Kate's here.

I found her talking to Maeve in the kitchen when we got back from town, which was slightly unnerving to say the least. I don't want my name blackened before she's begun. But she looks happier, and there's an air of calm about her that matches the grace of her body.

We've done the job description and all that jazz, and she seems at ease with the informality of it all. I'm now sitting in my wheelchair in front of my desk, and Kate has perched herself instinctively on top of it. Her back has remained admirably straight and her exquisite legs dangle over the side in a rather distracting manner. She is wearing a simple T-shirt with a white lace skirt. Her hair is tousled, and her shoes have fallen lazily off her feet during our conversation leaving her barefoot, which makes her look more of a country girl today.

'So, to recap, then. You start next week. Ten until six, Monday to Friday. And you're happy with the salary?'

'Yes, perfectly.' She smiles. 'Thank you.'

'My pleasure. Great. Okay,' I say, ferreting around for a pen and some paper. I'm a bloody writer and I never seem to have a single functioning pen in the house. 'I just need to take down your personals.'

'What do you mean by that?' Her legs go rigid.

'Nothing, nothing.' I feel suddenly nervous myself. 'I just meant nothing. It's bad phraseology.'

She still looks tense.

'Forgive me. I seem unable to open my mouth without uttering a *double-entendre* at present. It's as if I've been possessed by Benny Hill or something. It's very embarrassing.'

She shakes her head. 'No, Max. It's not you, it's me. I'm the one who should be apologising. I'm easily threatened by men at the moment. But it's okay, I don't feel threatened by you – not really.'

'Thanks very much.'

'I mean, you're hardly likely to go chasing me around the office with a wicked glint in your eye and a spring in your step, are you?'

'I don't suppose I am.'

'I didn't mean that. Now, don't go using your disability to gain sympathy.' She places her hand upon mine in a reassuring manner to prevent me taking offence. 'That's the second time you've played that game in the short time I've known you.'

'Well, it was a bit insensitive. I suppose your Séan was the sporty type.'

'What's that got to do with it?'

'Nothing,' I mumble sulkily.

'He was, as it happens. Great body, very fit, big into Gaelic games.'

'You're not still in love with him after he left you penniless, are you?' I ask incredulously. Why does this bother me?

'Love? What is love, exactly?' She sighs. 'Anyway, when I said you weren't going to chase me around the office, I was paying you a compliment, if you must know. I've had a lot of problems with men behaving in a certain way towards me. It's good to meet a man who's being nice, just because he's being nice.'

Half of me feels instantly guilty. The other half of me feels fine because, for some reason, I would genuinely like to help this woman.

'Besides, I'm too old for you.'

'Pardon?'

'A little bird told me you go for younger women.'

A little bird? A great big gossiping dried-up shit-stirring Irish buzzard more like. 'Don't believe everything Maeve tells you. She's prone to exaggeration. Anyway, how old are you?'

She places a hand to her bosom in mock horror, her fingers splayed perfectly evenly. 'Is that the sort of question a gentleman asks a lady?' she says, blinking rapidly.

'It is when you're about to employ her.'

'Twenty-one.'

'Or thereabouts,' I challenge.

'Give or take seven years.' She giggles.

'I can't take seven years, Kate. Otherwise I'd have to give you work breaks to use the potty! Twenty-eight? If you think that's old, then I'm about to throw away my chair and crutches to be presented with a gold zimmer frame.'

She laughs again, and it's infectious. Her nose wrinkles and her shoulders rise. She looks like a naughty schoolgirl. 'Can a lady ask a gentleman,' she begins, regaining her composure, 'what enormous age he has managed to survive to?'

'No, she bloody well can't!'

'That's not fair,' she complains.

'Put it this way, I'm close enough to that age where the propaganda tells you life begins, yet you can't help yourself taking a morbid interest in hearing-aids, false teeth and engraved slabs of marble.' I look her straight in the eye.

'I hadn't realised you were that old.'

'I'm not that old,' I insist, defensively. 'Just so I'm prepared, are you in the habit of asking lots of personal questions?'

'I'm told it's a bit of a habit of mine,' she confesses.

'I bet you generally get an answer too, don't you?'

'Mmmm,' she hums, in the affirmative.

'In that case, before you ask any more, what I suggest you do is this. Go and find Maeve and get her to give you a guided tour of the spare bedrooms. You can choose which one you like best, as long as you don't criticise the décor.'

'Seriously?' she queries.

'Yes. And don't go listening to Maeve's tittle-tattle. Cliff Richard's debauched, according to her.'

'Why?'

'His eyes give it away, apparently.'

'I understand.' She nods. 'Okay, I'll go then, shall I?' She slides fluidly off the desk on to the floor. Then she crosses to the door and opens it. Before she exits, she stops. 'Is it okay if I move in at the weekend? Otherwise I'll have to sleep on a park bench somewhere.'

'Yeah, that's fine.'

'Thank you, Max. Honestly. Thanks for everything. You're a nice guy.'

I've waited a long time for a woman to tell me I'm a nice guy and now it's happened I hate it. Nice guys are boring. Nice guys are not sexy. Nice guys you walk over.

I slap myself mentally for being stupid. I am attracted to Kate, whereas she likes me because I'm so obviously safe. Let's face it, a woman who's turned on by a sporting all-rounder would hardly be interested in a man who needs a four-wheel-drive to get about both outside and inside the house.

One of the reasons I attract younger women is because they are impressionable. It makes them blind. Gives them a disability to match my own. But Kate isn't impressed by my fame. And women who aren't can see clearly and are not impressed by a man in a wheelchair.

Eugene is at the table with Caroline and Nigel. They are eating, but a quick glance tells me that Caroline's bowl of pasta has barely been touched.

I've been feeling a bit unsettled since my chat with Kate. It's probably just that we seem to have doubled the number of people living in this house within a few days. I'm not used to all the bustle. So I've come down here for a cup of coffee.

'So you see,' Eugene is saying to the children, 'by making the tights "barely black" and making one of the women a half-caste, your detective can solve the murder. What d'you think?'

They're staring at him. Caroline is open-mouthed and Nigel's brow is furrowed. He speaks just as I roll up to join them at the table.

'Blue tights?'

'Blue?' Eugene queries, a look of astonishment on his face. He's not the only one. I'm looking at Nigel in a startled manner myself.

'Yeah. Then the vicar . . .'

'Priest,' Eugene corrects, sounding a touch brittle.

'Whatever,' Nigel continues, 'writes the word "Navy" on the wall. One of your women can be a Wren, and we all think she did it, when really it was the other one who wore the blue tights.'

Eugene is staring at him in silence. Is he contemplating, I wonder, researching his book by taking off his shoe and seeing if it's possible to strangle someone with a sweaty, old, grey sock?

'That's – that's brilliant, Nigel!' he says at last. 'Why didn't I think of that? Why didn't you, Max?' He turns to face me.

'It takes a certain kind of brain, I suspect,' I reply.

'Can we go to our rooms now?' Caroline asks.

'What? Again? Every time I come into the room, you two bugger off upstairs. I could take this personally, you know.'

They sit there, a study in misery.

'There's no meat in pasta.' I point at Caroline's full bowl.

'I know.'

'Then why haven't you eaten it?'

'I don't like it,' she says stubbornly.

'Well, what do you like?'

'England!' she screams.

'Well, sod off back there then, and starve yourself to death.'

'*I am not anorexic!*' she screams at me, before making yet another dramatic exit.

Nigel is looking at me wide-eyed and terrified.

'Sorry, Nigel, but I've got to get her to eat something.'

He says nothing.

'Can you have a word with her for me?'

He nods.

'Okay, off you go.'

He sprints for the safety of their bedrooms.

'You handled that well, boy,' Eugene comments, which really gets my goat.

'You're about as much help as your missus is, Eugene,' I snap at him.

'Me? What have I done?'

'Going on about your book like that.'

'I was just trying to make polite conversation, so. Help them relax a little,' he pleads.

'Polite conversation? Filling their heads with tales of shag-happy priests who get strangled with a pair of Pretty fucking Pollys?'

'There are no parrots in my book that I know of, Max.'

'The tights, you ignoramus! Maybe we should call the brand chameleon, as they seem to be able to change colour every five minutes.'

'You don't like the tights idea, do you, now?'

'It's got nothing to do with that. But you can bet Caroline's going to keep hers under lock and bloody key every time you're around.'

'Ah, no! You don't think—'

'She's so strung up as it is, she'll probably scream blue murder the next time she sees a man in a dog-collar.'

The usually placid Eugene straightens his back in anger. 'Now, then! I won't hear that. There's not a priest in the whole of Cork will lay a finger on her.'

'Maybe.'

'Can't be saying the same for young Nigel, now . . .' Eugene adds.

'Don't go filling his head with that stuff. Shit! That's all we need!' I shout at him.

'I'm only trying to help,' he shouts back.

I sigh. 'Will you listen to us? Five minutes ago, we were all co-existing with a reasonable degree of harmony. Then the kids arrive and we're at each other's throats like pit-bull terriers.'

'It's not the kids, it's just little Miss High and Mighty,' Maeve cuts in, having appeared magically from nowhere to clear up the dishes. She's good at that – creeping up unexpectedly.

'No problem with young Nigel's appetite, now.' She scrapes the contents of Caroline's plate into the pedal bin. 'He's always sneaking down past his sister's searchlights and tucking into a mighty ham sandwich or six in the kitchen, so.'

'Is he?'

'He is. Mind you, I could put all my origami skills into practice and fold Madam Caroline's lettuce leaves into the shape of the Dáil, and she'd still cock her snooty nose up at it.'

I take a cigarette out of my packet and place it in my mouth. I've started smoking again. Two days of balletic secretaries and parenthood and I'm puffing my way into an early grave. Two days in my care, and Caroline and Nigel start subscribing to the Marlene Dietrich School of Agoraphobia. It's enough to drive anyone back to the fags.

'Nigel's a fine young lad,' Maeve continues. 'He's me toy-boy.'

'Is that so?' Eugene asks, raising his eyebrows.

'Strange taste in men you have,' I tell her, patting myself up and down in search of a light.

'No worse than your taste in women. Though I have a feeling yours might be after improving soon.'

'What do you mean by that?'

'Nothing, so. Try your jacket pocket.'

I go to my jacket pocket and find my lighter.

'Anyway, my niece is coming up on Saturday night to take the young majesty out for a spin.'

'Julie, you mean?' Eugene asks, suspiciously.

'I do.' Maeve sits down opposite me. 'You see, young Julie is a spirited lass, a little on the feisty side. She'll stand none of your nonsense from little Miss Uppity.'

I look to Eugene for confirmation. He has his eyes closed and is slowly shaking his head.

It's one o'clock in the morning and I'm lying in bed, thinking of how much easier everything will be when Kate moves in. I believe I'm looking forward to it, but I shouldn't be, should I? I mean, I only need a secretary, that's all.

Oh, well, at least all's quiet on the western front.

I'll get comfy. Try and get some sleep.

I hear the scream.

At first I think I'm dreaming it. Or that I'm trapped briefly in that state of half-consciousness, so that my mind could be playing tricks on me.

But this is real. I open my eyes and I see the clock: four forty a.m., it blinks at me in infra-red. I reach for my crutches, which are propped up against my bedside cabinet. I take time to steady myself, let my brain send a message of strength to my arms, then move as fast as I can out of my bedroom door.

I'm confused, disoriented by sleep. Then I hear it again and, recognising its tone, I know where to go. I move down the corridor as fast as I can, which is still frustratingly slowly.

The door to Caroline's bedroom is open, the first person I see is the boy, his back towards me.

Caroline is lying on the bed. She has stopped screaming but she is sobbing, shivering, gulping for air.

'Caroline? What is it?'

'She's been having her nightmare again,' Nigel tells me.

'She's done this before, then?' Feeling shaky myself, I sit on the bed.

'Yes. Since . . . you know.'

I nod.

'Caroline?' The shivers and sobs continue. I don't think she sees me. I must comfort her I know, but I don't think I can. I've never had to deal with anything quite like this before.

I press my back against the headboard, then use my arms to swing my legs on to the bed. Hesitantly, I pull Caroline towards me. Then I put my arms around her. She leans her head into my chest, and her legs draw themselves up into a foetal position.

She's holding me, gripping me.

I feel I should pat her in some way, reassure her, but instead I look at Nigel and tap the other side of the bed. He perches on the very edge of the mattress, and for some reason I ruffle his hair.

Caroline's left arm is round my waist. It's strange to admit, but it feels ... good. As if she needs me.

'Don't let them get me! Don't let them get me!'

'Who, Caroline?'

I look at Nigel and can see that he, too, is freaked by this. I wink at him.

He half smiles.

'Don't let them get me!' Caroline's chant is weakening.

'I won't, Caroline. I promise. Max is here. I'm not going anywhere. Nothing will dare get you with the Old Weirdo himself around, will it? You can sleep now. It's all right. I'm here.'

I go for broke and stroke her hair. Not in the way I might have stroked Justine's hair. I do it purely to calm her. Her breathing slows as her body relaxes. Her limbs become heavy as she drifts back to sleep.

14

I'm shattered. I stayed with Caroline for an hour or so last night, which meant it was six o'clock by the time I left. It hardly seemed worth going back to bed. So, I shepherded Nigel back to his room with a few consoling words, then went up to the office. It was then I had my brainwave and called my solicitor on his home phone number. A sleepy voice answered. 'Hello?'

'Paul?'

'Yeah. Who's this?'

'It's Max.'

'Max? Bloody hell! You on a different time-scale over there or what?'

'Sorry to ring so late – or is it early? Listen, there's something I want you to organise for me . . .'

At eight I went down for breakfast with Maeve and Eugene, after which I sent Eugene out on an errand. Maeve was steeling herself for an act of bravery: serving Caroline Linda McCartney vegetarian sausages for breakfast. It's all part of a cunning ploy she has to persuade her to start eating meat. She looked a bit tired today actually, did Maeve. Having Nigel trailing after her must be wearing her out. I suggested she paid the doctor a visit and she told me to stop mothering her. Ha!

I'm now in the drawing room, going through the chapters I wrote last night. It's become a new habit, coming in here with a pot of coffee, as has playing 'Scheherazade' as I work. Either I'm playing this because I am now permanently tense, or it has developed some other connotation since Kate's arrival.

It's about ten thirty a.m. or thereabouts, and I can feel my eyes beginning to glaze over. There's a knock on the door.

'Come in.'

'I'm just after reporting that the mission is accomplished, Max,' Eugene says, wheezing and hacking breathlessly.

'Good. Where have you put them?' The kids' suitcases have returned from their summer break and Eugene's been to Cork airport to collect them.

'Nowhere yet. They're in the hall. I thought I might have a reviving cup of coffee first, or perhaps try to talk Maeve into giving me a full body massage before I pull what few muscles I have left dragging things up those endless feckin' stairs.'

'Fair enough. Though you're a braver man than I am, Gunga Din, if you're really going to let Maeve smooth out your knots.'

He winks at me. 'Ah, you'd be surprised now.'

'Well, you can't leave them lying in the hall. Why don't you take them up to their rooms now and have your rub-down after?'

'Determined to finish me off, aren't you, Max? Why don't you just put a bullet through me head? At least do for me humanely,' he puffs.

'You'll live,' I tell him, and I laugh.

There's another knock on the door, which is still open.

'Sorry, I didn't realise you were busy.' It's Caroline.

'Come in. Eugene's got to carry something upstairs, anyway, haven't you, Eugene?'

'Yes, master. Right away, master,' he replies, as he leaves.

'Cup of coffee?' I ask.

'Yes please,' she answers, and she suddenly smiles.

Good grief! She actually smiled. Not a big smile, but nevertheless I feel as if I've just received a gong for persistence in the face of bloody-mindedness.

I'm not sure why, but Maeve always brings in a massive tray with three or four spare cups and saucers.

'Take a seat,' I tell Caroline, and she comes and sits directly opposite me. 'Milk and sugar, madam?'

She nods. I do the honours, hand over her coffee then top up my own cup.

'Now, what can I do you for?' I enquire.

'Nothing, really. I just thought I ought to say thank you.'

'It was a pleasure. And what did I do, exactly?'

She smiles – again!

'You know what I mean. For taking care of me last night,' she says, a little awkwardly.

'You don't have to thank me. And you don't have to talk about it, if you don't want to.'

She sips her coffee.

'Ironical, really, when you think about it,' I say to plug the silence. 'I comforted you because you had a nightmare, then I went into my office, made a few phone calls and carried on writing books to scare the hell out of people.'

'Are they really scary?'

'You haven't read one?' I say, clutching at my chest in mock-horror.

'No,' she confesses.

'I don't blame you.'

'I'm not frightened of everything, you know.' She's aggressive again suddenly. 'I might like to read one, one day.'

'There's plenty of copies floating around, if you're serious.

Mind you, I'm not sure your dad would approve of you reading one of my – Sorry, Caroline, I didn't mean to say that.'

'It's fine.'

But it isn't. 'I don't think sometimes. Look, I'm sorry if I've made you feel uncomfortable or unwelcome for the past couple of days. I'm . . . inexperienced, I suppose. I've never had kids of my own, let alone seen one grow into a young woman. That's why I'm so clumsy. I'm not trying to take the place of your father, honest. I couldn't live up to that if I tried.'

I see tears in her eyes. Oh, Lord, I've made things worse.

'Well, you did okay last night, I suppose,' she says, as they spill over her lower lids.

'Oh, come on! Don't cry on me,' I say. And I open my arms to her, before I've really thought about it. She walks tentatively over to me and perches self-consciously on my lap.

'It's okay,' I say reassuringly, and she collapses against me. She's curled her legs up and thrown her arms around me, and she's hugging me tightly.

She's still wearing my T-shirt, which she sleeps in and it's ridden up to her waist. Being squeezed by a nubile teenager displaying lacy black knickers is terrifyingly disconcerting, I can tell you. But, as Jamie's stand-in, I'm not committing a crime here, am I? A father is still expected to hug his scantily clad teenage daughter, right?

'I've not been very nice to you since I got here, have I, Max?' she whispers in my ear.

'The truth?'

She nods and her hair brushes against my face.

'You've been a bad-tempered, moody old cow.'

'I'm sorry.' She wipes her tears on my shirt.

'It's forgotten.'

'Max?' she whispers again.

'Yes?'

'About my dream. They're ... well ... they're spiders.'

I feel myself freeze.

'I dream about them, hundreds of them, crawling across the floor to get me.'

'Really?' I reply hoarsely. I'm not overly keen on them myself.

'Stupid, I know. I just ... I've always been scared of them.'

'We're all terrified of something, Caroline. And those fears are often completely irrational.'

'Even you?' she asks.

'Of course.'

'What are you scared of, Max?'

'It's a secret.'

'Tell me.'

'You wouldn't believe me if I did.'

She's lifted her head and is looking into my eyes. 'What is it?'

I say nothing.

'You're joking!'

'Nope. Snap is the word I think we're looking for.'

'You're just saying this to make me feel better,' she claims, suspicion in her eyes again.

'Am I, bugger! You're lucky I didn't know you were dreaming about spiders on your bedroom floor. You wouldn't have seen my arse for dust, I'm telling you. I'd have set a new world record for the Man Running with Crutches event at the disabled Olympics.'

She smiles, briefly. 'But you write horror stories!'

'Not about spiders I don't.'

'If I dream about them again, I won't call for you. All right?' she promises.

'Yes, you will. Then I'll join you on the bed and poor old Nigel can spend three hours running round the bedroom bashing imaginary spiders over the head with his slippers.'

As if on cue, Nigel has barged in. He's in the Maeve camp of skipping the cursory knock on the door. She must be training him. He's fully dressed in his new sportswear. Caroline has sprung from my lap to her feet.

'What's going on?' he asks.

'I was giving your sister a hug. That's all right, isn't it?'

Nigel looks at his sister. 'I suppose.'

'I am her godfather, aren't I?'

'I suppose,' he repeats sulkily.

'So I'm not breaking any rules, then?'

'I suppose.' He pouts.

Jealousy? 'Do you want a hug?'

'No!'

Maybe not, then.

Hark! A knock on the door. It's Eugene.

'There's somebody here to see Caroline,' Eugene announces.

'Me?'

Into the room walks Caroline's visitor. It has cropped ginger hair, bleached T-shirt and dungarees. There appears to be a tattoo of some description on the upper part of the right arm.

'You, Caroline?' it asks.

'Yes.'

'Hi. I'm Julie. Did you not know I was coming?'

Caroline looks to me for guidance.

'Didn't Maeve tell you?' I say awkwardly. 'This is her niece.'

We both look at the girl, who stands with her weight shifted on to one hip, and both hands slipped inside the breastplate of her dungarees. She appears to be chewing.

'So?' Caroline responds, with deliberate indifference.

'Nice to meet you too,' Julie fires back.

'Why has she come to see me?' Caroline enquires, suspiciously.

'Am I invisible, like?' Julie asks, in a surprisingly deep voice.

'Pardon?' says Caroline, with a slight upturn of the nose.

'I was just wondering why you keep asking him, like I wasn't here or something.'

'Do I?'

'You do. You can talk to me, you know.'

'That's very good of you,' Caroline acknowledges, condescendingly. 'Max, why is ... sorry. Julie, why are you here?'

'I brought the car. I've come to take you out for a spin. Introduce you to a few people in town, like.'

Caroline shakes her head in confusion. 'Why?'

''Cause Auntie Maeve told me to.'

'Does everybody do what Maeve tells them to?' Caroline says, hostilely.

'Everybody except you, Caroline,' I cannot resist chipping in.

'So, are we going or what?' Julie directs at Caroline.

'No, we're not.'

I hold up my hands. 'Hear me out, Caroline. You're never going to find out if you like this area unless you look at it. You're always going to miss your old friends unless you make new ones. You're always going to feel like a prisoner here unless you grab the opportunity to get out while you can.'

'It's up to you. No skin off my nose, either way,' Julie grunts.

'I've nothing to wear,' Caroline says feebly, looking down at my crumpled T-shirt.

'That's what you think! Your suitcases have arrived. They should be in your room by now.'

'Great!' enthuses Nigel.

'I'll give you some money to spend ... And, no, I am not trying to buy you.'

'Just bribe me,' Caroline corrects me.

'Exactly. As a matter of fact I'll give you an allowance. Otherwise you'll have to keep running to me every time you need something. If you so choose, you can get a summer job once you've settled and pay me back,' I say, in deference to her pride. 'Come on, Caroline, us arachnophobes have got to stick together.'

'I'll see if I've got something suitable to change into,' Caroline says, heading for the door.

'Thank you.'

She pauses when she reaches Julie, who is still chewing gum. Then she turns, and walks back over to me. 'I'm really not sure about this, Max.' She sighs.

'Listen,' I begin, in a stage-whisper, 'any more complaints, I'll ask Julie to do the housework and I'll send you into town with Maeve.'

'Oh, no! I'm going, okay?' Caroline races out.

'What about me?' Nigel whines. 'Can I come?'

'Sorry, squirt, no shrimps allowed,' Julie tells him cruelly. 'Shall I follow her?'

'Good idea, I reply.'

She turns to go and Eugene catches her arm. 'Be good now, Julie, you hear me?'

'Yes, Uncle Eugene,' she replies, in a bored fashion as she leaves.

'What shall I do?' Nigel asks sadly, a lost expression on his face.

'Actually, Nigel,' Eugene intervenes, 'Maeve was looking for your help. She's a job she can't manage alone and I'm too busy. She's in the kitchen.'

Nigel walks away.

'I notice Maeve didn't show her face in here.'

'She thought it best to leave them to it.' Eugene's grinning.

'Has Maeve really got a job for Nigel?'

'No, but don't worry, she'll think of something.' He winks, then heads for the door.

It's Saturday afternoon and Kate is moving in. Eugene and I are

128

on the gravel to greet her as she drives up to the front of the house.

'Hi,' she says, as she gets out. She looks pale and tired, but no less beautiful.

'Everything okay?' I ask.

'Fine, fine,' she says, but I don't think it is.

I glance at the car and it looks surprisingly empty for someone who has just moved house. 'Where are your goods and chattels?'

'In the boot,' she tells me, and walks to the back of the car to unlock it.

'I suppose you'll be expecting me to carry it all upstairs,' Eugene whispers.

'Naturally,' I confirm.

'Well, just as long as you pay for the hernia operation,' he says, as he walks over to the car to join Kate. He fishes out two large suitcases on to the gravel.

'Is that it?' I ask her.

'Pretty much. There's a small box in front of the back seat with a few bits and pieces in it.'

'I'd thought there'd be more. You know, ornaments, bits of bric-à-brac, lampstands, a microwave,' I suggest, as Eugene grunts and groans his way past me with the luggage.

'No. It's mostly clothes, really,' she states, running her hands through her hair.

'Why don't you follow Eugene upstairs, do a bit of unpacking and I'll put the kettle on?' I suggest.

'Okay, thanks,' she says, limply, and steps inside the house.

I feel disappointed. I'd been looking forward to Kate's arrival, but her demeanour has made it a bit of an anticlimax.

It's nearly dinner-time. Eugene is upstairs cleaning himself up, Maeve is cooking, and Nigel is playing sous-chef. If I didn't know better, I'd think they'd been welded together.

I'm parked at the kitchen table, looking forward to this meal. It'll be the first time we've eaten together properly: myself, Maeve, Eugene, Caroline and Nigel and, of course, Kate. I've barely seen her since she moved in. She came down for a coffee, but seemed distant, distracted. Then she went back upstairs to finish unpacking. That was over three hours ago, which by my reckoning means she's taking about ten minutes per garment.

And there's something else: she's changed her mind about which room she wants. I have a house littered with empty bedrooms and she suddenly decides she'll sleep in the pokiest one of all – the room right next door to Maeve and Eugene.

Why? What have I done to make her feel threatened? The last time she was here she said I was only man who didn't make her feel nervous.

Keep your distance, Max. As always. Just keep everything at a distance.

Caroline's just breezed in wearing full makeup, short frock, the works. 'Has that woman moved in?' she asks bluntly.

'Yes,' I confirm.

'Why?'

'She's my new secretary.'

'So? Why's she living here?'

'Because she's nowhere else to live.'

'Oh. I see.'

Feeling uncomfortable I change the subject. 'Nice of you to dress for dinner.'

'I'm not here for dinner,' she replies rapidly.

'What are you here for, then?' Maeve asks.

'I mean, I'm not stopping. I'm going out.'

Maeve slams a saucepan down on the working surface. 'But I've cooked for you. So I'm supposed to feck your dinner into the bin?'

Caroline shrugs, and Maeve places her hands firmly on her

130

hips. 'There are people starving all over the world, now. Your portion could keep a refugee alive for a month, and you just cock your nose up at it.'

'So – mail it to them,' Caroline says flippantly, and Maeve's face begins to look alarmingly mottled.

'Caroline,' I butt in, 'give a little, will you? Just have a bite to eat before you go out, and we'll all feel better for it.'

'I am eating. I'm going out to eat.'

'Well, why in God's name didn't you tell me that, before I wasted all that food?'

'I didn't ask you to cook for me, did I?' Caroline screams.

'Come on, Caroline, it's common courtesy. You should have let Maeve know if you were eating elsewhere.'

'Don't you start,' Caroline rounds on me. 'You were the one who said I had to go out with Julie, start making friends. And she's your niece.' She turns back to Maeve.

There's the sound of a car horn.

'There she is. I've got to go,' and she flounces out of the kitchen.

There's silence. Then we hear the front door slam.

Maeve catches me staring at her and Nigel, who's been standing by her side throughout the conversation blinking, saying nothing, keeping it all inside.

'I know, I know, but I deserve a few manners, Max. That's all I'm asking for.'

I nod in agreement. 'That's the third night in a row she's gone out with Julie.'

'My plan may be backfiring a little,' Maeve concedes.

'Oddly enough, she always comes back at a decent hour. I don't know if she's playing by the rules Jamie set down when he was still around, but I don't think she's got home later than half past ten. Earlier sometimes. I don't think I've said anything to her.'

'I have,' Maeve declares, lifting the saucepan lid to check the food isn't spoiling. 'I had a word with Julie. Threatened her within an inch of her life.' She picks up a wooden spoon and stirs the stew.

I smile. 'Thanks, Maeve.'

I glance at Nigel and notice he looks sad, and a little twitchy. Of course, we've been going on about his sister in front of him again. And I mentioned his father. How stupid of me. I know he doesn't like to hear Jamie's name.

Kate has just glided into the room.

'Now, girl, you look lovely,' Maeve tells her.

And she does. Light makeup. Simple dress. Gorgeous.

'Thank you, Maeve.'

'Sit yourself down, now. Dinner won't be long. I'm just waiting for that man of mine to scrape the muck off his hands, then I can serve up.'

'Oh.' Kate puts her hand to her mouth. 'Maeve, I'm so sorry. This is so rude of me. I have to go out.'

'No!' Maeve exclaims. 'Not another one.'

'Another?' Kate enquires, glancing in my direction.

'Don't ask,' I say.

'What must you think of me? I should have said something, but what with just moving in and so on, it slipped my mind. In fact, I'll be out most evenings for a while. If that's okay?' She looks at me.

'Of course,' I lie. 'It's nothing to do with me. I'm just your employer.'

'Well, I must be off.' She stands up and picks up her bag. 'Listen, Maeve, don't worry about me. I can always get myself something later. And once again, I'm so sorry.'

'Don't worry, love. It's just unfortunate timing, that's all. Go on, be off with you. Have a nice time.'

Yeah, have a nice time, Kate.

'I'll try,' Kate replies. "Bye, everybody.' She slips out of the kitchen.

Most evenings? What does she mean she'll have to go out most evenings? I've just looked up to find Maeve sitting opposite me with Nigel behind her. She's staring at me, Nigel standing behind her.

'You don't like your woman being off out on the razzle tonight, do you?' she asks quietly, but directly.

I'm saved from replying as Eugene shuffles back into the kitchen. He looks around. 'Just us, is it?' he asks.

Maeve walks across to the Aga and we watch her stare into the large pot of Guinness and mushroom stew. 'I hope you're hungry, boys,' she says. 'I hope you're fecking starving.'

15

We're into July and the weather has been uncommonly good. The sun has shone gloriously, the damp has been vapourised from the air, and the green that dominates this land has taken on an altogether brilliant hue.

What a strange week it's been. Caroline is gradually becoming more friendly, particularly towards me, and I've occasionally caught her being almost civil to Maeve. She's out and about a lot of the time, floats around in mini-skirts as opposed to tracksuits and at bedtime the T-shirt has been replaced with baggy pyjamas. She's eating like a bird, but she is eating. It's also been some time since I last heard her call her brother 'stupid', which may have helped him settle down a bit.

Speaking of Nigel, now he's got his own clothes back he dresses like John Major. Something will have to be done about that. He spends most of his time with Maeve. He follows her round the house, goes shopping with her, visits her countless relations and, although he's still a long way from being verbose, he seems more relaxed. He may even be happy in his own funny way.

The big difference, of course, is Kate's presence. Or, rather, the lack of it. The calm, relaxed beauty I met when I interviewed her has become withdrawn, tense, timid. She's jumping at shadows, and her conversation is guarded and controlled. She's polite and charming, yet somehow she seems superficial, and the one thing I would have said about Kate is that she was anything but superficial.

And at six fifteen every evening on the dot, she disappears out of the house.

We're eating breakfast. Eugene has finished and is heading out of the door, Nigel is on his second helping. He never talks, just eats. Caroline is picking at some dry muesli and poor old Maeve has only just sat down.

I'm watching Kate, who is leaning against the work-surface, nibbling a piece of toast and Marmite while checking a piece of correspondence. I've seen her do this every working morning since she arrived. I don't know why but I'm transfixed.

I realise Caroline is staring at me. She's noticed me looking at Kate and her eyes type the message of disapproval on my mind. I wish she'd stop. It's strange, but I can brush off all Maeve's lectures about my behaviour with the Justines in my life as a minor irritation, yet Caroline's stare makes me feel cheap. I look away.

'Did you have a nice time last night?' Caroline's question grabs everyone's attention.

'I said, did you have a nice time last night, Kate?'

Kate slowly puts down her toast and lifts her attention from the typed letter. 'Sorry. Not especially. Why do you ask?'

'You looked as if you were having a nice time, that's all.'

'Did I?'

'Yes. Cosy, you know. A nice cosy chat. Just the two of you.'

Kate's turned pale. 'It was okay. I saw an old friend I hadn't seen for a while. We had a bit of catching up to do.'

'That's nice,' Caroline says with the smile of a crocodile.

'What business is it of yours, anyway, young lady?' Maeve butts in with her usual timely reminder of her presence.

'I was just asking, that's all,' Caroline protests sulkily.

'Well, I must be getting started. If you'll excuse me, please?' Kate glances at me, then leaves.

'What was that all about, now?' Maeve interrogates.

'Don't look so mad. I was only teasing her.' Caroline pushes away her bowl of muesli, and scowls.

'What about, for crying out loud?' I enquire.

'She's got a boyfriend,' Caroline reveals, and I feel my stomach knot. 'I saw her in Ballinkilty in the Druids Arms.

'And what were you doing in a public-house?' Maeve stabs.

'I wasn't drinking. I wouldn't. Alcohol is bad for you. Julie and I had arranged to meet some other friends there, that's all. It's right in the middle of Ballinkilty. We went on to Bandon to see a film.'

'So what on earth made you think Kate had a boyfriend?' I can't stop myself asking.

'Or that you've any right to embarrass the poor woman about it,' Maeve adds.

'It was just a joke.' A glint of teenage enthusiasm comes into Caroline's eyes. 'But you should have seen them. Heads together, talking, mooning into each other's eyes. It was horrible. He was all muscles and stubble, and he kept pawing her. She pretended she didn't like it, but you could see she did and—'

'Now that's enough.' I try to stop myself shouting. 'You've no right to make her feel uncomfortable by spying on her like that.'

'I wasn't spying on her. I just noticed her, okay? Anyway,' she continues, looking directly into my eyes, 'I can't see why everyone is making such a fuss.' She scrapes the remainder of her muesli into the bin, and stomps out of the kitchen.

Maeve turns to me. 'It's no business of Caroline's, or ours for that matter, what Kate gets up to in her own free time, is it, Max?'

'No,' I reply, after far too long a pause.

I'm more confused than ever. Why does it bother me that Kate goes out every night? She's perfectly entitled to her own life. Of course she can have a boyfriend if she so chooses. I just find myself wishing she didn't.

I had another run-in with Caroline over lunch and banished her upstairs. Then, an hour or so later, I started to feel guilty. Maybe I had overreacted because of her revelation at breakfast this morning. I wheeled my way grudgingly up the ramp, to make peace, and stopped when I then heard another voice coming from her room. I coasted down the corridor until I was between the two children's bedrooms.

'Don't be too hard on Max, Caroline,' I could hear Kate saying. 'He's brought you to live in a beautiful country. You'll not go short of money, or clothes, or food. And he's given you a fabulous house to live in.'

'I know,' Caroline replied flatly, 'but he always takes everyone else's side against me. Eugene's. Maeve's. Yours.'

'I'm sorry you feel that way,' Kate replied. 'Has Max told you about his mother?'

'No.'

'She died when he was younger than you and Nigel. She was knocked down by a car while saving his life, right in front of him.'

'That's awful,' Caroline responded. 'Did he tell you that?'

'No, but I have it from a very reliable source.'

I still haven't decided whether to hand-sew Maeve's lips together or cut out her tongue and hang it from my rear-view mirror as an example to others.

'I'm only telling you this because I thought you should know that he does have some understanding of what you're going through, even if he's not brilliant at communicating it. And he's a kind man underneath all that bluff. His heart's in the right place. He certainly rescued me.'

I don't think I've ever overheard anybody paying me a personal compliment before, especially a woman like Kate.

'Anyway, I must go and see if he's got any typing for me to do.'

Panic. I turned and ram-raided my way into Nigel's room, which was fortunately empty.

I'm sitting here now, trying to stop my heart racing, and thinking about what I've overheard.

Maeve is drunk! It's nearing midnight on a Sunday evening. Caroline and Nigel are in bed, and we grown-ups are in the dining room. All four of us. Sunday is the one night when Kate isn't gallivanting off somewhere.

It's only about the third time this room's been used since I bought the place. It's huge and ostentatious, the sort of ornate dining room seen in many a Hammer horror film of the sixties. The walls are painted deep Victorian red, and its high ceiling is crowned by a crystal chandelier. The table is long enough for the two people stationed at either end to have to shout to hear one another. The four of us are sitting somewhere near its centre.

It was Maeve's idea, this. Out of the blue, she suggested it would be nice if Kate and I joined Eugene and her for a proper dinner.

'I'll cook something special,' she promised. And she did, one of the most delicious salmon dishes I have ever tasted.

She's also been running around in her little nappy firing arrows at Kate and me all night. It's been highly embarrassing for both of us, but especially for Kate who has her man. Maeve must be off her trolley to think Kate's ever likely to ditch the 'body-builder of the year' for a man who has to carry a tin of three-in-one oil in his back pocket in case the damp rusts his back wheels.

'O' course he's done very well out of all that filth he writes, Kate. And he's got the self-discipline to keep them coming off the conveyor-belt. You have to respect him for that, now.' Maeve takes another swig from her glass, then turns to me. 'It's rare to find a high level of intelligence and beauty in a woman, wouldn't you say, Max? Usually the pretty ones have about as much brains as a boiled lobster, and the clever ones have faces like a recently beaten rump steak. Not like Kate here, eh, Max?'

I know what she means. I'm struggling to find fault with Kate, but apart from a tendency towards reckless driving, and of course her recent odd behaviour, she is pretty perfect.

'Finest thing that ever happened to me, marrying this ol' git next to me, Kate,' she says. 'Thirty years and I don't regret a day of it. We've got each other, you see. It must be awful growing old all by yourself, don't you think? And I won't last for ever. What's going to happen to Max when I pop me clogs?'

Kate doesn't reply. She's in the corner of the dining room now, setting up the CD player. She's definitely not my usual type of woman. For one thing she's mature. And she's definitely not the kind of girl you bounce round in an electric wheelchair. The light from the candles on the window-ledge frames her face, exaggerating the red tint of her hair. Her soft skin is contrastingly pale.

'Max, what's this little gem from your collection? It doesn't seem to go with the rest of your musical taste,' she asks, holding up a CD. She's wearing a light grey dress, subtlely decorated with small blue flowers. Its soft material clings to her body as she sways unsteadily across the room.

'That's *Fear of Falling*, the soundtrack of a film they made of one of my books. It's mostly fifties rock-and-roll.'

'Oh, yes!' Maeve screams, unexpectedly. 'Now that's my kind of music!'

Kate has pressed the button on the remote control and the music's thrashing out now. Maeve has dragged Eugene out of his chair and is jiving with him. I'm not one to go on about being disabled. In fact, I make a point of doing the opposite. But there are certain things you just can't do, and this is one of them.

Maeve and Eugene are giggling like schoolkids, and Kate is in a world of her own. She's perfectly still. It's beautiful just to watch her, or is it painful? I'm not sure. I want to dance. I want to dance with Kate.

It's several tracks later and Maeve is still going strong, even though her face is so red, it looks like a wilting poppy. Eugene has flagged and is slumped in a chair.

'Come on, Kate girl. Get up and dance wit' an old woman.'

'I'm sorry. I can't dance,' she states firmly.

'Stuff and nonsense! A young girl like you? I'm sure you're a beautiful mover.'

'No, Maeve. I don't dance. Okay?'

'Ah, come on! Loosen up a little, for feck's sake! Show Max what you can do. I'm sure Max would love to see you dance, wouldn't you, Max?'

'Yes. I would,' I confess.

'Look!' Kate snaps. 'I won't dance, okay? I just . . . can't dance. Now, please leave me alone and stop bullying me!'

It's an awkward moment, but we're saved by Bill Haley. 'Rock Around The Clock' strikes up, and this sends Maeve into a nostalgic frenzy.

I notice Kate's left hand is resting on the table. Instinctively, I place mine on top of it. 'Okay?'

'I'm fine.' She takes her hand away and places it on her lap.

'Right, come on, Eugene. It's time for the tricks,' Maeve announces loudly.

'Behave yourself, woman,' he warns her. 'We haven't attempted that in over fifteen years and I'm not about to break me back trying it now.'

Maeve's stamping her foot, scraping it along the floor, like a bull about to charge. Eugene stands up, quickly. 'Maeve, come on now. You'll kill the both of us, yer daft fecker, you.'

'Are you too old, Eugene? Have you lost your manly strength?'

Kate and I look at each other, wincing at this challenge.

Eugene wipes his sweating brow. 'I'll show you who's lost his strength. I'm not ready for the knacker's yard yet. Let's be having you, girl. Full routine now, mind.'

And they're off. Maeve's jumped up to Eugene's waist, her legs splitting either side in a flash of flesh-coloured stockings and Marks and Spencer's underwear. Eugene has swung her out – now to the left hip, now to the right – back on her feet, and as the music climaxed, she's rolled over his back.

I sit whooping and cheering, like a member of an American sit-com audience. Even Kate smiles and claps, forgetting her own distress.

Eugene has collapsed into a chair. Maeve is gasping for breath, leaning against the dining-table for support. 'There's no swinger like an old swinger,' she declares, between wheezes.

'And no fool like an old fool,' Eugene counters, laughing like a drain.

I've just seen Maeve flinch.

'You all right?' I ask, casually.

She's flinched again, clutching her chest this time. 'Oh, Max,' she sighs, 'didn't I tell you I wouldn't be around for ever?'

She's gone down like a stone.

Kate has rushed to her side. She's kneeling over her, listening, first to her breath, then to her chest. Mouth to mouth, Kate to Maeve.

'Oh, no, please, God!' cries Eugene. 'Oh, please, God! Don't let her die!'

Kate is moving away from her mouth, sliding down Maeve's body, straddling her.

'Not my Maeve, not my Maeve. Please, God, no. Please, God, no!' Eugene intones, rocking back and forth.

'Get an ambulance!' Kate screams. 'Get an ambulance. Now!'

I'm pushing myself towards the kitchen and the nearest phone as hard and fast as my shocked muscles will allow me.

As I leave the room, I look back over my shoulder and see Kate desperately massaging the old woman's heart.

Part Two

Storm Tossed

16

Maeve. I've been thinking of all the words I have used to describe her over the years – a naff, writerish thing to do, I know. I've called her stubborn, bullish, gossipy, bossy, opinionated, difficult. I realise now that these are all words associated with strength. Maeve is one of those people you expect to go on steamrollering their way through life. She's a real survivor, someone who will outlive us all. That's what I believed until three nights ago.

'Critical but stable', is what the hospital have told us. A phrase you've heard a thousand times, on hundreds of news bulletins, in a thousand episodes of medical soap operas through the ages. From *Dr Kildare* to *Dr Finlay's Casebook*, from *Casualty* to *ER*.

What the fuck does that mean? About fifty-fifty in Maeve's case, from what I can gather. Eugene travelled with her to the hospital. He refused to let either Kate or me go with him. He was surprisingly definite about that. Maybe he felt that if Maeve was going to die, it was a private thing between husband and wife. He might also have been protecting her fierce pride. He's been staying at the hospital for the last two nights.

I took an executive decision not to tell Caroline and Nigel. I figured they'd already had a bellyful of human frailty. On top of which, Nigel has become increasingly fond of Maeve. They share secrets. I thought news of her heart-attack might push him over the edge.

I informed Kate of my decision, and tactfully raised the subject over the telephone with Eugene. Luckily they both agreed with me. So I told the kids Maeve was exhausted and had gone away for a rest. I hinted it was better than her staying here and making our lives a misery.

Putting on a brave face for them has meant that today is the first time I've had a moment to consider how I might feel if Maeve dies. I don't know what I would do if she wasn't there to boss me around. The thought horrifies me. She's in charge, really, running the house like a matriarch. I've missed not having her here to lean on.

Caroline has deigned to take Nigel with her to Ballinkilty this afternoon, which is a blessed relief. And Kate has been magnificent.

Her prompt first aid saved Maeve's life, at least for the moment. And since Maeve's departure, she's taken on most of the domestic chores. She always manages to leave me and the kids something to eat before she does her six o'clock disappearing act. Generally she has held things together. I knew I was right to hire her.

Speak of the devil, she's just come through my office door.

'Sorry to bother you, Max. There's a delivery van outside and a guy is asking me to sign for things, but I thought you'd better come and check the tea chests first.'

'Okay. I'll be right down,' I say, saving the notes I'd made on my computer before I leave the room.

I'm downstairs now, in the hall, checking the paperwork. 'This is fine,' I verify.

'Right, then. Where do you want this lot?' the deliveryman

asks, indicating the chests as his colleague shuffles about behind him.

'Can you just lift the lids for me a minute?'

He does so grudgingly, and I take a quick glance at the contents of each.

'Kate?'

'Yes, Max?'

'Could you lead these gentlemen up to the kids' bedrooms for me? The chest on the left is for Nigel's room, the other is for Caroline's.'

'What exactly is in them, Max?'

'It's their personal belongings. You know, bits and pieces from their home. I thought they might like to have them.'

Kate is smiling warmly at me.

'What?' I ask.

'Nothing, nothing. Just full of surprises, aren't you, Mr Patterson? Would you like me to unpack them?'

'That'd be great.'

'This way, gentlemen,' Kate instructs.

'One little thing first. Sorry to ask.' The man speaks directly to me. 'But are you *the* Max Patterson? The writer?'

I nod.

'Would you mind signing one of your books for me, please?' He pulls a rather grubby-looking paperback out of his jacket pocket.

I look at the cover. The novel is rather horribly and ironically titled *The Bleeding Hearts Society*.

I'm back in the office, reading a fan-letter from the pile Kate left for me before she changed her job spec.

There's a knock at my door, followed by the entrance of a grey-looking Eugene. He's unshaven, and his cheeks have hollowed. His shoulders, usually proudly square, have become rounded by his burden.

'Hello, my friend. How are you?' I enquire.

'I'm fine,' he replies.

'And how's the patient?' I brace myself just in case he's come to tell me the worst.

'She's still hanging in there, Max, but the prognosis is not good. 'Twas a major heart-attack, and if she lives she'll never be quite the same. She'll need to take things very easy, so. Lots o' rest.'

'Of course.'

Eugene is shuffling, uncomfortably. 'I've been thinking, Max. Maeve's not a lot of use to you now. You might be best to be looking for replacements for us both.'

'Don't be daft!'

'I'm serious, now. You have to be practical about these matters.'

'I'll find something for her to do. I'll sit her in the hallway and she can bark every time the front doorbell rings. She's fiercer than an Alsatian, and she won't crap on the parquet flooring.'

He's almost laughing as he runs his hands through his hair.

'Look, Eugene, this isn't the bloody potato famine. I'm not the bastard English landlord who's about to evict you. Bugger me, I'm the last one to give someone a hard time for being physically incapable. You two have looked after me for years. When Maeve comes out—'

'*If* she comes out, Max,' Eugene interrupts.

'*When* she comes out,' I repeat, 'she'll still have a home here, with a living wage.'

He looks choked. 'You're a good man, Max. A bloody fine man.'

'Yes, well, keep it to yourself, will you? I've an image to

maintain. Spread that nonsense around Ballinkilty, and there's a grave danger that one of the locals will buy a book. Speaking of which . . .' I hand him a large padded envelope.

'What is it?'

'It's the first half of the first draft of my new manuscript. Take it to the hospital with you. Leave it lying around, or tell Maeve you nicked it. We can't have her realising I know she reads my novels, now, can we?'

'That we can't,' he acknowledges huskily. 'Right, I must get to work.'

'Oh, be serious! Make a list of anything urgent and I'll give it to Caroline and Nigel. The exercise will do them good. Then, for heaven's sake, have a shower and a shave, and put some clean clothes on. Otherwise, when Maeve sees you, you'll be on the wrong end of a rollocking for making the doctors think she's married to a knacker.'

He nods.

'Then get your arse up to the hospital again. As soon as Maeve's fit enough, move her into a private room. She'll moan about starving children and the waste of money to your face, then behave like Lady Muck the minute you're out of earshot. Okay?' I check to see he's taking all this in.

'Okay,' he whispers.

'Right, now sod off. I've got to get some work done to pay for all this.'

He stands and heads for the door.

'Oh! One more thing before you go.' I hand him a smaller, thinner envelope. 'It's a few notes I made about that book you're writing. I suggest the priest is stabbed in the chest, not the back. That way he has access to his own blood. He sees his killer clearly. He makes the sign of the cross on the wall. This is misinterpreted as the dying act of a religious man. Then change your killer from the society woman to the schoolgirl, Marie. She attends the convent. That's why the priest paints the sign of the cross. That's your resolving clue.'

He says nothing, but his mouth is frozen in a half-smile.

'Read the notes over during a quiet moment at the hospital. Give me a ring and let me know what you think.'

Eugene nods again and makes quickly for the door without speaking. It's not that he's ungrateful. I realise that he doesn't want me to see him cry.

So the Man in Black has a heart, after all, does he? I wouldn't bank on it. I just had a bit of time to think. It's good to do something constructive with it, that's all.

I hear the sound of clumsy feet running towards the drawing room. Caroline and Nigel tumble through the door.

Why is it that every time I sneak into the drawing room for a crafty whiskey, someone catches me doing it?

'Hello, you two. Good day?'

'Yes, thanks. How's Maeve?' Caroline comes straight to the point.

They're staring at me, their eyes daring me to lie. 'You know, don't you?' I ask.

'Julie told us,' Caroline affirms.

Why didn't I think? 'I'm sorry. I didn't mean to patronise either of you. I just thought—'

'Is she very sick?' Nigel asks. His complexion is pale and his hands are clenched.

'Yes, Nigel. I won't lie to you any more.'

'Is she going to die?' The tears begin to roll down his cheeks.

I pause.

'She is, isn't she? She's going to die.'

Caroline feels for Nigel's hand and he slips it into hers. He looks terrified. Distraught.

I search for something positive to say. 'I wouldn't underestimate Maeve,' I tell him finally.

'Can I visit her?' he asks, more hopefully.

'As soon as she's up to it.'

Kate has just joined the happy throng. 'Can I butt in a minute? Paul just rang. He wanted to check if everything arrived safely.'

Did Paul ring? Or did Kate see the children on their way into the drawing room and guess the score? Either way, she's arrived like the cavalry to remind me we have a way to distract them, maybe even cheer them up.

'Right, you two,' I say, slugging back my whiskey, 'Kate and I have something to show you.'

A few minutes later and the four of us are in the corridor outside their bedrooms.

'Open your doors and you may see some things you recognise.'

I watch Nigel as he dives amongst books, a model aircraft, and fingers the posters Kate has hung on his walls.

Then I wheel myself into Caroline's room, Kate behind me. Caroline is looking around at the cuddly toys, makeup, jewellery boxes and ornaments. Then she walks over to the wardrobe where the clothes she left at home are now hanging. She turns, and something about the way she stares at me is unsettling.

Some arms have just snaked around my neck. A soft warm cheek is pressed against mine. 'Nice touch, Mr Unemotional,' Kate says, and plants a kiss on my forehead.

A warm glow washes through my body.

17

It's Friday morning and I've the house to myself. It seems ages since this happened. Kate has taken Caroline on a quick flyer down to Ballinkilty to buy groceries and have an urgent hunt for 'blusher', whatever that is, and Eugene, at Maeve's absolute insistence, has taken Nigel out for the day. He'll drop him home late afternoon and pop up to the hospital to see her this evening.

I've got a little bit of work done, and have popped down to make myself a cup of coffee. Though, of course, it won't taste the same if there's nobody here to moan at for not making it for me.

I hear the familiar thud of post hitting the flagstones on the hall floor. No Maeve, no Kate, so I suppose I'll have to go and fetch that myself as well.

I wheel myself into the hall and stop abruptly. There's a man standing in the hall. He holds my mail aloft in one hand, and flicks ash on to the floor from the cigarette he holds in the other.

I tense. 'Don't they give you a uniform, these days?'

'I'm not the frigging postman,' he grunts aggressively, checking the top of one of my letters, 'Mr Patterson.' He tosses it back on the floor.

He's tall, but then most men look tall when you're sitting down. He strokes his unshaven chin, and as he does so he teeters unsteadily for a brief second. 'Where is she?' he asks. 'Where is the slut?'

I don't suppose he's talking about Maeve.

'I said, where is the *slag*?!'

He bellows the last word, and barges past me in the direction of the kitchen. His hip catches the handlebar at the back of my chair, causing me to tilt slightly, but he didn't seem to feel it.

I follow him into the kitchen. He's turning circles, pacing. 'Are you going to tell me where she is or am I gonna have to kick the shit out of you?'

His first threat of physical violence. I'm surprised it took this long.

'She's out.'

'Who is?' He grins.

'Whoever it is you're looking for.'

He laughs. A coarse laugh. An ugly laugh. 'You know who I'm looking for, *Mr* Patterson,' he snarls, in guttural tones.

He's right. I do. He's looking for the person who last emphasised '*Mr*' – on my answering-maching not so very long ago.

'Kate! I'm looking for Kate,' he roars.

'She's not here. I'm on my own.'

'She is here. They told me she's here. She's here, all right, so don't fucking lie!' He takes a slow, pointed look around the room. 'Nice place you got here, Mr Patterson. Be a shame to see it come to any harm, now, wouldn't it?'

I notice the muscles in his arms. Developed, yes, but not much more than my own. Upper-bodywise, there's little to choose between us.

'So, are you going to tell me where she's hiding, or am I going to have to tear this house apart looking for her?'

There's the sound of the door opening, a soft voice calling, 'We're home!'

The man draws a large kitchen knife from the wooden block on the work-surface next to the Aga. The glint of the blade as it catches the light tells you just how sharp it is. 'Not a fucking word, or you're dead,' he tells me.

I hear the footsteps approaching the kitchen from behind me.

'Two of our bags split, so I left poor Caroline chasing round the grounds trying to rescue all manner of goodies.'

'Nice of you to drop in and join the party, Kate,' the man says, as she enters the room. 'Me and Mr Patterson were getting worried about you.'

I hear the groceries fall from Kate's hands to the floor.

'Oh, dear God, Séan! What are you doing here?'

'That's a nice way for a woman to greet her man. Have you not a kiss for me?' He strokes the knife suggestively.

'Séan, for heaven's sake!' I hear the fear in Kate's voice. She's seen him like this before.

'I want the money. Where's the fucking money?'

'I'm doing everything I can, you know I am. Now, will you *please* leave?'

'I can't do that because these people are hassling me. They're hassling me, and you know I *hate people hassling me!*'

'Okay, Séan, okay. Are you all right, Max? Has he hurt you?' Kate steps up beside me.

'Have *I* hurt him? Are you serious? Jeez, I know you're partial to a good length of dick, but are you telling me this is your new man? Are you fucking cripples now, Kate? That's sick!'

'Séan!' Kate's face flushes.

'That's desperate. Does it still work, then, Mr Patterson? Is it not all shrivelled up like those excuses for legs you have there?'

'Oh, God, Séan, please,' Kate begs.

'I mean, Lord knows you love a screw. If anyone knows it I do.

But this man is a fucking spastic! He must be loaded, because he's shag all else going for him.'

I see the recognition light up behind alcohol-shot eyes. 'Of course, you're the feller that writes the books. You're filthy fucking rich, and she's whoring it for money. Well, she owes me. Ran out on me and left me up to my neck in shite.' Hate blazes in his eyes. 'I tell you what, Mr Patterson. You pay me the money owing and a bit to cover my expenses, and I'll let you keep her.'

'You don't own her,' I shout.

'Ah, come on. Do you really think she'd stay with you if I'd take her back? I'm strong and virile. Ask her. I can give it to her standing up, the way she likes it. You're hardly going to be able to satisfy her like that, are you?'

'I hate you, Séan!' Kate screams.

'Pay me the money and you can have her. She's all yours.'

'Back off, you foul-mouthed pig, or I'll—'

'You'll what? Look at you! You'll what? Run me over?'

Now he really shouldn't have said that.

He pulls back the hand holding the knife. 'Shit, if I threw this knife at your chest you'd be dead. How would you get out the way, you fucking half-man, you?'

Think, Max, think. You write about terror, about fear. Use it, for crying out loud.

'Don't hurt me,' I whimper.

'Oh, not so tough now, are we?' He smirks.

'Please don't hurt him, Séan. Please.'

He's walking towards me, brandishing the blade. 'I could do what I liked and there's nothing you could do about it.'

'Please, I'll do anything, anything,' I beg. Reel him in, Max. Reel him in.

'I bet you would. Anything. Right, Mr Patterson?'

'Yes, anything. Whatever you say, Séan.'

'Mr Brennan, to you,' he says, stepping closer.

Keep coming, keep coming. Just a bit closer. 'Yes, Mr Brennan. Sir.'

Shit! He's moved too fast. A burst of speed and he's stooped down and grabbed my shirt, the blade pointed at my throat, his face directly in front of mine. How drunk is he, I wonder.

'NO, SÉAN, NO!' Kate screams, sobbing.

'If you leave now, I'll give you your cash,' I whisper. He must relax, he must relax for a second.

'You'll give me any amount of money I ask for, won't you, Max?'

'Yes,' I promise.

More footsteps. Another voice. 'It took me ages to gather everything up. The wind had blown everything all over the drive and – what's going on?' I hear Caroline's voice rising with fear. But it's distraction enough.

As she enters, Séan looks up. His face is out of mine, the blade has moved to the left, and his upper body is now perfectly in line. I ball my fist and put my full bodyweight behind an upper-cut.

Connection. A beauty. Right on the chin. His head snaps back, and he hits the floor like a sack of coal, his head bouncing back off the flagstones, the knife skittering across the kitchen floor out of his reach.

'Oh . . . Jeez . . . fuck . . .' He clutches his lower jaw, then lies still.

'Max! That was fantastic!' Caroline yells.

'Sorry, Kate,' I find myself saying.

'Oh, God, Max, thank you. I wished I'd done that years ago.' She is crying and laughing at the same time. I want to hold her, to comfort her. 'Do you want this arsehole in your life any more?' I ask instead.

'No, Max. Please, no.'

'Right. Take Caroline into the drawing room.'

'Max, that was *fantastic*,' Caroline repeats.

'Take her into the drawing room and call the Guards.'

'No,' Séan groans from the floor, 'not the Guards. I'm drunk, I'm just drunk.'

'Okay, Caroline, let's go,' Kate urges, and they leave.

'Now, my friend.' I concentrate on Séan. 'I reckon we have ten minutes max before the Guards arrive. You're up for breaking and entering, assault, and threatening behaviour with a deadly weapon, to name but a few. You've some fast talking to do, especially if you want me to tell the Gardai that it was all a misunderstanding.'

He sits up, still holding his jaw. Eyeing me suspiciously, he senses a way out. 'All right,' he begins. 'What do you want to know?'

The Guards have gone, taking Séan with them. He's been charged with being drunk and abusive, and will get away with a strong telling-off, no more. 'Unless there's anything else you'd like to tell us, Mr Patterson,' the Guards say, as they leave.

Kate has come into the kitchen. I've just poured myself a celebratory coffee from the filter machine.

'Can I come in?' she asks.

'Of course you can.'

'I thought you might not want to see me.' She hovers in the doorway.

'Why ever not?'

'I think I'd better leave,' she suggests. 'I just nearly cost you your life.' She is breathing erratically and nervously.

'I didn't go through all that just to lose another secretary-cum-cook-cum-childminder, so don't be bloody ridiculous!'

'At least let me explain, Max. I owe you that.'

'Grab a coffee, and come and sit down.'

She crosses to the filter machine.

'How's Caroline?' I ask, as she pours herself a cup.

'Fine, except now she thinks you're John Wayne.' She walks across to join me at the kitchen table.

'Her knight in shining wheelchair, eh?'

She smiles. It's such a lovely smile. 'I met Séan in England,' she begins. 'He wasn't as he is now when I met him. He was very sweet, and full of charm, and ... sober. I didn't notice the drinking. Maybe I didn't want to. It didn't become a problem until we moved here and bought the smallholding together. Suddenly he didn't want to work. He drank, gambled, stole. Then he became violent. We had to sell the farm because we couldn't make it pay.'

'The way land prices are around here, you must have made a profit, surely?' I enquire.

'Yes, but we didn't have it long enough to make a huge difference, and by then Séan had run up enough debts to soak up any equity left after the mortgage was paid back.'

I take a sip from my cup.

'It didn't end there. We split up but we had a joint bank account.'

'And Séan's run up an overdraft of ten thousand on it,' I interrupt to save her pain.

'How did you know?' she asks, astonished.

'I had a word with your man.'

'He's not my man. He hasn't been for ages. I know Caroline saw us together in the bar, but we were just talking. The bank are chasing us, and Séan wanted me to pay his half as well. I've been working at the pub as a barmaid to get the extra cash to try to resolve the situation.'

'Haven't you talked to your bank?'

'Yes, but it's a joint account. They don't care who's paying it back, or who's spent the money, and Séan just keeps turning up and threatening me.'

She's sobbing.

'Please don't cry, Kate. I hate to see you cry.'

'Oh,' she says, taken aback by the honesty of my statement. 'Do you? Sorry.' She takes an exaggerated breath in an effort to stop.

'Right. Here's what's going to happen. I'm going to pay off the overdraft.'

'That's so kind of you, Max, but I can't possibly let you do that.'

'You can't really stop me. It's a joint account and Séan had no trouble accepting the offer. As you said, the bank couldn't give a toss who pays the money back as long as somebody does.'

'Max—'

'I don't want you to have to pay it back, but if it makes you feel better, I'll stop a bit out of your wages every month until it's paid off and, remember, I won't be charging interest.'

'Ten thousand. That could take years.'

'Five thousand. The other half is down to Séan.'

Kate shakes her head. 'He'll never pay you back a penny, Max.'

'It doesn't really matter. I've insisted he signs a legal document stating he owes me five thousand pounds. I also told him I might be inclined to forget chasing that money, as long as he never comes near you again without your permission. If he does, I'll bankrupt the son-of-a-bitch.'

Kate lets out an explosive giggle, before putting her hand to her mouth to stop it. 'Oh, Max!' she says. 'Thank you.' She puts her hand on top of mine.

'My pleasure. I hope you don't think I was taking liberties.'

She's still smiling, but her eyes narrow a little. 'You knew exactly what you were doing when Séan threatened you, didn't you? When you acted scared. You wanted him to get closer so you could hit him.'

I open my eyes wide. 'Now what makes you think I would be that devious?'

'You were pretending, weren't you?'

I sigh. 'I believe when Muhammad Ali fought George Forman he called it rope-a-dope.'

She giggles again, her pretty nose wrinkling.

'Anyway, I only clobbered him to save my backside,' I inform her.

'Really?' she queries.

'Naturally. I have a nasty streak in me.'

'Or a protective one,' she counters firmly.

'Maybe,' I concede, but I have to look away from her as I do so. You see, I can't stop thinking about what Séan said to me. The plain truths he shouted in drunken anger. Maybe it *is* sick for a woman like Kate to want to make love to a man in a chair. I never thought about it before. I couldn't take her standing up, and I might not be able to satisfy her, or protect her as easily as he could.

I am suddenly terrified that one day there will be another Séan, and this one will not only be strong and virile, but kind and loving too.

18

A wind of change has swept through the house since Séan was given his marching orders. With Maeve absent, Kate has become 'the woman of the house'. The large scrubbed-pine table in the kitchen is covered with a fresh blue-and-white checked table-cloth and, at its centre, a vase stands filled with wild fuchsia, Rose of Shannon and harebells. Napkins are folded elegantly into wine-glasses and instead of conversations in which various factions try to negotiate the peace after a civil war, there is laughter and warmth during mealtimes.

Over the last few days, this new atmosphere has spread through the house faster than fleas off a cat's back. Vases of flowers became visible in the drawing room and in the hall, and they even put in the odd guest appearance in the downstairs loo. And the heavy curtains I have always kept closed have been swung open to let in the soft Irish light.

It's more than this, though. Kate's natural air of calm and ease has returned. It's as if the house and those who reside within it are gradually waking up. Becoming alive.

Perhaps none more so than the owner.

So, in response to this and the way certain people have coped with recent traumas, and to the uncharacteristically hot West Cork weather, I've made the ultimate sacrifice. Despite screams from across the pond from my publishing house, I've abandoned working for the day and nobly decided to accompany Kate, Caroline and Nigel to the beach.

Kate has been filling the children's heads with beauteous descriptions of a large beach called Inchydoney, two miles from Ballinkilty. I've sent everyone off to get ready and it's taken them hours. I'm now rolling around the corridors rallying the troops. As I head for the children's rooms, Nigel emerges in blue Bermuda-type shorts and grey T-shirt.

'What kept you?' I ask as he passes me.

'I'm here now, aren't I? See you downstairs.'

'Is your sister nearly ready?'

'Dunno.' He carries on walking.

I knock on Caroline's door. 'You nearly ready to roll, Caroline? Only I was a young man when I suggested this trip.'

'Come in a sec.' A voice beckons from within.

I use the front wheels of the chair to push the door further ajar and enter the room. Caroline stands before me in a plain, Persil-white bikini.

'What do you think, Max?' she asks.

'About what?'

'Only, I can't decide—' She is standing in front of a full-length, free-standing mirror, which is tilted slightly backwards. She is twisting and turning, looking at herself from all conceivable angles. She then contorts herself to try and catch a glimpse of her backside.

'Exactly which monumental decision are you wrestling with, Caroline?'

'I don't know which one to wear.' She is still playing a solo game of Twister in front of the mirror.

'Which bikini, you mean?'

'Yes.'

'Wear the other one,' I instruct her firmly.

She turns from the mirror to look at me. 'But you haven't even seen it yet.'

'I don't have to. You're thinking of going for a swim.'

'Of course.'

'Then that costume is a no-no. It'll be completely see-through by the time you come out.'

'Max, you prude.' Her reflection grins at me from the mirror. 'It doesn't matter, does it?'

'Not on a beach in Spain. But if you walk out of the water at Inchydoney showing off your bits and pieces, it's a bit different. The women will immediately brand you a hussy, and the men will have to go to confession and declare impure thoughts.'

'The trouble is,' she moans, looking at herself again, 'my other bikini is too small. Look. I'll show you.'

And she takes off her bikini top.

I don't know where to put my face. Luckily, she isn't looking at me. Instead she searches for her other bikini under her duvet, then bends down and ferrets under the bed.

If I wasn't so completely lapsed, I might be at the head of the confessional queue this week. However, I defy any man to have a pretty blonde topless teenager in front of him and be able to control his response completely – unless, of course, he is related. And that's the point. Technically, I'm not.

'Here it is,' Caroline announces, retrieving the bikini top and, to my great relief, putting it on. 'What do you think, Max?'

'It's perfect,' I bluster.

'Really?'

'Absolutely.'

'Oh. Okay. I'll change the bottoms on the beach as we're in a rush. And don't worry, I'll wrap a towel around me,' Caroline says before I can object. She picks up a sun-dress and slips it over her head.

'Come on then, slowcoach.' She turns to me and smiles. 'Now you're holding everybody up.' And she heads for the bedroom door.

It could be that, as a young thing of the nineties, Caroline has no hang-ups about nudity. It could be a sign that she is beginning to accept me as a father substitute. A sign she is settling down.

Alternatively, she might have known where the bikini top was all along and simply been testing my reaction.

Nah! My imagination is running away with me.

We're at Inchydoney beach. It's a large expanse of fine, light-coloured sand, edged by cliffs. The sea beyond is rarely less than restless, and often aggressive.

The tide is a long way out, and as you walk towards it, the sand changes to hard and firm and uneven, as if a thousand tractors had raced on it the night before. Or so I am told. I don't venture very far myself.

I sit here watching Kate and Caroline making their way towards the water. I'm not swimming myself. With no functioning legs to give me the necessary propulsion, I'm generally reduced to flapping my arms about and turning round in circles. I have company, however.

Nigel is in front of me, sitting on the sand through which he sulkily runs his toes.

'Why don't you brave the water as well, Nigel?'

'Don't want to.'

'Why not?'

He shrugs. Does a lot of shrugging, does Nigel.

'Go on, it'd do you good.'

'No.'

'Keep you fit,' I suggest.

'So?'

'Build your muscles.'

'So?'

'Stop you getting fat.'

'So?'

'You never know your luck, Nigel. There may be some gorgeous piece of totty out there, desperate to be rescued.'

'No, Max,' he snaps, throwing a shell he's been toying with into the distance. 'Look! I can't swim. Satisfied now?' There's a mixture of shame and anger in his voice.

'Sorry. I didn't know.'

'Well, now you do,' he says, looking away.

'Didn't they teach you at school?'

Pause. 'I used to take a note,' he confesses after a while.

I have an image of Jamie racking his brains for eight years once a week for viruses that would be made critical by contact with water. The sudden memory of my friend sends a shudder of sadness through me. I remember he is dead. Drowned. I look out to sea, and then at Nigel. Jamie couldn't swim either.

'If you've never had a lesson, how do you know you can't swim?' I query, when things have steadied down inside me.

Another bloody shrug.

'You might be a born fish, for all you know.'

'Not bothered.'

'Look, you'll never get anywhere in life unless you try, Nigel. I mean, you can't even fail gloriously unless you have a go.' I catch my breath. I'm actually sounding like a caricature parent now. 'I tell you what. There's a new leisure centre in Ballinkilty. I'll pay for you and Caroline to join. You can take swimming lessons. Find out if you're any good at it.'

'Maybe.'

Two ladies are sprinting towards us at championship speeds. Correction. One girl and one woman.

Kate looks gorgeous. I must confess, after I left Caroline I considered knocking on Kate's door, hoping she was having difficulty choosing a bikini as well.

Now she stands before me, next to Caroline, dripping and shivering. There is not an ounce of spare flesh on her. Her lithe, petite body is toned and in perfect proportion. I can't take my eyes off her. It's as if she were a mirage conjured up by my mind, and that if I were to lose concentration she would break up and disappear. As they reach us I become aware that most other men on the beach are watching her too.

'Nigel, could you pass us our towels, p-p-please?' Kate asks, through chattering teeth.

'Touch chilly, was it?' I ask, smiling.

'Freezing,' Caroline affirms.

I needn't have asked. The nipple count tells the story. 'Tell you what, get changed and I'll take us back into town and buy everyone a drink to toast your bravery.'

Convulsive nods in response.

'I'll start the long haul back to the car now. Meet you at the top.'

'Won't you need some help?' Caroline asks, with concern.

'I'll take Nigel. He can bail me out if necessary. That okay with you?' I ask him.

'S'pose,' he mumbles, standing up.

'That's what I admire about you, Nigel. The way you refuse to do things under sufferance.' I claw my way upright, and lead with my crutches.

I can't stay, not while they change. I'm too embarrassed and, if I'm honest, I feel suddenly shy. And this time it has nothing to do with Caroline.

*

We've discovered why Ballinkilty is so busy: there's a country-and-western festival.

Ballinkilty has a thriving live music scene. When they're not playing cowboy crap, there's a couple of decent local bands. But today they're playing on the streets, and in just about every bar in town. Hot dogs and baked beans are being cooked on the pavements, people are wearing Stetsons and tasselled jackets, and toting six-guns. For a change, I don't look out of place. If you gave me a waistcoat to go with my hat and the rest of the black I am wearing, I'd look ideal on the fake 'Wanted' posters plastered all over town.

Anyway, all this has given me the excuse for a bit of a pub crawl. We've been into two or three bars, and as Caroline found Julie and a crowd of friends at the second pub, it's now just the Three Musketeers – Kate, Nigel and, by this stage, a quite nicely soused Max.

There's a large crowd in front of one particular pub, and the sound of cheering and clapping. I lead the way forward to discover what's going on. One advantage of being in a chair is that it has the same effect as shouting, 'Lady with a baby!': people get out of your way. I've never been quite sure if this happens out of compassion, pity, embarrassment, or whether they just don't want you to break their toes as you run over their feet. If you add to this the fact that it's a rare visit to town by the wicked Man in Black, they move twice as quickly.

As I and my party are allowed through to the front of the crowd, I see a bucking-bronco machine – in other words, an electronically operated saddle that whips and spins to simulate the movement of an unbroken stallion. There's a rather fat lady, squawking and hanging on for dear life, as we watch. She falls off, not surprisingly, on to the large area of mats designed to cushion the fall.

Big applause and laughter.

'Right, who's after trying their luck next, then?' barks Jack the Lad in charge. 'Any man in the mood now, after a couple o' pints for a short, sharp ride? Any lady wish to put her years of experience to the test by breaking in another stud?' He reels off the patter with indigenous charm.

I have an idea, and I look closely at Nigel. Even though he's among us, he never actually feels as if he's with us. It's as if he's withdrawn inside himself to deal with his worries, and his grief.

'Nigel, my man,' I begin, smiling at him, 'you're the lad for the job. Why don't you show them how it's done?'

'Very funny.' He frowns.

'I'm serious. I have every confidence in you.'

'Just leave it.'

'Come on, Nigel, it's only a bit of fun.'

'Not to me, it's not.'

'You can do it.'

'Says who?' He folds his arms across his chest.

A twenty-something butch sod has finished the ride, still astride it, to cheers and chants from his friends.

'Who's next, then?'

If I get this wrong, I'm never going to drink another pint or six of Beamish Red as long as I live. 'Right, then,' I say, as I wheel myself forward.

'Max, where are you going?' I hear Kate cry from behind me. 'Max!'

'Ah, no!' Jack the Lad objects as I approach. 'I'm not insured for someone like you, now.'

'Someone like me!' I cry. 'Don't be so ... *wheelist*! That's discrimination. There's a law against that, you know.'

'Is there?' He appears confused.

'Indeed. I could take you to court over that.'

He's looking around him, scouting the crowd for a superior to confirm or deny this. 'I just don't want you to hurt yourself, so.'

'Don't be daft. My legs are shot to pieces as it is. There's less chance of me injuring myself than all these other dozy gits.'

He's still unsure, so I brandish a tenner. 'I don't need your insurance. Now keep the change and help me on to this bloody thing.'

He does as he's instructed.

I'm up. After a fashion. The trouble is, I can't grip with my legs. Neither am I going to attempt to wave my hat in the air with my spare hand. Both my arms will be strictly reserved for the function of hanging on for dear life.

Whoa! Here we go.

'Max, hold on, just hold on!' I hear Kate scream above the general hubbub.

Actually, it's not too bad. It's a sort of rhythmic circle and if you concentrate it's – Oh, bloody hell! It's speeding up.

At this point it's a toss-up which way I shame myself first: (a) fly arse-over-tit immediately; (b) vomit over the two-year-old girl in her brand-new party dress at the front of the crowd; (c) give public credence to the myth that all people in wheelchairs are incontinent.

And the winner is?

A!

I hit the mats with a sickening thud. Uncertain applause peters out around me.

'Are you all right? Are you hurt?' Kate is kneeling beside me, and I glow at her obvious concern.

'Of course I am. I only fell three feet.'

'A *tour de force* of grace and balance.' She applauds.

Jack the Lad helps Kate load me back into my chair, shaking his head as he does so.

Before I can thank them, Nigel is beside me, his face flushed with anger. 'You stupid, stupid man! Why did you do that? Why?'

'Because—'

'You could have been seriously injured,' he shouts. 'You could have been killed!'

'Hardly, Nigel.'

'You knew you couldn't do it, didn't you? Not without legs that work. You knew you couldn't do it!'

'No, not exactly. How could I? I'd never tried. So I had a go, didn't I? And who knows? I might have been wrong. I might have taken to it like a duck to water, Nigel. And at least I bloody well tried!'

We're glaring at each other now. For the first time since he arrived, his eyes look bright and alive.

'All right, all right!' he says. 'I'll take the swimming lessons, okay? Just don't do anything like that again.'

'You're the boss,' I reply. 'Now, is anyone going to help me out of this crowd? Or are you going to bring me my pint out here?'

'Come on, John Wayne. Now you've got off your horse, let's get you some milk.' Kate smiles an open, generous smile. It's an offer I can't refuse.

19

It's early evening and I am nicely mellowed out on a mixture of Beamish Red and a very acceptable South African Pinotage. If I'm bruised after my tumble earlier today, it is anaesthetised by just the right levels of alcohol swimming around the relevant areas of my brain.

We eventually located Caroline in a pub garden in the midst of a group of cider-swilling teenagers.

'I thought you didn't like alcohol,' I barked at her.

'I don't. I'm drinking Cidona,' she said, offering me her glass to sniff. She was telling the truth.

It was then I noticed a young oik had his arm around her. I shot him a withering glance and he let it slip from her shoulder.

'And who was he?' I asked her as we left.

'Alan.'

'Well, you just behave yourself, young lady,' I warned her.

'He's just a friend. He was only giving me a hug. Not jealous, are you, Max?'

'Why would I be?'

'No reason,' she replied. 'He's good-looking, though, don't you think?'

'I wouldn't know,' I replied.

'Oh,' she said softly. 'I just thought you might have noticed.' And she hurried on ahead of me to where Nigel was beating the trail.

Then we headed back home and Kate, bless her, cooked us a meal. So now we're eating supper together. The four of us.

I watch Kate serving mounds of pasta on to the plates and I feel a sudden empathy for normality. Mum, Dad and two kids. How it must feel to glance up suddenly and notice how the one you care about is looking after you.

The thing is, I never ate a proper meal with my own family. I would be fed separately by my mother before my father returned to claim her from me, and then I was sent off to play by myself. So this is rather nice.

Anyway, there's something I need to discuss. 'Listen, you two, what are your feelings about school?'

I watch them turn to look at each other. It's a what's-he-getting-at-now look. A we'd-better-be-careful-what-we-say-here telepathic exchange.

'It's fine,' replies Nigel.

'I've never been that struck with it myself,' Caroline confesses.

I refill Kate's wine-glass as she places our supper on the table to make me feel less guilty about topping up my own.

'I don't mean in general,' I continue. 'I'm talking specifically about your schooling. From this day forth, as it were. I've had a letter from your boarding-school. They want to know if you're going back next year. I wondered how you felt about that.'

Nigel is looking at his feet, as if he were in the presence of an ancient emperor.

'We . . .' Caroline glances at the top of Nigel's head. 'I don't know. I hadn't thought about it.'

I sense Kate observing the three of us, as if trying to decide whether to follow her natural instinct and help, or remain quiet.

'If the letter hadn't arrived the other morning, the subject would never have entered my head either.'

'Why do the school want to know about next year? I mean, what about September?' Caroline asks.

'Well, you have to give a term's notice. I suppose it was just presumed you would go back for this coming term.'

'Oh,' she says, quietly.

There's an awkward silence. I take a mouthful of food to plug the hiatus.

'Out of curiosity,' Kate says, feigning ignorance, while kick-starting the dialogue like a theatrical prompt, 'what exactly are the options, Max?'

'Well,' I begin, picking up my cue, 'as I see it, either you go back to your old school or you can go to school here.'

'It's a tricky decision, though, isn't it?' It's Kate again. 'I mean, poor Caroline and Nigel have only been here five minutes, and now you're asking them to decide whether they want to stay here in Ireland or go back to England in term-time.'

There's a change in the air. Nigel is still staring blankly, but Caroline's stare is more searching.

'It's up to you,' Nigel submits.

I feel Kate squeeze my hand under the table, which startles me. I realise it's a warning.

'Tell you what. Why don't you to go back to your old school in England in September as per usual? If,' I qualify hastily, 'this would make you happy. In the meantime, I can investigate the options here. Then, when you're both a bit more settled, we can sit down and kick it around again when we have all the facts at our disposal. How does that sound?'

'Fine.' Nigel gives his familiar shrug.

I catch Kate's expression from the corner of my eyeline. She nods in agreement, and also encouragement.

'Actually, I might like to be in Ireland,' Caroline says. 'I mean, it's not good for us to keep moving from country to country, so it might be better if I stay here, wouldn't it, Max?'

I stay. Not *we* stay.

'Wouldn't it be better? If I stayed? Wouldn't you like that, Max?' Her gaze is oddly intense.

'May we leave the table and go to our rooms now?' Nigel asks, taking a retrograde step.

Caroline flashes an annoyed glance in his direction. It's usually Caroline who plays this hand.

'If you like,' I reply.

They slink away from Kate and me, thanking her politely for the supper as they go.

'Oh, God! I'm not up for this parenting malarkey. I'm so ham-fisted with it.'

'You don't seem to be doing such a bad job from where I'm sitting,' Kate informs me.

'Really?'

'Seriously. It was nice of you to give the kids the option. I seem to remember having a distinct lack of say in such matters when I was their age. It's a difficult time though, your teens. You're neither a child nor an adult, so nobody can baby you, but they can't give you the freedom to make your own decisions either.'

'I hadn't thought of it like that,' I disclose, taking a consoling mouthful of South African grape.

'That surprises me, frankly, because most of the things you've done for Caroline and Nigel seem well thought through.'

'Not really.'

'I'm referring to you shipping their personal possessions over here, comforting Caroline after her nightmares—'

'Who told you that?'

'I have my spies everywhere,' she replies, smiling. 'Look at your performance today,' she continues. 'That act of foolish bravery on the bucking bronco. Didn't you know what you were doing?'

'You're being very sweet, Kate. But the facts are—'

'That you are not the bastard you pretend to be!' she declares, with a firmness that makes me catch my breath. 'Why do pretend you are, Max?'

'I don't,' I reply, reeling.

'Yes, you do, and I can't understand why. Look at what you've done for Caroline and Nigel.'

'I haven't—'

'Not to mention the way you've responded to Maeve and Eugene's crisis.'

'I've only done what I thought was right to people who have been decent to me – to Jamie and Maeve. Some sense of duty, or something . . .'

She runs her fingers around the rim of her wine-glass. 'Why won't you admit you care, Max? What would be so wrong with that?'

Now I'm fingering my own wine-glass in agitation. 'It's just not me, that's all.'

'But it *is*, Max. Everything I've witnessed since I came here tells me that. What's wrong with emotions? Why won't you allow yourself to – to feel?'

'I do. Well, maybe I don't. I just can't handle these things very well.'

She looks directly into my eyes. 'Is it because you blame yourself for your mother's death?'

I'm glowering at Kate. Why did she say that? What fucking business is it of hers? I look away from her.

'I'm really sorry, Max. I warned you what I was like. I've gone too far.' I hear her chair scrape the ground as she rises. 'I'll go to bed.'

'No. Don't go. Please. I'm being oversensitive. I guess I'm in the habit of being defensive about it. Please. Stay.' I lift my eyes to look at her again.

'Okay.' She sits back down. 'I really didn't mean to be nosy. I just want to help.'

'Do you?' I ask, wanting to believe it's true.

She nods.

There is a pause while I steel myself. I look into Kate's eyes, wondering if it's right to admit to something I've never told another soul.

'You're right. I have spent over thirty years believing I'm a murderer, that I killed my mother and destroyed my father's life.'

'Max, Max.' Kate leans over, puts her arms round my shoulders, and kisses me lightly on the top of my head. The tenderness of her gesture causes a blockage in my throat, and I feel the back of my eyes begin to sting. 'You're so hard on yourself, sweetheart. I've watched the way you are with Caroline and Nigel, and you're doing a fantastic job in impossible circumstances. You'll make a wonderful father yourself one day.'

'Sweetheart', 'wonderful father'. Instead of 'bastard', 'useless son'.

'I'm sorry,' I say, forcing the words up past my aching throat. 'Too much booze.'

'Don't be afraid to show emotion, Max. I know men are scared by it but,' she takes my hands in hers, 'don't be. Follow your heart for a change.'

'Really?'

'Yes.'

I'm looking into her eyes, moving my face to meet hers, shaking, sinking, without a life-jacket. And I'm not sure I can hold my breath long enough ever to surface safely again. I watch the soft lips part slightly. And then I kiss her.

Suddenly she pulls her mouth away abruptly and stands up. It is the first graceless movement I have seen her make since she arrived.

'Oh, God, I'm sorry Max, I shouldn't have . . . I mean . . . it's not your fault . . . I'm just . . . I'm sorry. Please forgive me.'

She runs from the kitchen. As she exits, she collides with Eugene in the doorway. A brief apology, and she's gone.

'Not interrupting, am I, now?'

'No!' I reply, too abruptly.

'I was just after wondering would I be in time to steal a morsel or two of dessert off your plates?'

'Sit down and help yourself.' I feel devastated. It's the booze, I tell myself. It fools our brains, hearts and bodies into responding to the emotion of a given moment. Once that moment has passed, we're left with the cold, clinical facts, however unpleasant they may be.

Eugene, a plate loaded with cake, sits in the chair opposite.

'How's Maeve?' I ask.

'She can come home in a couple of days, Max. But she's not the same, you understand. The woman needs rest and care and attention.'

'Of course.'

'Look, Max, you've been very kind, but—'

'Listen to me, Eugene, Maeve will come back here. This is her home. We'll all rally round. Me, Kate, the kids. We'll ship in outside assistance, if necessary. Now stop worrying.'

'She'll not be a help but a burden to you now.'

'Yeah, well, she's carried me for long enough. Now, cut the self-pity. Lord knows, there's far too much of that in this house as there is.'

He stares at me briefly, then nods and slaps me on the shoulder. 'Goodnight, Max,' he says, as he too goes upstairs to bed.

20

The dragon woman returns today.

There's an air of apprehension in the house. Kate has scrubbed the place from top to bottom, roping the kids in to help. She has also filled Maeve's room with beautiful flowers.

Nigel is completely overexcited. In a dour, static, Nigel sort of a way but, nevertheless, he has actually shown signs of life, tripping over his words as he speaks, and from time to time allowing his face to break into a smile.

Kate has moved out of the room she occupied next to Maeve and Eugene in case she disturbs them, and into the Medieval Room, which just happens to be the bedroom opposite mine.

There's been no repeat of the other night, which is just as well. No excess of alcohol almost tricking people into behaving recklessly.

There's a knock on the drawing-room door.

'Come in,' I call, though I know who it is. Caroline and Nigel no longer bother knocking. Kate's head has appeared. 'Maeve and Eugene have arrived, Max.'

'Oh, good. I'm on my way.' I wheel myself into the hall, but I can't see much as Kate, Caroline and Nigel are directly in my line of vision.

I can hear the chorus of voices welcoming her home, and over Caroline's shoulder I can see Eugene's tall figure. He looks strained and flushed. I wink at him and he smiles wanly. 'Would you mind letting yer man through?' he asks everyone.

It's ridiculous, really. The hall is massive yet everyone is bunched in just a few feet of it.

I wheel myself forward until I am faced by Maeve. And I mean faced. Her eyeline is but an inch or two lower than my own. Her brown eyes are blackened and hollow, and her skin is like dried parchment. She looks considerably thinner and very frail.

I confess to being shocked. Not by her physical deterioration, but by something else altogether. You see, the reason she is almost at the same height is because she is sitting in a wheelchair. This has thrown me out of kilter somewhat. I suspect the incongruity of the situation has just hit her too.

The difference, of course, is she will get out of that chair one day. It is merely a sign of her present physical weakness. But I won't and, for a brief moment, I hate her for it. A second later, I loathe myself for being so fucking selfish.

'Snap!' I say.

There's a small smile in return at life's little ironies.

'Welcome home.'

'Thank you,' she replies softly.

'I suppose this means you expect me to let you off cooking supper this evening?'

'If you wouldn't mind, now?'

'Seeing as it's you. It's good to have you back. I sort of missed you.'

'Is that right?'

'Yes. Well, I've had to wash my own socks, haven't I?'

'You have not!' Kate cries, giving me a playful tap on the head.

179

'Oh? Washing your socks for you now, is she, Max?'

I smile. 'I see your recent health problems haven't loosened your grip on that wooden spoon of yours, Maeve.'

She nods.

Eugene senses Maeve's emotional discomfort. 'If it's okay with you, Max, would it be all right if I took her for a bit of a lie-down? It's been a big morning for the ol' girl.'

'Eugene! Let the poor woman get in the door before you rip her bloomers off, will you?'

A genuine smile from Maeve. 'I see that mind of yours is as depraved as ever it was,' she tells me.

'Well, I've not had you around to spring-clean it for me. And you know how filth settles if you don't take a duster to it occasionally.'

'Right, I'll lead the way,' Eugene announces, as he points the wheelchair in the direction of the ramp next to the stairs.

As Eugene wheels Maeve past me, I notice she's crying. I've never seen her do that before. Not in ten years.

I turn my chair around and see Nigel leaning against the wall. He looks pale.

'You all right?' I ask.

He nods, though I'm certain he's lying.

'Come on, don't write the old buzzard off yet. I'm relying on you to cheer her up.' I crook my finger in a gesture of beckoning and he crosses over to me. 'Let her have a quick rest,' I whisper into his ear. 'Then I'll get Kate to make a bacon sandwich. You take it up to Maeve, and pretend you cooked it yourself, right? That way she'll eat it.'

'Okay.' He stands straight and looks me in the eye. I can see the faintest twinkle.

'We're going to have to box very clever, you and I, if we're going to get that stubborn mule running this house again.' I wink at him. 'Off you go. Come and find me in about an hour's time, okay?'

It's about half past eleven at night and I've spent the day trying to work, but my concentration has collapsed, fragmented. I keep worrying about Maeve, and Kate keeps creeping into my inner vision. I can't seem to stop thinking about her, wondering what she's doing, where she is, what she's thinking.

I was just about to get into bed, and then I realised I've left the manuscript of today's work back in the office. I want to check through it before I go to sleep. So, feeling energetic, I grab my crutches, teeter my way out into the corridor – and bump into Kate. She's just returned from the bathroom, and is clutching a sponge-bag under her left arm. She's wearing a long creamy nightdress, and is barefoot. Her hair flows around her shoulders, and her face, lit by the soft light in the corridor, shines with beauty. She looks lovely, more innocent than any fictional virgin I have created, more sensual than any heroine.

'Why are you staring at me like that, Max?' she asks me.

'I'm sorry. I've never seen you in your nightdress before,' I reply stupidly.

'I should hope not, otherwise I'd be checking my bedroom walls for peepholes.'

I smile nervously. There is a short pause.

'Goodnight, Max. Sleep well.' And she gently blows me a kiss from the palm of her upturned hand. Her bedroom door closes.

I've shut my eyes in frustration at the sense of an opportunity, a critical moment, slipping by.

I haven't slept properly for the last three nights. I think I'm going mad. I can't settle to anything. I can't write. I've stopped eating. All I do all day, all fucking night, is think about Kate.

I've just pushed another full plate of food away. The children have made breakfast this morning, under Eugene's supervision. It's a special treat for Maeve, who takes a lot of coaxing out of her room.

As the plates are being collected, scraped and smashed by Nigel, Maeve has whispered into my ear. 'Would you be kind enough to do us a favour, Max?'

'What's that?' I ask.

'Could you spare us half an hour? I could do with a break from all this care and concern. I'm beginning to feel like a child whom the grown-ups don't want to talk freely in front of. Do you understand what I'm saying?'

'I know exactly.' I smile wryly. 'Have they started talking above your head yet? Or speaking slowly and loudly to you as if English were your second language and the batteries in your hearing-aid were low?'

'Yes!' she confirms, a flicker of relief on her face at the discovery of an ally.

'Right, my angel.' Eugene claps his hands together. 'Will yer come wit' me upstairs and sort out your medication?'

'Will you feck off? Can you not see I'm in the middle of a conversation?'

Eugene looks startled.

'Maeve and I are going to have a pot of coffee together in the drawing room, Eugene.'

'Fine, fine. I'll make the—'

'Why don't you go and give the grass a long-overdue mow, and I'll make sure Maeve takes her narcotics,' I promise him.

He fidgets uncomfortably. 'Will I bring a pot of Supervalu's finest blend through to you?' Eugene asks, a little nervously.

'That would be very good of you, my man,' I say, grandly.

'Well, now, I'll just wheel Maeve into the drawing room.'

'No, you won't,' I tell him, firmly. 'The lazy bugger can do it herself.'

Maeve looks at me in surprise.

'Right, Mrs MacEoin, it is time for your first driving lesson. These are your engine,' I instruct, holding up my hands to illustrate, 'which you place on your steering-wheels, here.' I put my hands on the metal hoops which run around the outside of my wheelchair. 'To go forward you spin the wheels this way, and to reverse the opposite way.' I give a brief, practical demonstration. 'To turn left, you spin the right wheel. To turn right, you spin the left wheel. Is that clear?'

'No,' she replies.

'Well, don't worry, you'll pick it up as we go along. The most important thing to learn is the emergency stop. This is achieved by pulling one's hands on the steering-wheels in the opposite direction to which you are travelling. *Comprende?*'

'So simple a chimpanzee could master it.'

'You will initiate the emergency stop upon my signal, which I will give to you now. WATCH WHERE YOU'RE BLOODY GOING, YOU DOZY COW!'

She's laughing.

'Okay, Mrs MacEoin. I want you to reverse away from the table, checking over your shoulders before you start the manoeuvre.'

She does this and crashes straight into the Welsh dresser.

'I see I'm dealing with someone with natural aptitude here. Okay, left-hand turn.'

This becomes a right-hand turn.

'Left Maeve, left! You're facing the wrong way.'

'What do you expect, you fecking slave-driver? I'm not wearing my wedding ring,' she notifies me.

'What's that got to do with it?' I ask.

'How else does a girl tell her right from her left, you ignoramus?'

'It's the opposite way, trust me.'

She turns, one hundred and eighty degrees.

'Perfect.'

No, it's not, she's still going. Turning full circle.

'What are you doing, woman? We're trying to get into the hall, not forming a bloody formation dancing team.'

'I'm trying, you impatient swine!' she says, giggling.

She's steadied the ship and is progressing in the right direction, to a spontaneous round of applause.

'Ten-four, rubber duck. We got us a convoy!' I announce as I follow her out of the kitchen. 'Easy, easy. Left hand down a bit.'

Crunch!

'Maeve!'

Crash!

'Other way. Other bloody way!'

Scrape!

'Keep this up and your old man will spend the next six weeks with a paintbrush in one hand and a tube of Polyfilla in the other.'

Slam!

'MAEVE! WATCH WHERE YOU'RE GOING, YOU DOZY COW!'

She's stopped on a sixpence and I've slammed into the back of her.

She regards me smugly over her shoulder. 'I'd get your brakes looked at if I were you.'

'You been taking driving lessons off Kate?'

'I heard that!' a voice rings out from the top of the stairs, as Maeve and I make our way recklessly to the drawing room like a pair of blind Formula One racing drivers.

We've both calmed down. Maeve frightened me for a minute. Did a lot of digging for breath, and I thought I'd taken things a bit too far. But after a cup of coffee her breathing eased, our laughter subsided, and the conversation has taken a more serious tone.

'How do you cope, Max? How do you manage, boy?'

'Manage what, exactly?'

'Disability. Imperfection.'

I sigh. 'I've adapted to it over a long time. You've still got your L-plates. Besides, there's nothing wrong with your legs. You're not exactly confined to that thing, are you? I don't mind you playing with it till you get your strength back, but don't go milking it, all right?'

'I won't.' She smiles, and briefly presses her coffee cup against the side of her face. 'It's not just a bit of infirmity. It's more than that, Max. It's the way people change around you. All this mothering. They are so feckin' patronising! It's as if you give up freedom of choice the moment you get sick. "Now don't be silly, Maeve. Of course you must take your medicine. It's good for you." "Now, you must eat your dinner, Maeve, as you have to keep your strength up." I'll be honest with you. Since the heart-attack, I've felt less like a woman and more like a feckin' poodle with every passing day.'

I groan in sympathy and sip my coffee.

'Why do people treat us this way, Max?'

I shrug. 'Part ignorance. Part concern. But mostly because they're frightened.' I put my cup down on the table, and lean forward slightly. 'I think it's a case of "There but for the grace of God go I", a realisation that it's no more than a roll of the dice, that it could still happen to them, one day. It terrifies people. Our imperfect physicality makes them face their own mortality, their mental frailty. The only way to deal with that is to remove it a step or two, distance themselves from it. That's why they end up treating you like a second-class citizen. It's easier to cope with if they can see you as something foreign, alien. So, either you become invisible to them, or they go overboard in the other direction.'

'Could be,' she acknowledges, finishing her coffee and resting the cup on her lap.

'One other thought. I can't vouch for this because I've never had anyone close. I mean, I'm not married, and I've no brothers or sisters. But I think those who love you might be frightened of losing you, and it makes them want to wrap you in clingfilm. Keep you fresh for as long as possible.'

'I'd prefer cotton wool, if you don't mind. There's no need to bring perversion into the conversation.'

I smile.

'I'll be honest with you, Max,' she declares, shaking her head, 'I can't settle to being a burden. I'm dependent on himself for everything. I can't wait to get my strength back. Get out of this thing and back on my feet. Jeez, if I thought I had have to live in this thing the rest of my days, I'd as soon be dead, and that's the truth.'

I fail to hide my flinch.

'Oh, Max, love. I'm sorry, I wasn't thinking straight. I'm so sorry . . .'

'It's all right. I used to think that too. Still do sometimes. Having the writing career has made a big difference. And, more recently, the kids have helped. A sense of responsibility. You were right about that, Maeve. I've started to feel people are depending on me. I suppose it looks as if it's just me doing things for them. Yet, in a funny sort of way, they've done a lot for me, brought me out of my shell a bit.'

'And Kate, Max. Don't be forgettin' Kate.'

'Kate?'

'You heard me,' she says, pointedly.

I don't want to think about this. 'Well, I suppose we'd better send for your knight in shining armour.'

'Eugene? Oh, Jeez! Your man's driving me mad!' she declares, lifting her hands in the air. 'Find him jobs, Max. Invent them if you have to. Just get him off my back, for feck's sake!'

'But he loves you, he's missed you. And you were in that hospital for almost fourteen nights.'

'Max Patterson, you've a dirty, filthy mind.'

'I know. It's what you missed most about me, wasn't it?' I say, winking. 'Come on, let's go and locate your drugs. The way I'm feeling I might just try to score a few off you. I tell you what, on the way we'll try to knacker a few skirting-boards, strip a bit of paintwork, and knock over a few vases. I can't have you croaking through sexual exhaustion, can I?'

'MAX!'

'Welcome to the biannual Dunworley vintage wheelchair rally,' I begin, as we exit, Maeve cackling behind me.

21

It's mid-afternoon and, yet again, I have just tossed the day away. I sit at my computer as I have done all week writing sod-all while a woman soaks through the pores of my skin making me question everything I believe in.

I switch off the hardware in a fit of pique, wheel myself to the tiny window and stare out of it, desperate for distraction.

Eugene is still mowing one of the far lawns, bless him. I can almost see the beads of sweat springing from his brow even at this distance. I have only just noticed, for the first time in ten years, how beautiful the garden and grounds of this house are. Eugene has performed miracles, and nurtured a blaze of strong colours to set against the emerald green of the lawns. The garden is ordered, neat, precise, and he has tended it with the same loving care, the same passion, that my mother used at the back of the home we shared.

I can see Nigel is walking Maeve about in the grounds. We had our chat and I appointed him Maeve's official physical trainer, gave him strict instructions and told him that, above all, he mustn't let Maeve know what he is doing. He's taken his task very seriously.

Closer to the house, a large blanket is spread beneath the remains of a picnic. Caroline is standing and dusting crumbs from her skirt. She speaks briefly to Kate, then makes her way back towards the house. Kate remains lying, stretched out along the blanket's length. A pillow supports her head as she reads her book, a large straw hat protects her eyes from the sun, her dress is rolled high enough for the sun to caress her thighs.

A scene, a painting almost, of complete peace and tranquillity. I stare secretly at Kate, at her beauty.

Why can't I buy into this atmosphere? Why can't I break through this barrier of pain I built to protect myself all those years ago, and go and become part of the garden? Why do I watch the people who matter to me from a dark and dusty attic?

Sod it! I spin down the ramp, race into the drawing room and pour myself a hurtling great whiskey. 'Scheherazade' is thrown on to the CD player at full volume, thank you very much, and half the contents of the tumbler are tossed into the back of my throat.

That's better.

I've decided. I can't take this. Kate's got to go.

The window is open, and a breeze is drifting into the room. Sunlight follows the wind, I wheel my chair over to the square of light the sun's rays have painted on the floor, and I bathe in it, relieved to have reached an inevitable decision.

I open my eyes and look out of the window. I watch Nigel help Maeve wrap a shawl around her shoulders, and lead her back towards the house.

The music fills the room, and I watch Kate roll into a sitting position. She remains very still. I watch her back, and admire its strength.

Unexpectedly, she tosses her hat into the air, into the distance, and her hair tumbles down. Then she stands. She begins to walk in a circle, carefully placing her feet, leading with her toes. Her eyes are cast downwards. Then I see her suddenly lift her head to the sun. She opens her arms to its embrace . . . and begins to dance.

I am aware of the music that is playing as I watch her, transfixed. I am captured by her grace and elegance, by the sheer passion of her movement, by her co-ordination and retention of the through line. The heady mixture of control with freedom of expression.

I can almost taste her joy as she dances. And I know, finally, certainly, and with terrifying clarity, that I am in love with her. That I love Kate.

And I am filled with despair.

Kate deserves perfection and I am not worthy of her. The reality is that, stuck in this wheelchair, I could only drag her downwards.

She finishes her dance, and I can see her shaking with laughter and release. Next, the transition seamless, she weeps a little, wiping her tears with the back of her hand. Then she turns and sees me, and knows I have been watching.

I take a rose from the vase Kate has placed on the window-sill in front of me, and I throw it out of the window in her direction. She smiles and performs an exaggerated curtsey and I blow her a kiss goodbye.

It's about ten thirty p.m., I think. I didn't go down for dinner tonight. I couldn't. Instead, I have lain here rehearsing my speech.

I'm propped up on my bed wearing a navy-blue towelling robe, having had a bath. I hoped it would help me relax.

There's a knock on my bedroom door. It's Kate.

'Sorry to disturb you, Max,' she apologises, as she creeps round the door. She's wearing her nightdress. 'I just came to see if you were all right. When Caroline said you weren't coming

down for dinner, I wondered if you might be sick or something.'
She fidgets nervously as she says this.

I take a deep breath. 'Kate, there's no easy way for me to say this . . . I want you to leave.'

She's silent as my words slowly sink in.

'Why?' she asks finally, and I can't bear to see the confusion and hurt on her face.

'It's nothing to do with you. Really. It's me. It's my fault.'

'In what way?'

'It won't help either of us going into detail. It's simply better if you go, that's all.'

'Look, you've just fired me and I'd like to know why. Is it my typing, my cooking, my flower-arranging, my dress sense, Max? What exactly have I done wrong?'

'Nothing! It's not you, Kate. You're wonderful, and very, very special. In fact, you're perfect.'

'So you're firing me because I'm perfect?' She shakes her head. 'I don't understand. You see, I thought . . . Well, I thought you liked having me around.'

'I do. I admit it. But you're bad for me, Kate, bad for my work and I . . . I haven't been able to think about anything but you for the last two weeks.'

'Oh,' she says quietly.

'I'm so sorry. I've tried to stop myself and I just can't. You're my first thought in the morning and the last of each night, and in between you fill my dreams. That's why you have to leave. I simply can't cope being around you when I know there's no hope—'

'How do you know that?' she asks, taking me by surprise.

'Oh, come on. I kissed you the other night, and you ran away from me.'

The anger fades from her eyes, and I watch them fill with a

look of determination. 'Why can't you cope with my presence in this house?' she asks, walking closer towards me.

'I suppose because I'm scared of—'

'Face your fears – isn't that what you taught Nigel?'

'Yes, but—'

'What if I don't want to go? Supposing I admitted I felt something for you too?'

I stare at her. 'Do you?'

'And if I did?' she asks, sitting on the edge of the bed. 'Would it make a difference? If I admitted that, after Séan, I was scared too? And that was the only reason I ran away?

'Do you think I was unaware you were watching me today? That I had no idea who was playing that music? You made me want to dance again. I never believed I would. I danced for you and you alone, you silly, silly man.'

There is a silence.

'Do you still want me to leave?' Kate asks.

'No,' I reply. 'I can't bear to be without you.'

'Really?' Her mouth breaks into a soft smile. 'Are you absolutely, unequivocally, irrevocably sure?'

'I don't know what I'd do without you.'

She walks towards me until she is standing next to the bed. She traces my face with her fingers. I take her hand in mine and kiss it before she takes it from me.

Her nightdress is removed in one simple movement – a moment of grace and extreme sexuality. It stops my breath.

She perches lightly on the end of the bed and begins to untie the belt of my robe. I stop her.

'What's wrong?' she asks.

'I'm embarrassed.'

'What about?'

I don't speak.

'Max?'

'My legs.'

'There's nothing wrong with your legs. Look at them.'

And I do. They're underdeveloped, slightly scrawny, but they don't exactly look as if they belong to Tiny Tim Cratchet.

'Maybe you're right,' I say, as she lays herself down next to me, and folds her body around mine.

I have never flowed like this before. It is the only time since the accident that I have had complete freedom of movement. It felt so natural, so right. There has been no clumsiness, no restrictiveness.

We are making love and every time I have turned, or twisted, I have found another part of Kate's body I want to know, to discover, to explore. Every inch of her seems soft and exciting and sensitive and alive. Her scent is different, her taste is different, her touch. I want to own her, and possess her, and set her free all at the same time. I experience an unbelievable mixture of tenderness, and almost unbearable electricity.

As she lowers herself on to me and takes me inside her, I feel wonderful, and, for the first time ever, I feel privileged. She's giving so much of herself to me, and I want to give the same to her.

She's shuddering on top of me now, and as I come I want to pour everything into her. Everything I am, everything I own, and every single ounce of love I am capable of giving. I want it all to be hers.

22

We've talked. We've kissed. We've held each other tight. I've not felt so heady since I played Spin the Bottle and Kiss the Girl at a friend's birthday party when I was seven years old.

We held a board meeting in bed and decided that *we* – God, I love saying that – should keep our relationship quiet for a day or two.

Our reasoning is this: we live in a house riddled with upheaval. To spring our happiness suddenly on Caroline and Nigel in particular may unsettle things even further.

I am both exhausted and exhilarated. I've chased Kate round the bed as best I could all night. Not in a let's-do-it-again type of way, but more in an I can't-bear-to-let-you-go style of pursuit.

Having said that, as I watched her dress for breakfast at the foot of the bed, I knew that if I was capable of dragging her back under the duvet, I would have. I never realised that watching someone you love put their clothes on could be as big a turn-on as watching them undress.

Mind you, I haven't been brave enough to voice my feelings yet. I keep thinking, I love you, in my head, but I haven't managed to trip the words off my tongue. Still, plenty of time for that.

It's weird. After a night of loving, passionate, erotic sex, people say their legs turn to jelly. My problem is that mine wobble on a daily basis, but if the rest of my anatomy is anything to go by, I understand what they mean.

Consequently it has taken me fifteen to twenty minutes' worth of effort to get as far as swinging my legs over the edge of the bed and sit upright.

I grab my crutches, drag myself over to the stool in front of the dressing-table and flump down. Then I stare at my reflection and try to recapture my usual grumpy face. I can't do it. I think of Kate and my face crumples into a smile.

Breakfast was one huge ball of frustration. I kept wanting to touch Kate, to hold her. When she sat next to me, I wanted to caress her thigh under the table. Every time she spoke to me, I wanted to stop her mouth with a kiss. When she bent over the table to clear things away, I still don't know how I stopped myself playfully biting her bottom.

Instead of which, the raciest thing we managed was to hold hands briefly under the table in a quick, loving squeeze of reassurance.

People departed, and Caroline and Nigel took a taxi into Ballinkilty. Kate tells me it is time to give them some trust, some freedom.

She left the kitchen just after them with an exaggerated roll of her eyes and a heart-melting smile.

Now Eugene has sidled up to me, dragging the chair recently vacated by my love along with him as he moved. 'Max, I'm a worried man.'

I snap myself out of my daydream. 'Why's that?'

He runs his hand through his grey, wiry hair. 'It's Maeve.

She's so depressed, so feckin' maudlin. Every positive is answered with a double negative. I'm at me wits' end.'

He looks it.

I brush my fist lightly against his stubbly chin. 'Come on, Eugene. We'll sort it. What exactly do you think is the problem?'

He screws his face into a ball, then shakes his head.

'She's giving up, Max. She's convinced she's gonna spend the rest of her life huffing and puffing and shuffling around like an invalid. There's nothing I can do to convince her otherwise, I'm telling you.'

I sigh. 'What has the doctor told you?'

'That she has to take care. Have lots of rest, take it easy to begin with, not too much excitement. He says it was a bad attack and there's no guarantee it won't happen again. But—'

'She's abusing the privilege,' I suggest. 'You're scared she's going to live the rest of her life in fear and that she will never have fun again?'

'Exactly,' he declares. 'I feel awful bad asking you this, but I must find a way to convince her that she can lift her face into the air again.'

I feel suddenly inspired – creative, even. A day ago, such an outrageous idea would never have found its way into my imagination. 'Do you trust me?' I ask.

'Do I have to?' he enquires suspiciously.

'Leave it with me, Eugene. I can't promise anything. I'm not a miracle-worker. If I was, I'd be giving Michael Flatley a run for his money instead of sitting here.'

'Okay, Max. I understand.' He stands up. 'Just give it some thought, eh? Let me know if you've any bright ideas.'

'I will.' I watch him leave. The minute he is out of the room I cross to the telephone and put in my first call.

*

I've plucked up my courage and made a request.

We fetched the ghetto-blaster from the dining room, where it had lain unused since the night of Maeve's heart-attack, and it's now playing in Kate's bedroom, the volume low, the bass high.

I've asked her to dance for me. Tonight, of course, is different from the last time she danced to 'Scheherazade'. I am lying on her bed, and she is naked and moving above me, astride me. I would not have believed it was possible to be so blatantly sexual and still remain so feminine.

I cannot deny that the sight of her is building me up to uncontrollable levels of desire and passion. Yet, at the same time, these emotions are blending with warmth and love and pride that one so gorgeous has chosen me. I feel her thighs clasp the outside of my own, and her hair tickle my face as she stoops forward to kiss me.

'Max? she says, planting butterfly kisses on my neck. 'Why can't you walk?'

'Because if I try, I fall over.'

'But why?' she asks, kissing my chest. 'Was it an accident?'

'Yes. My mother's, actually.'

She sits up and looks at me.

'Were you hit by the same car?' She flattens the palms of her hands and runs them up and down my body, from chest to groin.

'Yes.'

'And that's the reason you can't walk.'

'It's psychological, so the doctors tell me.'

'I don't understand.' She takes my erection in her hand.

'Apparently I have post-traumatic paralysis.'

'You mean, there's no physical reason for you to be in that chair?' she asks, as she plays with me.

'No.'

'You're a fraud, Max Patterson. You pretend to be a bastard, when you're really a sweetheart. You pretend to be indifferent, when you care deeply. And you sit in that chair when really you can walk.'

'I can't walk, Kate. Honestly. I've tried and I really can't.'

'I didn't think I would dance again until I met you. Maybe I can make you walk again.'

'One miracle at a time, Kate. One at a time.'

She begins to lower her head.

'Kate?' I stop her half-way.

'Yes?'

'I – nothing. Please, don't stop now.'

She closes her mouth around me and I feel bliss and heat and surrender. Then I hear the knock on the door.

My eyes flash in its direction before glancing down at the horrified stare on Kate's face.

'Nigel!' Kate whispers, and dives off the bed, taking the duvet with her.

Another knock.

'Kate,' Nigel calls.

I feel a bit exposed and glancing around, discover my T-shirt, which was tossed on a pillow in a moment of passion. I place it over my stubborn erection.

I now look as if, on my lap, there rests a tent for a resident of Lilliput.

'Just a moment, Nigel,' Kate answers, pulling on her dressing-gown.

'What's he doing here?' I ask.

'It's been a regular occurrence ever since Maeve's heart-attack. When she was in hospital I'd find him outside my door crying.'

'So what happens now?'

'Same as always.'

'Kate,' Nigel whines again.

'On my way,' she calls softly. 'I'll do what I always do. Take him downstairs for a cup of tea and a quick chat, then tuck him back up in bed.'

'How many times have you done this?' I ask.

'Four or five.'

I smile at her. 'You're amazing.'

She returns my smile. 'Back soon.' She kisses me and makes her way out of the room. 'Come on, Nigel, let's get the kettle on,' I hear her say, as she closes the door behind her.

Is she right? Can she make me walk again? She's made me feel, and made me love again, although she doesn't know that.

I reach for my crutches and swing my legs over the edge of the bed. I use them in conjunction with the strength in my arms and upper body to haul myself upright. I grit my teeth, will myself to succeed.

Right here goes. I let the sticks fall ... and I follow them, crashing to the floor in a crumpled heap.

I feel a stinging in my eyes. What's the use, I curse, what's the fucking use?

23

Tonight I have organised an outing to the pub in Ring. Thankfully, Justine has never worked evening shifts. At night she waitresses in Ballinkilty.

We're all going, with the exception of Caroline who refused to attend. I could have insisted, I suppose, but I'd have been given the I'm-not-a-child-any-more routine and, frankly, I didn't want a sour-faced teenager poohing on everyone else's fun.

Maeve took a lot of persuading. In fact, I bullied her. She told me she didn't want people staring at her. I said that if she didn't want that she should wear a large silly hat like I do, and then people could stare at that instead. Maeve said she didn't possess one, so I suggested she go naked. At this point she gave in grudgingly.

Eugene has driven us down here, Nigel has come along as Maeve's unofficial nurse, and Kate came because I told her I didn't want to go anywhere without her. She's sitting opposite me across the table in the pub, and occasionally sneaks a bare foot up the inside of my trouser-leg and smiles a warm, tender, secretive smile as she does so.

She's wearing white jeans and a sleeveless top, and she looks absolutely edible. I'll tell her I love her tonight, when we get home, I promise myself.

Maeve has sandwiched herself on the bench between Kate and Nigel to 'stop myself keeling over', as she put it. Eugene is next to me, and I remain on wheels. Sod 'em, let them stare. I'm still wearing my hat, though.

We've been here an hour and a half and for most of this time Maeve has been moaning and groaning about her age, her health, her appearance, other customers, pubs in general, etc.

She has, however, cheered up considerably in the last ten minutes due to a couple of hot ports. The pub has been filling steadily and there's a buzzing, friendly atmosphere.

'I've got to start trying to enjoy what little's left of the rest of my life, haven't I, Max?' she's asking.

'Oh, *please*. You'll be around to torment me for a good few years yet,' I tell her.

'Of course you will. Don't be so depressing, woman,' Eugene chips in.

'She always been bloody miserable,' I say.

'Max!' Kate reprimands me.

'It's nice to know one's friends and loved ones have a high opinion of you. What's this?' Maeve asks, as the barman places a piece of paper and a pencil on the table.

I take a quick look. 'Enter team name, it says here.'

'Team name?' Maeve repeats. 'Team for what?'

'A tug of war, I think.'

'Oh, Jaysus, it'll kill me! Is it compulsory?'

'Calm down, Maeve. I'm only joking. It must be quiz night,' I scan the walls until I see a handwritten poster. 'Yes, it is. Look.' I point to the evidence.

Another hot port is placed on the table in front of Maeve, along with the rest of our drinks.

'Feckin' great. Just what I need. The whole bar can see I'm a physical wreck, and now they're about to find out how ignorant I am too.'

'We don't have to enter, Maeve,' Nigel says protectively.

'Oh, come on,' I argue. 'It's only a bit of fun. In a pub this size it's going to look a bit snooty of us if we don't join in.'

'It is a team game,' Kate reminds us. 'You don't have to answer any questions if you don't want to, Maeve. We can all sit back and let Max make a fool of himself. We'll make him team captain.'

Maeve grins at me. 'I'm really beginning to like this girl, Max.'

'We'll need a name,' Eugene points out. 'What'll we call ourselves? The Horror and the Housewives?'

'Kate's not a housewife,' I object.

'The Cook, the Author, the Dancer, the Odd-job Man and the Schoolboy,' Kate suggests.

'Sounds a bit like one of those art-house soft-porn films.' I am unable to resist giving her a loving wink.

'Fierce bleedin' mouthful as well,' Maeve remarks.

'We'd better be thinking of something quick,' Eugene urges, as the barman starts to gather entries from other tables.

I scribble something hastily, just as he arrives to collect the papers.

'I want to go home.' Maeve is sulking.

'Right, now, ladies and gentlemen and peasants,' the barman announces, as he climbs on a chair. 'I have here the names of the teams, which I will read aloud to you now. As always, when you hear your team name, would you be giving a big cheer so the opposition can be seeing what an ugly bunch of feckers they're up against.'

Jeers, cheers and laughter echo around the pub.

'Right, so. We have the Philandering Farmers.'

There's a roar from a robust-looking bunch of men in the

corner. 'The Naughty Nineties.' A muted cheer comes from a collection of old duffers of mixed sex. 'The Thirtysomething Virgins.' Raucous cackles from a group of dubious-looking girls, accompanied by cries of 'In yer dreams', 'Believe that you'll believe anything', and 'more like fortysomething slappers' from the rest of the bar. 'And, last but not least, the Dodgy Tickers!' I am the only one who cheers, which makes the rest of the pub piss themselves laughing, including our table. Even Maeve grins.

'You're a swine, Max Patterson,' she informs me.

'Now, then,' the barman continues, 'tonight we have a theme.'

I hear the muttering. I look around and see people mouthing the words 'theme quiz', and looking bemused.

'And tonight's theme is music.'

'Fantastic,' Maeve states. 'They'll be asking me questions about classical composers whose names I couldn't pronounce, even if I feckin' knew them.'

'Well, if I'd known, I'd have bribed the quizmaster to ask questions on basic household detergents,' I tease, and receive a poked-out tongue in return.

'As always, the winning team takes home a bottle of whiskey and gets a free cooked lunch,' the barman shouts. 'Now, I know most of you can barely mark your cross, let alone write your names, so can you please shout out the answers. The team with the biggest gobs stands the best chance of victory. Right. First question. I want artist and song here. Which Margaret sang about a raging temperature?'

I hear cries of 'What?' and see much scratching of heads.

'I know it,' says a quiet voice from across our table.

'Pardon, Maeve?' I say.

'I know the answer,' she tells me.

'Well, don't keep it a secret. None of the rest of us have a bloody clue.'

'What if I'm wrong, boy?

'Maeve, it's a game! Shout it out before some other bugger gets it.'

'Peggy Lee. She sang "Fever", so she did,' Maeve shouts at the quizmaster.

'Is right! A point to the Dodgy Tickers!'

Cheers from us. Friendly boos from the opposition.

'Next question: who had a hit on a small mountain named after a pie?'

'I know it again.' Maeve has a small but satisfied smile on her face.

'Speak up, then,' I urge.

'Fats Waller. "Blueberry Hill".'

'The Dodgy Tickers again! Who showed his metal, while singing about a miserable colour?'

'Oh, God, Oh, *God*!' Maeve intones, clearly racking her brains.

'Come on, Maeve, we're relying on you,' I urge her.

'It's on the tip o' my tongue, now.' Yet another hot port lands in front of her. 'I know, I know,' she announces, becoming suddenly animated. 'The feller with the mouthful of teeth.'

'Ken Dodd?' I suggest.

'No.'

'Janet Street-Porter.'

'*No*. It's a man.'

'Champion the Wonder Horse?'

'Fifties, he's a fifties pop star. I've got it!' she shouts. 'Tommy Steele, "Singing The Blues".'

'Again, the Dodgy Tickers!'

And so it continues.

'Name a group called after a schoolboy stain.'

Maeve: 'The Ink Spots.'

'What black rhythm and blues star threw fruit?'

Maeve: 'Chuck Berry.'

'What fifties and early sixties pop idol was an angry ol' goat?'
Maeve: 'Billy Fury.'

I look around and notice that one or two people in the pub are failing to see the funny side of this *tour de force*.

It's the last question. It doesn't matter. Maeve has trounced the opposition single-handedly. Tonight she's a bloody star!

'Who flogged a stick of candy from inside a detention centre?'

'*Elvis Presley! "Jailhouse rock"!*' she screams, waving her arms like an overexcited Muppet.

Whoops, cheers from her team, and, in fairness, all around the pub. A large bottle of whiskey and two vouchers are thrust into her hand from the quizmaster.

I look across to the Thirtysomething Virgins' table, and one of their number returns my stare.

'It's a bloody fix!' the woman hollers at Maeve.

'It was not. You be taking that back now,' Maeve retorts, in a slightly slurred voice.

'Ah! Come on! How else would an ol' bugger like you know all them answers?' the woman snarls.

I feel tension gathering around the table.

'I may be getting on in years, but I could still give you a sound slapping, girl, unless you find a civil tongue in yer head.'

'Jeez, it's obvious it's all been rigged just to make an old crock feel better.'

'Ol' crock, is it?' Maeve says, standing. '*Ol' feckin' crock, is it?*' She bangs her fists on the table.

'Can't you take a joke, missus?' The woman raises her hands in surrender.

Thankfully, Maeve sits back down. 'All mouth and no knickers, that one,' she declares, grinning.

I look at the barman and, as if on cue, the music strikes up. 'Jeez!' cries Maeve. 'It's Bill Haley, I love this song!'

One of the Philandering Farmers strides across and gives her a hug.

She notices my look of disapproval.

'Ah! Cheer up, Max, you miserable fecker! When are you going to learn to enjoy life?' She raises the remainder of her hot port to her lips as our table becomes surrounded by well-wishers and admirers of tonight's star guest.

The hooley's over.

Eugene has finally persuaded Maeve it's time to go home and helped her into the car. I'm waiting on the roadside between Kate and Nigel.

Eugene approaches. 'You're a wicked man, Max Patterson.'

'Me? Why? What have I done?'

'A theme quiz? Fifties music? "Rock Around The Clock" the first song played on the jukebox?'

'I can't be blamed for life's little coincidences,' I protest.

He bends down and gives me a breath-removing bear-hug. When he stands, the daft bugger has tears in his eyes. 'I'll never be able to thank you enough,' he says.

I shake my head. 'You've got a nasty suspicious mind, Eugene MacEoin. Now get us home before we're arrested for loitering with intent.'

We're in the car. Maeve's in the front with Eugene, and they're singing traditional Irish songs at the tops of their voices. Kate is holding my hand, but keeping a safe distance to avoid detection. This is easily achieved, because Nigel is slumbering between us.

'Okay, I give in. How did you manage all that?' Kate whispers.

'Bribery. I knew they had a regular quiz night. So I telephoned the landlord and had a word. Some of the teams play every week – the farmers, for example, and the Thirtysomething Virgins. He already knew Eugene because he drinks in there quite regularly. The rest was just a matter of waving a cheque-book under his nose.'

'But all those questions on rock and roll?'

'That was the easy part. I am a writer, after all. Took a bit of research, mind.'

Nigel is beginning to snore.

'It nearly went horribly wrong for you, though, didn't it?'

'Did it?'

She raises an eyebrow. 'What would you have done if that woman had punched Maeve on the nose?' I see the concern in her eyes, and detect a slight edge of criticism in her voice.

'It would never have happened.'

'How do you know that? It could have.'

'I'd have had to get the landlord to slip her another twenty quid if I'd wanted her to actually fight Maeve,' I say, stroking the inside of her palm with my index finger.

Kate's giggles grow in intensity as the truth sinks in.

Home sweet home. We've teetered, or in my case, swerved from side-to-side through the door. Coats have been discharged, and a sleeping Nigel carried upstairs by Eugene.

'Am I hearing things?' Maeve asks.

My brain belatedly registers one hell of a racket coming from the drawing room. 'Christ!' I yell angrily. The Cure is being played at such a high volume you can't tell the music from the speaker feedback. I wheel my way in the direction of the uproar and burst through the door like a Wild West sheriff, with the rest of the posse in tow. The sight that greets my eyes is astonishing.

Bodies writhe everywhere: on chairs, on sofas, on the floor, among empty beer cans, bottles and fag ash. Mouths appear to be glued to each other by the power of suction and the welding of tongues. The music is so loud, and the teenagers are so engrossed in their activities, that hardly anyone has noticed we are here. One or two acne-ridden youths straighten their clothes in embarrassment, but that's it.

Maeve stops the music and Kate turns on the lights. Everyone's frozen. By now, even Casanova on the floor has realised he's got an audience.

'Bloody hell fire!' I shout. I've just noticed that the bare-breasted blonde at my feet is Caroline. 'What is going on here?'

No reply.

'Caroline?' I glare at her, and she blushes as she pulls down her T-shirt.

'What is this? An AGM for the hard-of-hearing? No one want to give me an explanation? A pathetic excuse, even?'

My sense of smell takes me back to my university days, and I turn to my left. On the chair next to me, dressed in white, some bearded lout is smoking a joint. I snatch the roach from his whiskery gob.

'Cool it, man,' he says.

'"Cool it, man?" What do you think this is? A revival of *Jesus Christ Superstar*? Now, piss off out of my house.'

'Oh yeah?' He snorts. 'Like you're gonna make me, right?'

'If he doesn't, I will,' Eugene, who has now arrived in the room, growls threateningly. 'You feck off home, Michael Brady, before I call your mammy to come and get you.'

Talk about magic words. Suddenly the room is frantic with kids searching for shoes, knickers, handbags and jackets. Within minutes they are scurrying out of the room, racing down the hall and out of the front door. Eugene is hot on their heels, a size-eleven boot cocked and ready to use if necessary.

'Feck of a walk home for most of 'em,' Maeve remarks, looking suddenly tired, as she parks herself in a chair.

I turn to Caroline. I am furious. 'No wonder you were so determined not to come to the pub tonight. You obviously preferred to stay at home and re-enact the last days of the Roman empire, complete with orgy. What in God's name do you think you're playing at?'

'I'm sorry,' she whispers, fidgeting.

'Sorry? That's it, is it? Not "It'll never happen again, Max"? Supposing Nigel had walked through that door with us and seen you on the floor with lover-boy?'

She bends down so that her face is inches from my own. 'I'm only following my godfather's example, aren't I, Max?' she hisses. 'How dare you judge me, when everybody knows you're screwing her?'

Kate's face has turned pale.

'That's a terrible thing to say,' I roar. 'How can you possibly draw such a comparison? Kate is a grown woman, fully in charge of her emotions. You're fifteen, and below the age of consent.'

'I'm not that much younger than Justine, and age didn't seem to bother you then.'

'Go to your room, Caroline. And you can stay there until you are able to make a full and sincere apology to us both.'

We watch in silence as Caroline slams the door and bounds up the stairs.

'Kate, I—'

'I'm sorry, Max. Maeve. If you wouldn't mind excusing me.' Kate speaks with stilted politeness. And she, too, walks away. Every step she takes hurts.

I realise I am being watched. I turn my head to see Maeve's craggy, and now rather weary, features staring at me. I look into her eyes, and I steel myself for a bollocking. Her eyes half close with exhaustion. She looks suddenly tired, drained.

'Are you okay? You didn't overdo it tonight did you? Only I didn't—'

She holds up a hand. 'I'm fine.' She smiles at me. 'Don't go taking this too seriously, Max. It'll blow over.'

I shake my head. 'I'm not so sure.'

'I'd be a liar if I said I was the president of Caroline's fan club, but she's been good for you. Both the children have. They've made you think about someone else's problems, rather than wallowing in your own misery. Actually, I think you've done a grand job with them.' She shifts uncomfortably in her seat, then winces visibly, which frightens me. 'You've changed, Max. For the better, I might add. You've stopped burrowing your head in the little world you created, and you've joined the rest of us miserable devils in the real one. I'm proud of you.'

'Thanks,' I say, more than a little embarrassed.

'Mind you, Caroline had a point about your disgusting behaviour with Justine, among others.'

'I know. I haven't exactly set a good example, have I?'

'But she was wrong to compare all that with what you feel about Kate, wasn't she?' Maeve tilts her head to one side and looks into my eyes. 'How long are you going to go on pretending you're something you're not, Max Patterson?'

I smile at the vivid memory of Kate saying almost the same thing not too long ago. 'Isn't that a case of the pot calling the kettle black?'

She nods slowly. 'That's what I'm trying to say. We're like two peas in a pod, you and I. Why do you think we argue all the time? I don't find it easy to show affection, either. It took me years to tell Eugene I loved him. I used to feel foolish, and frightened. I was lucky he was so stubborn.'

'He's a braver man than I am.'

'Until we came here, Max, life was all about work and worrying about debts. I was always frantic about whether we could keep a roof over our heads and I never seemed to find time to show Eugene how much I cared about him. But you don't have those worries. The only thing missing from

210

your life is love. You must tell Kate how much you feel for her.'

I sigh. 'You're right. I don't know why I find it so difficult.'

'You had a bad start to life, and you've built a wall around yourself ever since. But you have to allow yourself to be vulnerable. If you love Kate, you have to take the risk that you might lose her. I'll not be around to bully you for ever. God only sends the right one along just the once, Max. Grab your chance with both hands, boy. Promise me now.'

'I will. I promise.'

Maeve's eyes are streaming with tears. I've never seen her like this before. 'Maeve, please don't upset yourself.'

'There is something else. These last ten years have been the happiest of my life. Living here with you in this wonderful house. Now, who am I to be sitting here preaching to you about showing your feelings, when I've not told you how I felt in ten years? Max Patterson, you're an awkward, complicated, difficult man, and I love you very dearly.'

I sit here open-mouthed, while Maeve takes a handkerchief from inside her sleeve and wipes her eyes.

Eugene has just strolled through the door and Maeve cheers up. She doesn't want him to see she's been crying.

'Right,' he announces. 'Not a rampant teenage hormone left on site, with the exception of herself upstairs.'

'Thanks,' I say.

'Ah! Don't be too hard on her, Max. Sure if it weren't for girls like Caroline embarking on a voyage of discovery you and I would have spent our teenage years turning ourselves blind.'

'Eugene MacEoin, you're disgusting! Get up to bed now, you shameful man!' Maeve cries, as he pulls her upright.

'God save me, I love it when she's forceful,' Eugene says, raising an eyebrow at me.

'Out!' she tells him.

As they leave, Eugene looks over his shoulder and mouths, 'Is she all right?'

I nod reassuringly as they disappear out of the door.

24

It's been two weeks since the quiz night and Caroline has apologised to Kate, but there remains an air of tension between them.

It's a glorious day, the sort of sunny day that makes you think you've been transported to Greece or Spain or some other sunny European clime. I've said knickers to the writing and taken a few weeks off. It's been a pointless exercise anyway. On the rare occasions I smashed through the barrier, my heroine began to turn into Kate, and my villain couldn't bring himself to harm her. He developed a conscience, for crying out loud, and started being ... nice. My fans would have had a pink fit.

We've been to Simon's cove for a picnic – well, all except Caroline, who is at her boyfriend's house. Disapprove, render something unobtainable to a teenage girl and you make it all the more attractive and exciting – this much I have now learned.

Maeve and Nigel climbed uneasily down the slope on to the slippery moss and rocks that line the sea and went for a paddle. From above they looked sweet. Hand in hand, walking close together, they resembled Winnie-the-Pooh and Piglet. In fact, Nigel's ears are not dissimilar.

Maeve still looks grey and rather frail, but we've had no more tears since the quiz night. In fact she's become uncommonly cheerful; another almost Jekyll and Hyde transformation.

Kate lay on the rug sunbathing, her dress billowing periodically in the wind, and I suddenly realised how much she has changed me. For the first time in my life, I am completely happy.

I haven't told her I love her yet. I feel so exhilarated by her presence in my life, and Maeve's right, I'm terrified of frightening her away. I simply cannot come to terms with the fact that she actually wants to be with me. I try not to dwell on this and, instead, live each wonderful day as it comes.

Anyway, picnic over, back home, and we're now in the grounds of the house having an impromptu game of cricket. It was Nigel's suggestion. He's batting, of course, and I am the umpire – what else? Kate is wicket-keeper, and Eugene is learning to bowl as well as fielding everything from silly mid-on, to boundary. His face reddens, and you can hear him wheezing as he runs around retrieving the tennis ball we are using.

Maeve brought out the interval drinks, a jug of orange juice, and is now sitting on the bench in the sun, and watching the rest of us make fools of ourselves.

So, Eugene is bowling – or should I say 'hurling'? The ball changes the parting in my hair from left to right.

'Watch what you're bloody doing, man!' I grumble.

'Sorry, Max. I'm almost after getting the hang of it, I promise you.'

Maeve cackles from her seat in the pavilion.

'And what you laughing at, girl?' Eugene grins back at her.

'Ball games were never your strong point. You're not gifted with a natural flair, so you're not.'

'Give it time, give it time. I'll make the first fifteen yet,' he tells her.

'Eleven, Eugene. There are eleven players in a cricket team.'

He looks around the garden. 'Not in this team there's not,' he observes.

'Just bowl the ball, will you?'

Nigel is performing miracles in managing to hit some of the missiles Eugene is lobbing at him. The ball whizzes under my nostrils for the third time.

'Eugene, you're supposed to be bowling at Nigel, or more precisely the wicket, not slinging it at him like David having a bit of a tiff with Goliath, for God's sake!'

'Bloody daft English game anyway,' he whinges, as Kate retrieves the ball and throws it back to him.

'Just remember what I taught you. Talk it through in your head.'

'Fair enough. I take the ball behind me,' he shouts out loud, 'and bring my arm over the top.' He practises doing this as he instructs himself. I look across to Maeve, who shakes her head in mock disbelief.

'And release the ball . . .'

Maeve has just blinked, quite violently.

'. . . as my arm makes its descent—'

She's just done it again, and emotions are registering on her face. Surprise. Shock. Fear.

'Now, let's try one.'

Her back has arched, and her left arm has tensed.

'Here it comes, ready or not,' Eugene is shouting.

Maeve's eyes have widened.

'Take that!' Eugene roars.

Maeve looks across at me, smiles, then puts a finger from her right hand, slowly to her lips.

And for some reason I smile back.

'Would you look at that! He's smashed it in the air!' Eugene screams.

Maeve has stopped smiling. Her mouth has slackened, her left arm is limp, and she leans, slightly to the left, her head resting on her shoulder.

'Maeve, did you see that? Did you see how hard young Nigel battered that ball? Where the hell did it go?'

Kate has frozen. Eugene stops suddenly and sits down on to the grass, his legs too weak to support him.

Only Nigel moves. He runs over to her.

The rest of us remain where we are. This time we know.

The picture of Nigel calling Maeve's name and beating her chest in frustration will remain with me for a very long time.

25

It's the day after Maeve's death. I'm in the drawing room, and Eugene is opposite me.

Although he's been here for at least five minutes he just can't speak. Every time he tries to open his mouth his eyes fill with water. I watch him trying to control this. I see his throat tense with the ache of fought-back tears.

I haven't rushed him, or touched him. I didn't think I should. I've just waited.

'Max,' he finally manages to croak huskily, 'Max, I want to leave.'

'Don't be daft.'

'You don't understand. I can't stay here. This house . . . it's too full of memories . . . too full of . . . her.'

'That's exactly why you must stay. This is your home, and it was Maeve's. She loved this house. She told me so herself a few days ago.'

He's nodding.

'Oh, Eugene, don't leave us. We've just lost Maeve. How would we cope if you left us too?'

'But – I can't stop – thinking about her all the time.'

'Maeve wouldn't want you to. She'd be furious if she thought any of us would forget her, let alone you.'

There's a brief flicker of a smile.

'It will get easier in time, Eugene.' I tread out the well-worn phrase, which I of all people do not believe is true.

'How would you know?' he shouts, in a sudden burst of anger. 'You've never loved anyone! You've never loved anyone like I loved my Maeve!'

I put my finger to my lips. 'Maeve would never forgive me if I let you leave, Eugene. I'd have to spend the rest of my life dodging the thunderbolts she sent down from heaven if I let you trot off into the wide blue yonder.'

He gives a cross between a laugh and a sob in response. 'You would too, and that's a fact.' The anguish returns to his face. 'I blame myself, see? I never earned much and I never provided . . . I mean, I gave her such a hard life before we came here, Max, and I think it may have killed her.'

'Now, just stop that!' I say, very firmly. 'How do you think I feel? I set up that quiz night. I organised Nigel to take her on long walks. I allowed her to do a few bits and pieces of light work. If anyone should be racked with guilt about her second heart-attack it should be me, not you.'

'Don't say that, Max. Why, if it wasn't for you, boy, I don't know where we'd have been. We had ten wonderful years together here. She loved this place, and she loved you, Max. Maeve used to say that you were the son we never had. You mustn't blame yourself.'

Now my throat is constricting. 'I won't blame myself if you don't blame yourself either,' I tell him. But I will. I can't seem to help it.

Eugene nods again. 'I remember the first time I saw her. It was at a dance. I saw her across the room and I just stared at her. I stopped talking to my friends and I watched her, and oh, Max, I could have watched her all night. She was beautiful. Long curly chestnut hair, gorgeous womanly figure, dazzling eyes. It was the first time the pounding in my heart was bigger than the lust in my groin, and after that, after the first time I met her, I couldn't stop thinking about her. I knew I was in trouble the moment I clapped eyes on her. It was as if . . . as if it was love at first sight. Do you know that feeling, Max?' He is lost in his own memories.

'Yes,' I say. 'I think I do.'

'I remember the day I proposed to her, in the back garden of her parents' house. I was so scared I had to get drunk to give myself courage. I got down on one knee and toppled over because of the drink. And she laughed at me, and she said, "Of course I'll marry you, you big soft git," and I hadn't even managed to ask her yet and she—'

He's sobbing, head in hands. 'Oh, Max, I did a terrible thing. I never showed her how much I loved her. I never told her how important she was to me. I fooled around and hugged her and looked after her, but I was too stupid, or . . . And now it's too late. I can't tell her – and I want to!' he screams.

I've crossed over to him and his head is on my shoulder. Through the tremors that pass from his big bear-like body into mine, I feel his pain.

'Maeve told me she thought she hadn't shown *you* how much you meant to her over the years, so you were both as daft as each other. She knew, Eugene. Of course she did. I promise she knew how much you loved her.'

The funeral is tomorrow. In Ireland, people are gift-wrapped, boxed up and put in the ground virtually before they're cold. It's the only thing that happens quickly in the entire country. You may have no roof on your house, but sure what's a bit of soft rain to worry about? You'll be okay for another couple of weeks. But die, and you'll be interred with a speed and efficiency that would stagger a multi-million-dollar Japanese conglomerate.

She only passed away the day before yesterday, for heaven's sake! Still, the funeral is tomorrow morning, then there's a hooley of a wake from lunchtime onwards at the house. We'll send her off with a major thrash.

How are we all? Eugene is devastated. I hope he can find a way to get through the burial. Caroline seems to be largely unaffected. She didn't see it happen, and Maeve and she were not exactly bosom buddies. I think she's finding consolation in her boyfriend's arms. Kate has been magnificent. She was the first to recover from the shock and has coped with the fall-out from the rest of us.

And Nigel? He worries me.

He's just not speaking. He nods, he grunts, he functions, but it's as if he's suddenly deaf, dumb and blind. It's like living with an alien.

My heart goes out to him. His parents die, then the first attachment he allows himself to make after that drops dead right in front of his eyes.

I'm not sure what to do. I don't want him to grow up and become one of those wanky adults who blame all their problems on their disturbed childhood. In short, I don't want him to grow up like me.

And how about you, Max? I miss Maeve. I really miss her. But I have Kate to hold on to in the middle of the night, which is a big help. Because of her I'm okay. I think I'm coping.

Maybe Kate has taught me how to unleash my feelings. Because I've cried too – not for my mother, or my father, but I cried for Maeve.

I told you I don't do death. I do life now, though, don't I? And, since Kate, I do love as well.

*

220

Unlike the last time, I actually went to this funeral. And I listened to the priest describe a woman I didn't know. A woman who was kind and considerate, tolerant of the weaknesses of others. A gentle woman, despite the difficulties of her formative years. I met brothers and sisters and nieces and nephews and cousins and friends. I sat by the graveside and watched as they lowered her in. God, it was depressing.

I mean, is that it? All life's struggles and the best accommodation you're offered at the end of it is a six-foot hole with a roof garden. Where were the flights of angels? The golden staircase leading upwards? The kind, bearded face smiling and opening arms in greeting? Maybe I should have read the Bible more, instead of getting my ideas about heaven from old Hollywood movies and *Tom and Jerry* cartoons.

I threw my handful of dirt on to the coffin and wheeled myself away, determined to grab my chance of happiness. Then I came home and got absolutely fucking plastered.

As the whiskey slipped down my throat, I heard a familiar voice, saw a familiar finger wagging at me, heard the words, 'God only sends the right one along just the once, Max. Grab your chance with both hands, boy.'

'I will, Maeve. I promise,' I found myself whispering, and hoped she'd been assigned as my guardian angel.

26

I'm in the drawing room, staring at Caroline. We sit opposite each other, I in a chair, she flopped on the *chaise-longue*, glaring defiantly back.

It's about a week after the funeral and Caroline has been out with her boyfriend.

I said I wanted her home by ten thirty and she walked through the door at about one thirty. I've been having a nervous breakdown, which was not helped by Kate giggling and teasing me about it.

I begin the interrogation. 'What time do you call this, Caroline? Shall I tell you? It's half past one.'

'So?'

'So, I told you to be home by half past ten. Didn't they teach you to tell the time at that boarding-school of yours?'

She shrugs.

'I asked you to be home by a certain time and you disobeyed me.'

'So?'

'You say "so", just one more time, young lady, and I'll bend you over my knee and give you the slapping of your bloody life!'

'Promises, promises, Max.' She winks.

GOD GIVE ME STRENGTH!

'And cut out the *Lolita* act. It's not working. What have you been up to?'

'Nothing.'

'Where have you been until this hour?'

'Nowhere. In his house. At his friend's. In his car.'

'Getting up to what exactly?'

She raises her eyebrows and widens her eyes. 'What do you think I've been doing?'

'I shudder to think after the sideshow you put on at your illicit party.'

'He never touched me,' she says, running her hands through her hair. 'The point is, I don't know about ... sex.'

'Bullshit, Caroline. Do you think I'm a complete idiot?'

'No,' she says, lowering her eyelids coyly.

'You're winding me up.'

'I'm not.'

But she bloody well is.

'I'm just starting to feel things. I'm not a child any more. But I know one thing. I know I could get pregnant and I don't want that.'

Nor do I. She's got me there. If there's even the slightest chance she's telling the truth and she goes and gets—

'Tell me, Max. Please. Look, what if a boy ... Oh, God, this is embarrassing.' She blushes, on cue.

'You're embarrassed?' I counter.

'Can I get pregnant if he touches me ... you know, down below?' She times her glance to perfection.

'Depends what he touches you with,' I shout, interrupting to save myself from squirming on the end of this line a minute longer than I have to. 'Then if he uses that and you haven't used any contraception, Bob's your uncle, he's a daddy, and you're up the spout. Simple as that. Thank you and goodnight. Glad I could be of help. I'm going to bed.'

'Max?' she's giggling loudly and swinging her legs in the air. 'I'm none the wiser.'

'What's the joke?' Kate has just walked in.

'Oh, nothing.' Caroline stands up. 'Max was just telling me about sex, that's all.' She brushes past Kate as she leaves the room.

'Have you, indeed?' Kate says.

'She just asked me to explain the facts of life to her.'

'And you think a teenager knows nothing about sex?' Kate asks.

'I couldn't take the risk, could I? I am her godfather.'

'You're also her hero. That girl has a major crush on you.'

I steer myself towards the whiskey decanter. 'Oh, be serious.'

'I mean it. You need to be careful there.'

'She's only fifteen,' I state, pouring myself a large one.

'*Max!*'

Why is it that every time I reach for the whiskey somebody catches me? It's a sodding curse, I can tell you.

Caroline has rushed into the room, breathing erratically.

'I thought you'd gone to bed,' I snap.

'It's Nigel. He's not in his room. Or mine, or yours, or Kate's, or Maeve's. He's not anywhere. He's gone, Max. Nigel's gone.'

How can somebody like Nigel disappear off the face of the earth for nearly twenty-four hours?

If I was to use a single word to describe him it would be 'conspicuous'. He manages to achieve this simply by doing everything he can to be inconspicuous. The way he huddles in corners, the way he dresses. The way he never attempts to involve himself in conversations. All these things make Nigel infinitely noticeable. They draw attention to him for all the wrong reasons, attract all the negative emotions and responses to him. Nevertheless, in a totally perverse manner, they give him an aura.

Both sexes will react differently to Nigel for the rest of his life: men will want to punch him; women, if I can coax him into abandoning those magnifying glasses he wears as spectacles in favour of contact lenses, will be desperate to mother him, to help him, to bring the best out in him, and show him how to have fun. Once he's old enough to realise this, he'll take full advantage of it and get the kind of women into bed that you'd never believe was possible.

Having said that, if he's lying dead in a ditch now, his future's academic. It's my job to find him and haul his arse back here so he can live long enough to prove my theory correct.

I'm terrified. Not for me but for Nigel. As I've said before, 'Jungle Jim' he ain't. If he's still alive when I find him, I'm going to murder the little swine!

What *is* going on? Just weeks ago my life was well ordered, set. Now all I seem to do is lurch from one emotional trauma to the next. I hope this is the last. I pray life hasn't got another rock hidden in its fist to hurl at me when this one is over.

The telephone's ringing, which makes my stomach turn. I'd better answer it, in case it's the Guards with news.

It's the following morning and there's still no sign of Nigel. The Guards have combed the entire area. Yesterday the four of us split up into two cars to search, Kate and I in one, Eugene and Caroline in the other.

I should have stayed with Caroline. She's distraught.

It's funny how families are often all about sibling rivalry until the shit hits the fan when the blood-is-thicker-than-water cliché suddenly becomes a reality. Life imposes a crisis upon you and it's amazing how clear and unmuddied love becomes.

225

Today all four of us are in the Range Rover. The trouble is, Nigel could have hitched his way to Galway, or Dublin, or Belfast. He could have stowed away on a ferry to England. We just don't know.

This morning we've covered Inchydoney beach, Dunmore, Ardfield. We've swung back on ourselves and combed Rosscarbery and Skibbereen. And found nothing.

So, we're heading home. Although none of us is hungry, it's lunchtime and we must eat to keep up our strength.

We've passed through Ring, and taken the slightly longer way home up towards Dunworley and beyond. As we arrive at a junction on the road, I stiffen.

A memory – a recent one – a flashcard whipped in front of my eyes by my brain or my heart is delivered with tenacity and compelling force. Perhaps it's what I believe is termed instinct. It's all new to me, all hokum – before Kate.

'Take a right,' I tell Eugene, who is driving the Range Rover.

'Now?' he queries.

'Right. Turn right.'

'Why?' he asks.

'I don't know. Just do it.'

Eugene looks at me. Can he see it too? Does he see the old cine-film, a hair trapped in the gate, stretched irretrievably across the frame, the captured moment in time: a young boy and an old woman, Winnie-the-Pooh and Piglet, laughing together, hugging each other on a rocky beach.

'Simon's Cove? Where we were the morning Maeve died?' he checks.

There's a sudden air of anticipation in the car. The two girls exchange glances, the first signs of hope tinged with fear. None of us is certain of what we may find there.

We all swing our legs and bodies out on to solid ground, me relying on the carved and whittled wood of my crutches.

We call Nigel's name as we scan beach and sea and, despondently, the horizon. We stop in unison, to await the faintest of whispered responses. The exercise is repeated, then, as the silence replies deafeningly, we stand still in despair.

I remain in the centre of the group, the rivet that holds together the minute and hour hands, while the others spread to various points on the clock-face. Eugene, at nine o'clock, overlooks the beach. Caroline, at four o'clock, searches the area from the car to the jagged rocks on her left. Kate, at twelve o'clock, walks to the cliff-top, her eyes panning straight ahead across the ocean.

This is my fault, I tell myself. I built up everyone's hopes.

'Max?' I'm disturbed from self-recrimination by the calm and certain tones of Kate's voice. 'Would you mind swinging your legs in my general direction?'

'Why?'

'I want you to confirm or deny whether I am overdue an appointment at Specsavers.'

I make my way slowly towards her.

'Cross your fingers,' she instructs.

'Bit awkward.' I indicate my crutches.

'Make a wish, and look down.'

I do as asked.

Yes! That's him all right.

'I'm not fantasising?' she enquires.

'Kate, you have just spotted a young boy, perched on a ledge, twelve feet or so below us, who could topple, or fall, or hurl himself on to the rocks below at any moment.'

'Thank you.' She sighs with relief. 'For one awful moment there, I thought I'd turned Greek.'

'Pardon?'

'Lost my marbles.'

227

I rest the side of my face against hers, then tenderly kiss her neck. 'No. We're both sane. Sort of.'

'Can he hear us, do you think?' she asks me.

I listen to the sound of the waves battering against the cliffs, and the wind roaring in my ears. Then I look down at the top of Nigel's head, and watch his small form shivering.

'I don't think he can. He must be terrified, not to mention freezing. We've got to move fast. Any ideas?'

'Time to dial the emergency services, wouldn't you say?' she suggests.

'Good idea. Fish my mobile out of my pocket, will you?'

Kate does so, and I watch her face fall.

'What's wrong?'

'There's no network up here, Max. Look, I'll take the car and drive into Ring.'

'Just a minute, Kate, let me think a second.'

Kate looks directly and unnervingly deep into my eyes. 'I'll go with you on this, Max. Trust your instincts. They've been right so far.'

Turning, I see Eugene and Caroline making their separate ways towards us.

I stumble and swing my way from the cliff's edge, sensing Kate as she follows my lead.

Damn! I'm now being asked to be both heroic and decisive at the same time. Neither are qualities I would rush to put at the top of my CV.

We all meet six feet or so from the cliff's edge.

'Okay.' I fake a commanding air of authority. 'It's like this: below the cliff-top behind us, some twelve or fourteen feet down, is a ledge. It's about four and a half feet wide, and about three feet or so deep. Now, don't ask me why, but upon this dangerous precipice some dozy, four-eyed teenager has decided to park his irritating little arse.'

I see shoulders sinking with relief, tears welling, words forming and I raise a finger to my lips.

'There's no network on the mobile phone. Besides which Nigel must be tired, dehydrated and disorientated. If we leave him there by himself and helicopters and life-boats start arriving, I'm scared he'll panic. Believe me, he's got precious little room for error down there. So we need to help him ourselves. Are we agreed?'

Eyes look at the floor. Which basically means, we are, but if this goes pear-shaped, you're on your own, pal.

'Fine. Eugene?'

'Max?' he says, still not raising his eyes from the ground.

'Is the tow-rope in the back of the Range Rover?'

'Yes.'

'Good. Right, well, one of us will have to be lowered down to the little monster.'

'I'll go,' Caroline says firmly. 'He's my brother.'

'That's the problem,' I inform her. 'He's your brother. Nobody can drive you closer to the edge than those you're related to. It's too risky, Caroline. And if you go over the edge with him, I'll probably end up in the slammer for it. I know how much you want to go. But, no. I won't allow it.'

'Oh, for feck's sake, there's no contest!' Eugene declares. 'Would you be looking at the facts, now? I'm an ol' git. My wife has gone. I've feck-all to lose. I'll do it. I've always fancied myself as a bit of a super-hero anyway. Come on, now, give us a chance to get me picture in the *Southern Star*. Ah, Max, you wouldn't deny an ol' friend his moment of triumph, would you, now?'

''Fraid so, Eugene. Someone will have to reverse the car. I'll explain why in a minute. I can't drive it, of course. Caroline can't, because she doesn't know how to and this is not the time for her first lesson, and Kate can't, because I've seen her drive before.'

'Oh, thanks very much,' Kate retorts, the faintest of smiles on her lips. 'So it looks like it's up to me.'

I shake my head at her.

'Why not?' she asks.

I lean forward and whisper into her ear: 'Call me a sexist pig, but there's no way on God's earth I'd even consider letting you go down there.'

She opens her mouth to protest.

'Anyway,' I say, raising my voice so the others can hear, 'you've got bigger muscles than me. I need Mrs Popeye keeping a tight grip on the rope at the top. Caroline, the minute I'm on the ledge with Nigel I want you to take the mobile and run as fast as you can back towards Ring. Telephone the emergency services the minute you get a signal. Better still, bang on the door of any house you come across, but get that call through.'

'Right.' She nods. 'And that's after we've lowered you?'

'Max!' protests Eugene. 'You're crazy. Face facts, boy. You are a—'

'Cripple? Ten out of ten for observation, Eugene. Which means I can't drive that car, I can't run into Ring, and it won't surprise you to discover I was never picked for the tug-of-war team at school. So, we tie the rope to the Range Rover's bumper, and, Eugene, you'll reverse the car to get Nigel back up here after I've put the rope around him. Very carefully, mind. Kate and Caroline will help you support the rope to get me down there. Agreed?'

No one bothers to argue.

'Right. Right,' I repeat again, the second time with considerably less confidence than the first. 'Let's do it.'

I have a rope around my waist. And, oh, Lordy, Lordy, I am now being dangled over the edge of a cliff.

The Range Rover is parked at the top, hand-braked, in gear

and the other end of the tow-rope is tied to the vehicle. Eugene has joined Caroline and Kate on the rope to lower me down, due to my weight. He can leap into the car when the moment arises.

'Okay.' I swallow. 'Let's get on with it.'

'Max, please take care,' Kate says.

'I fully intend to, don't you worry.'

Backwards and forwards and in and out I go, twirling as they lower me. A human yo-yo. Below me I can see a mass of craggy rocks with edges like serrated blades, and an angry sea leaping up at them, like a hungry animal waiting for its supper.

I have no idea if Nigel is aware of my presence as I descend the dozen or so feet to the ledge on which he is sitting. He certainly hasn't acknowledged it.

The rope is biting into my waist. This was no time to pretend I was a thirty-two when I was really a thirty-four, but it had to be tight.

Trouble is, if your legs don't work, abseiling is a bit of a bugger as I can't really steady myself.

All I can do is dangle in a somewhat ungainly fashion as the—

My head has just collided with the rock-face and I've closed my eyes against the pain. I open them as I swing back again and put my arm out for protection. I've hit my elbow and my left arm has gone numb.

I'm getting closer, or at least closer to Nigel, even if I am swinging several inches away from the lip of the ledge.

There's just a few feet to go. It's time to break the ice.

'Well, fancy meeting you here,' I announce loudly.

He looks up at me slowly. His eyes are glazed, and his small face is deathly pale from exposure to the elements.

Maybe he hadn't heard us. Perhaps he was too lost in his own pain.

'Max?' he says incredulously, and who can blame him? 'What are you doing here?' His voice is hoarse and faint.

'Trying to get my bronze medal for the Duke of Edinburgh award. How about you?'

Silence. He's shaking with both cold and fear, I shouldn't wonder.

'Eugene! Kate! Can you get me closer to the ledge? I need to go down about four feet,' I shout.

His eyes start to droop. He's in danger of falling asleep and I can't reach him. 'Wake up, Nigel. I will now do my world-famous impression,' I announce, letting my arms and neck go as floppy as my useless legs, as I sing, 'Here come's Muffin, Muffin the Mule!'

There's no response.

'No? Bit before your time? What about this? *Aw!* Flubalub,' I speak in best Flowerpot Man voice. 'No?' I move my hands and head, backwards and forwards in more rigid, robotic gestures, 'Here come's Spot the dog. The biggest spottiest dog you ever did . . . Whoa, horsy, fecking whoa!' I scream, but too late. The rope twists as they lower me too quickly, and I spin from left to right, a few feet away from Nigel.

My back hits something solid, and I feel the skin tear and open from the base of my spine to the nape of my neck as my body is slithered down the rock. The sticky sting of spilled blood warms my back. I'm aware of my legs folding somewhere beneath me, before the welcome relief of my buttocks once again touching *terra firma*.

We're alongside each other, about three feet apart, staring forward.

'Nice view,' I observe.

He's dangerously close to the edge of the ledge. I try to reach him but he's on my left-hand side and my arm is still injured from colliding with the rock-face.

'I shouted and shouted and shouted, but you didn't come,' he mutters, his eyes closing once again.

232

'I'm here now, aren't I? No, Nigel, don't go to sleep. Not after I took all this trouble to drop in on you.'

'You don't love me,' he hisses accusingly.

'Why am I here, then? Why is the rest of the posse here? They're up there waiting for you, Nigel. Eugene, Kate, Caroline—'

'Not Maeve.'

'Is that why you ran away? Because of Maeve?'

'Don't know. Can't remember. Too tired . . .'

He slips towards unconsciousness, and his body begins to tilt to the left, towards certain death.

'*Nigel!*' The sound of my voice jerks him upright with seconds to spare.

'If you're too tired to talk, Nigel, then just listen to me. You know I used to be a maudlin, morose, miserable git like you. I was like that when you first arrived, do you remember?'

He stares at me, forcing his eyes open.

'I really resented you and Caroline waltzing into my bloody life and preventing me from wallowing in self-pity. But then, after a while, I started to find you a distraction from my tendency to abuse the privilege of self-pity. A few weeks later, I was forced to confess to myself that I rather enjoyed having the two of you around. And today, I will have to admit that the reason I have just slid down a cliff like a low-budget stand-in for Sylvester Stallone is because I wouldn't know quite what to do with myself if you weren't around to annoy the crap out of me any longer.'

A small smile appears on his blue-tinged lips.

'I'd miss you, mate. You can't go falling off a cliff and leave me to deal with your stroppy sister all by myself. I need another man in the house. I need moral support. The lads have got to stick together,' I suggest, giving him a friendly nudge.

'You'll leave me, Max. Everyone I care about leaves me.'

Does he care for me? This strange, sad boy?

'Mum and Dad left me, and Maeve left me too.'

'They didn't want to leave you, Nigel. Your parents didn't want to die young in a boating accident, and Maeve didn't want to have a dodgy ticker.'

'Then why did they die?'

'I don't know. I write horror stories, when I'm not rescuing people off cliffs. I can't give you the meaning of life. You have to live it yourself. Glean as much as you can as you go along.'

A large sigh.

'Look, Nigel, I'd never seen Maeve happier than after you and she became friends. I mean, she started smiling instead of snarling. Asking, instead of ordering. Manners instead of downright rudeness. I mean it was ... horrible!'

Big smile now. 'Do you mean that?'

'Yes,' I reply honestly.

'I can't love you, Max. I swear I'll never love anyone again,' he states determinedly.

My mind spins back in time and I hear another strange little boy making himself that same promise after watching his mother die under a car.

Silence.

'Come on, Nigel,' I say at last. 'Let's get you home. I want you to stand up, and take a few steps towards me. Just get close enough for me to tie this rope around you.'

'No,' he replies.

'Don't be so dozy. You're so cold you've turned blue. Stick a white hat on your head, and you'd look a dead ringer for Papa Smurf!'

'I can't move, Max. I'm too scared.'

'Nigel, you have to. I can't get to you.'

'*No!*' he screams hysterically.

'Nigel, please. If you won't do it for me, do it for Maeve. She'd want me to take you home.'

He stands, whimpering as he does so, and takes a step towards me, then another, then another ... and I've got him. He's slumped down next to me, sobbing. Physically painful though it is for me to do so, I put my arm around him.

'It's all right, Nigel. It'll soon be over,' I say, as I untie the rope from around my waist with my good arm and adjust the noose.

'Stand up, slowly and carefully.' He does so without complaint. 'Now, slip this over your head. How the hell did you get down here in the first place?'

'I fell. It was dark,' he replies simply.

'Are you hurt?' I ask.

He shakes his head.

I reach up and tighten the rope around his waist. 'Right, here's what happens next. You turn and face the cliff-face. Eugene gets into the car and reverses it, slowly. You won't have to do much work. Hold on to the rope with your hands, and sort of walk up the rock. Just don't let go. Okay?'

He nods.

'Calling International Rescue!' I holler. 'Scott Tracy, can you hear me up there?'

'Yes,' Kate screams back.

'Okay. Nigel's roped up. Tell Eugene to start reversing the car.'

'Roger!' Kate shouts in reply.

'"Roger"?' I say, smiling at Nigel. 'That girl has got to stop watching so much television.'

The rope begins to tug at Nigel, and he panics.

'Off you go, Nigel. Stay calm and let the car do the work. You just take a vertical stroll. Hold on to the bloody rope!' I remind him as he starts to ascend.

'Arghh! Max, help me! Help me! Arghh!' He's hysterical with fear, his feet are lashing around wildly, and his left boot is clattering into my ear with an almighty thud.

'Keep calm, Nigel. Hold on to the rope,' I scream, as he clatters into the rock-face.

'*Arghh!* ARGHH! ARGHH!'

Something's snapped. His terror must have built up overnight. One thing's for certain, he's wide awake now, all right.

'No, *no*, NO!' he screams.

'Nigel, remember the bucking bronco!' I call after him.

'I'll try,' he sobs.

I've shut my eyes. I'm praying I don't feel a sudden rush of air, accompanied by a scream as he falls past me.

It felt like hours. But judging by the whoops and cheers emanating from the top of the cliff, I presume the mission is accomplished.

I'm shaking as I realise the level of responsibility I assumed in all this.

'Max! I'm sending the rope back down.'

'Listen, I'm hurt—'

'What?' Eugene shouts back.

'I don't know if it's—'

'I can't hear you, Max.'

The ocean and the roar of the wind seem to increase in volume tenfold, deafening me. There's the sound of an engine. I look up and see it's not the elements but a helicopter that's making all the noise.

Caroline must have found a working telephone.

27

What a week it's been! The newspaper headlines have been amazing.

EXTRA! EXTRA! READ ALL ABOUT IT!

'Novelist in Cliff-face Rescue Drama.'

'Godfather of Gore Drives Ward Over the Edge.'

'Forty Stitches as Horror-writer Saves Son of Dead Friend.'

And in one notoriously tacky tabloid, 'Wacko Wheelchair Writer Wobbles Willingly over Whopping Waves to Rescue Weird Waif Godson.'

English press, Irish press, television, RTE, BBC, you name them, they've covered it. There's also been lots of shots of my undignified and bleeding arse being hauled off the cliff-face in a winch, but you can't have everything, I suppose.

Depending on which paper you read, or news bulletin you watch, I am either irresponsible, a hero or a total nutter.

My agent and my publisher are in seventh heaven. 'Wonderful publicity, darling,' they've all cried down the phone.

Fortunately I've been locked in the tender, protective, and, of course, privately paid for, bosom of the Bon Secours hospital here in Cork City. Actually, I've been here rather longer than was necessary. I've told the troops that, although my arm has healed, my back injury is infected, but strictly speaking that's not true.

I had a chat with the doctor – about my legs.

I explained my situation. He wasn't much use personally, but flash a glamorous enough credit card and the relevant specialist appears like magic.

I went through my story with him in great detail and he gave me an examination. He rolled me over and felt my spine. Then he picked up both my legs, one at a time and waved them about in a variety of different directions.

Then he took a large spike from his pocket. It looked vicious. Before I had chance to ask him what exactly he thought he was going to with it, he ran the sharp point along the sole of one of my feet.

'Feel anything?' he asked.

'No. Should I?'

He repeated the exercise on the sole of my other foot.

'Anything at all?'

'No.'

'Concentrate, Mr Patterson. Look at the spike.'

I did.

'Now. Again?'

'No.'

The other foot.

'Now?'

'Ouch!' I flinched.

'Feel that?'

'Yes.'

He looked at me intensely. 'Once more?'

'Ouch! That hurt,' I yelped.

'Really?' He paused in thought. 'Okay. I'd like to run a few tests, with your permission.'

'Granted.'

'It means we'll have to keep you shut in here for a few days more, if that's okay.'

'Fine.'

'I'll get you organised, then. In the meantime, I want you to try to wiggle your toes. Keep sending messages down from the brain. Don't get discouraged if nothing happens straight away. Just keep trying. Okay? Good. I must dash.' And he disappeared.

Two days of needles, bloodtests, urine samples, X-rays, and endless, endless trying to persuade my stubborn feet to respond passed agonisingly slowly.

On the third day, the specialist breezed in again.

'Okay. Good news, I think. You have no permanent damage that we can detect. There's some muscle wastage through lack of use, but that's to be expected. Your nerve endings are a bit sleepy and need waking up. But, in theory, you could walk,' he announced.

'I wiggled my toes. I can wiggle my toes! Look!'

And I demonstrated.

'Good, good,' he said. 'Right, here's the score. You're going to have to do lots of mental exercises to wake up these nerve endings and reopen all the relevant communication channels, as it were, then hours of intense physiotherapy with a complete sadist in a white coat. You game?'

'Yep,' I said, giving my toes a twirl.

'Okay. I'll pop back tomorrow afternoon. Discuss a schedule with you.' He breezed back towards the door.

'Out of curiosity,' he said, turning before he left, 'I always like to ask. What made your toes move for you in the end?'

I smiled at him. 'I thought of something nice.'

'Hmmm. Yes, I think I'll leave that there, judging by that grin. Good-day.'

I did think of something nice. I thought of Kate. I thought of dancing with Kate. And that made my toes dance too. It made them curl up with pleasure.

The mere thought of her made a small miracle occur.

I've been back home for two days. Reaction to my reckless and foolhardy stunt has been varied. Eugene keeps asking if 'Action Man would like another grape', or 'Is it okay if I have the afternoon off tomorrow to visit the dentist, Mr Diehard'?

Caroline is fawning. 'You're so brave, so kind, Max.' 'Wow! what an amazing man.' 'You're my hero.'

And Nigel? He never mentions it, but he is visibly more settled, more relaxed than at any other time since his arrival.

And Kate? She has just smiled and bathed my wounds and shagged me senseless, which is by far and away my favourite reaction.

It's lunchtime and I've taken Caroline and Nigel to the pub for a large, celebratory meal. We've agreed that next month Nigel buries himself down a disused mineshaft, and the month after that Caroline takes novice vows for a nunnery to escape the devil-worship her godfather is subjecting her to. Then we split three ways any extra profit the publicity brings.

'I need the toilet,' Nigel announces, before slipping off his stool and strolling off.

'He's getting better, I think,' Caroline states, as he disappears from view. 'He wouldn't be here at all if it wasn't for you, Max. I'm so grateful. If there's anything, anything at all I can do for you, just ask,' she says.

'Actually, Caroline, there is something.'

'Oh?' She leans slightly closer across the table towards me.

'I need a co-conspirator. A confidante and ally. Can you keep a secret?' I ask.

'For you, Max, anything.'

I'm not sure she's telling the truth, but Caroline is the only one who can help me, all things considered.

'When I was in the hospital I had a major breakthrough.'

'Did you? What happened?'

'I moved my toes.'

'Max!' she shouts.

'Sssh! It's a secret, remember?'

'Sorry. I'm just so happy for you.'

'I've embarked on an intensive physiotherapy campaign. There's a chance I might walk again.'

'Fantastic!' she yells.

'Caroline!'

'Sorry,' she says, taking a sip of her Cidona. 'I'm over-whelmed,' she adds, waving her free hand in front of her face. 'What do you want me to do?'

'I don't want anyone else to know about this—'

'Not even Kate?' she interrupts.

'Especially not Kate,' I confirm, and she smiles. 'Nothing's guaranteed, it might not work out. I don't want to disappoint anyone. On the other hand, if I pull it off, I quite fancy pulling the big surprise number.'

'When do you start the physio?' Caroline asks.

'It began while I was in hospital. The thing is, I really want to go for it. So it's going to be a heavy programme. I've arranged to do most of it in Cork, so I'm going to be disappearing off quite a bit and I may need you to cover for me.'

'I'll be happy to,' she says.

'Perhaps you could come with me a few times, give me a bit of moral support.'

'I'd love to,' she chirps.

'Also, if I'm going to speed things up, I'll need to work in the gym at home.'

'How exciting.'

'I may need you to get Kate out of the house occasionally.'

'I'll think of something.'

'I may also need you to sneak down to the gym and help me with one or two of the exercises. I don't want to involve Eugene, you see. I want to surprise him as well. Cheer him up after Maeve's death.'

'I'm really looking forward to it.'

'You on, then?'

'Definitely. When do I start?'

'This afternoon. I'm off to Cork – officially to have my wounds checked.'

She taps the side of her nose.

'I've a new piece of kit arriving to put into the gym. Kate has to be out of the house.'

'No problem.'

'And remember—'

'Don't worry, Max. It'll be our little secret,' she assures me, smiling in a slightly disconcerting way.

I glance over my shoulder and see Nigel returning across the pub floor. I turn back to Caroline and she gives me a wink, which I return.

I feel great. Everything's organised, in place. I've decided, you see. I'm going to tell Kate I love her on the day I take my first steps.

Then maybe, just maybe, I'll have a chance.

Three days of torture later and I'm knackered. I ache all over.

Today Kate asked me why Caroline suddenly wanted to be her best friend, which unnerved me a bit. 'Does she?' I asked.

'Yes. She keeps asking me to go shopping, or out for a drink. It's most odd.'

I had to think fast. 'Maybe that lecherous, pimply boyfriend of hers is doing her some good, after all. You know, calming her down or something.' I changed the subject faster that a Formula One team changes wheels. I must tell Caroline to be more careful. She has all the subtlety of a cart-horse farting.

Twelve days on and I'm euphoric. I CAN STAND – for about three seconds.

It may be no big deal to you, but to me it's one jump from doing an Irish jig while turning somersaults.

I must say Caroline has been fantastic. She's distracted Kate in order to allow me to slope off to Cork and see the physio, kept lookout, and generally covered my back. She's even come to Cork a few times and cheered me on. She's pulled on the outfit I bought her from the sports shop when she first arrived, which hadn't seen the light of day since her own clothes arrived from England. Then she's come down to the basement and waved my legs around for me and helped me on to bits of kit. I'm a big fellow to lump around, but she's stronger than she looks. We've laughed about it together – I couldn't have done it without her.

There's just one slight problem. Yesterday, Kate caught us coming back up from the gym. Caroline was in a tracksuit, looking all sweaty.

'What have you both been up to?' she asked, suspiciously.

'Caroline is getting fit.'

'I hardly think you need to lose weight,' Kate said to her.

'It's a secret,' Caroline blurted, and I think my heart stopped for at least a full minute.

'What is?' Kate asked.

'From my boyfriend. There's a race, over at Bandon Water. We're going down the rapids on a raft. He's entered a team, you see, and they think they're going to win. So Julie and me and a couple of others are going to enter another raft and beat the crap out of the boys.'

Kate's eyes narrowed. 'Bit dangerous, isn't it, Max?'

'No, it's okay. There's plenty of people there to fish them out if they fall in.'

Kate sighed. 'If you say so. Do you two athletes want a drink?'

We said yes in a nervous chorus. One Coke and a beer were requested as Kate headed for the kitchen.

'Brilliant,' I whispered to Caroline. 'How did you think of that?'

'Something I learned at school,' she replied. 'If you're going to make up an excuse for not doing an essay, make it as complicated as possible. More chance of getting away with it.'

Kate hasn't mentioned it since, so I assume that's just what we did.

Day fourteen.

Caroline cornered me alone in the kitchen while I was making a cup of coffee. 'Kate asked me where I was going today.'

'When?' I asked.

'As we were on our way out to the hospital, and while I was looking for my purse. She'd just seen you going out of the front door.'

'Damn! What did you say?'

She widens her eyes and raises her palms upwards. 'I just said I was going out with Max.'

'Why in God's name did you say that?'

'What else was I supposed to say?'

'You were quick enough with the raft story.'

'Sorry,' she snapped, half whispering, half shouting. 'I can't be brilliant every time. I'm doing my best.'

'Of course you are,' I assured her.

This can't go on much longer without us being rumbled.

Day eighteen.

A magical moment in Cork today. I got out of the chair and

244

walked between two parallel bars. It's not really walking because you can use the bars to support your weight on your arms. But I was upright, with my feet beneath me and I can't begin to describe how wonderful that felt.

Kate's asleep in my arms.

We had a dangerous conversation before she nodded off.

'Max, is everything all right?' she asked.

'I think so, why?'

'You just seem distant. Preoccupied.'

'Do I? I'm sorry. Just a few things on my mind. Work pressures, you know.'

'We don't seem to talk the way we used to. And you're always going off somewhere without me. Where do you go to?'

'There are people I have to see, that's all.'

'In Cork?'

'Yes. It's just a bit of business I have to attend to, concerning this house,' I lied.

'What about this house?'

'I can't tell you. It's a secret.'

'Max?'

'You'll know very soon, I promise you. It's a surprise. It'll ruin it if I say any more.'

'If you're sure,' she said, searching my eyes.

'I am. I'm going to give you the biggest surprise of your life.'

'Okay,' she said uncertainly.

'I'm sorry if you think I've been ignoring you. Give us a cuddle, please?'

She turned her back and snuggled into me, her bottom pressed against my groin. It feels sexy, yet comforting and loving at the same time. Definitely a mixture I could learn to live with.

It's nine thirty a.m. I'm in the gym, and I've the house to myself for a change. Well, almost. Eugene has driven to Cork to pick up a spare part for his ride-on lawnmower and he's persuaded Nigel to go with him. Kate has driven into Ballinkilty to top up on stationery supplies. And Caroline's here, but still in bed. She seems converted to that long-standing teenage tradition of never dragging your arse out of bed before lunchtime unless absolutely necessary.

So I've popped down here by myself. I'm lying on my back on a bench doing a few simple exercises. It's a hot day, and I'm just in shorts, but I'm still sweating, even in the basement. If this keeps up I may be able to walk again but I'll have lost so much body fluid I'll look like a stick of pasta.

Caroline's just come into the gym. She's dressed in the leggings and the halter-neck top I bought her.

'Morning, sleepy-head. Bit early for you, isn't it?'

She doesn't appear to be listening. She walks barefoot across the gym floor and presses her back against the wall.

'I didn't think you'd be up and around for hours,' I tell her.

'I couldn't sleep. It's so hot.' She pulls at her halter-neck top – to let in air, I presume.

'You should try counting pigs.'

'Pigs?' she queries, licking her lips.

'Less attractive than sheep. More of an incentive to nod off. There's nothing even vaguely idyllic about a pig trying to frosby-flop over a farm gate.'

She sighs slowly. There's something wrong here.

'Anything bothering you, Caroline?'

She glances at me, then looks away.

'Caroline? I said. 'Is there something wrong?'

She takes a deep breath, as if steeling herself. Then she turns to face me. 'Don't you know?'

'Afraid not. I got a D minus for telepathy at the Doris Day School for the Occult.'

'Okay.' She pauses, then looks directly into my eyes. 'It's you, Max.'

'Me? What have I done now?'

'Nothing. That's just the point.' She begins drawing pictures on the floor with a big toe as she speaks, as if she were trying to spell something out for me. 'You must have noticed.'

'I wouldn't bank on it,' I tell her.

'You're so kind and brave and good. I felt it the day of the country-and-western festival when you rode the bucking bronco. Then I fooled myself into thinking I was just being silly. But the day you rescued Nigel, I knew I'd been lying to myself and that it was true. I'm in love with you, Max.'

'*Bloody hell!* You can't be!' I explode.

'I am,' she whispers. 'We've had such fun together here, haven't we, Max? These last two weeks.'

'Yes, but—'

'We've not stopped laughing. We've loved being together, haven't we, Max?'

'Yes, but, Caroline, I'm your godfather. You're not in love with me. You just miss your father.'

'No, that's not it.' She runs her hands through her hair, suggestively, the way she's seen seductresses behave on television. The trouble is, she manages to trap one of her fingers in her hair-slide. 'Ouch!'

'You okay?'

'I'm fine.' She's trying to flick it off her finger, but it's refusing to budge.

'I'm an old man – well, compared to you.' I'm aware this is an irrational burst of ego.

'But you're so . . .' she's distracted by the stubborn slide '. . . so sexy, Max!' At last she frees it, and wantonly hurls it across the gym. 'You're very, very sexy.' She tosses back her hair and the top of her skull makes a nice cracking sound as it collides with the wall. 'Ow!' She rubs her head with her hand.

'Caroline! Stop this before you maim yourself.'

'I can't. When I lie in bed at night, when I'm in the bath, when I'm with my boyfriend, all I think about is you touching me, you kissing me, you making love to me . . .'

Good grief! She's running her hands over her breasts as she says this.

'Cut it out!' I shout.

'You've enjoyed me touching you, haven't you, Max? Here, in the gym. I know you have. I've felt it.' She begins to take off her leggings.

'Caroline! A young girl like you shouldn't be fantasising about some old fart who writes horror stories and who gets about the house in a glorified bloody shopping-trolley! It's not healthy.'

'But you won't be in that thing for much longer, will you? Don't you think I'm attractive, Max?' Her leggings are tight and they're sticking to her legs. She makes a noise like an American tennis player serving with each tug she gives them. It's like stripping by numbers. 'Don't you *grunt* think I'm *grunt* sexy?' She waddles towards me now, leggings stuck at half-mast.

Things are improving for me physically, but I still can't run away.

'I know you like young girls, Max. I've seen.' She hops, as one leg of the leggings is removed. 'I know they turn you on,' she gasps. They're off now, but she barely has the energy to throw them over her shoulder.

'I know they excite you.' She turns her attention to the button at the back of her halter-neck top. True to form, it's stuck. 'I know *I* turn you on.' She abandons her attempt to undo the button, and opts to lift the whole thing over her head instead. The button's too tight and it's got stuck around her forehead like a headband. She looks like she's wearing an outrageous hat. 'Let me make you happy, Max,' she asks, as she finally frees the top. 'Please, please! I love you.' She removes her knickers, which at least give her no problems.

She stands before me naked, panting, not with passion but with exhaustion. Her face is a mixture of red and blue, her hair is bedraggled and there are several scratches where she has caught her face with her nails.

It's like being seduced by someone who has just been toyed with by a playful leopard.

'Caroline! No!' I plead, raising my arms.

Christ! She's landed upon me, and is sitting on my lap. The trouble is, she's thrown her full bodyweight against me and I'm winded. Hell fire! She's pressed her mouth against mine before I've had a chance to breathe. I'm suffocating. Her tongue's in my mouth and now I'm choking.

'Good to see you're not neglecting any area of your goddaughter's education, Max.'

A voice. Kate's.

The world turns black.

Caroline jumps off me and I suck in air as if I had just risen from the depths, and broken the surface water of the ocean.

'Did you enjoy that, Max?' Kate asks, her beautiful eyes filling with tears.

'Now just hold on a minute, Kate. This isn't what you think it is.'

'So this is what Caroline's *really* been getting fit for?'

'No!'

Kate looks from my eyes to Caroline's naked body. For what feels like an eternity, she stands very still. Then she nods. 'Perfectly innocent. Any fool can see that.' She turns and leaves the room. I can hear her climbing the stairs.

'Pass me my crutches,' I bark at Caroline and she does so. 'Now help me into my chair.'

Again no argument.

'Now get dressed, for God's sake!' I scream at her, before setting off after Kate.

The climb up the ramp has taken aeons. Half of me has wanted to rush to Kate, the other half has wanted the journey to take for ever.

My stomach turns as I enter her room. Two suitcases are open on the bed. Clothes are being tossed into them in heaps – dresses, jeans, underwear, the lot.

'What are you doing?'

She doesn't reply, just continues to throw the contents of her wardrobe into the cases.

I begin to shake as the realisation hits me. 'Don't go, Kate. Please don't go.'

Silence again. She won't speak to me, she won't fucking speak.

'You're wrong. I swear you're wrong. Please listen to me!'

'I don't want to, Max. Not any more.'

'She jumped me!' I scream at her.

Kate spins to face me. Her eyes are red, and her cheeks awash with tears. 'For heaven's sake, Max,' she blazes, 'she's not even sixteen! Take responsibility for your own actions. At least be decent enough to do that!'

'I didn't *do* anything, Kate,' I say, pleading now.

'She was on top of you, Max. I saw it with my own eyes. How dare you deny it!' Drawers are emptying, suitcases are filling, the clock is ticking. 'I should have seen. I did see. I knew. I warned you. Business meetings in Cork. Hah! Hotel rooms with Caroline, more like.'

'That's not true. Listen, one minute she was telling me how great she thought I was, the next she was telling me she loved me, and before I knew it she was flying through the air at me, arms and legs flaying about like Bruce bloody Lee in *Enter the*

Dragon. She's a fatherless teenager, a mass of developing hormones. That wasn't an affair you witnessed, it was a clumsy mistake, an embarrassment —'

'Max, I've seen you both after a session in your gym. I've seen you come back up the stairs, faces red, covered in sweat. Now I know why!'

'Remember the surprise I said I had for you?'

'Oh, you had a surprise, all right. Men!' she spits, as she struggles to close the cases. 'Always excuses, always lies. You justify any behaviour you want, no matter the cost. Then expect to carry on as if nothing has happened. It's a pity you're in the wrong sort of electric chair, Max, because I swear, if you'd bought it from some southern American state, I'd volunteer to throw the switch myself. I'd send the volts through your pathetic body, you worthless bastard!'

Pathetic body. I shrivel inside.

'Maeve warned me about what you were like. But I trusted you, Max. You knew I'd been hurt. I thought you understood that I couldn't take it if—' She wipes the tears from her cheeks roughly with her knuckles. 'You're warped. Sick. She's fifteen, for pity's sake! She's your own goddaughter. You should get counselling before it's too late. Otherwise how long will it be before they start getting younger? How long before they lock you up for it?'

I can't speak. I haven't done anything. Why does the woman I love ... How can she think this of me?

'I believed in you, Max. I really believed in you. I thought you were the One. I thought I'd finally found a man I could trust, a man who would stay faithful.'

'Kate,' I begin huskily, 'I have something to say to you, something I should have been brave enough to say a long time ago.'

'No, Max! I don't want to hear it. I don't want any confessions—'

'You don't understand,' I whisper. 'The reason Caroline has been helping me is because—'

'Save it for the next idiot. I'm leaving. I don't need this pain.'

'Please don't go! I was going to tell you on the day I took my first—'

'I'll send for the rest of my things,' she cuts through me. She picks up her suitcases and heads for the bedroom door, where she pauses, and turns to me once more. 'You're a fraud, Max Patterson. You don't even need to be in that bloody wheelchair. You're not physically handicapped, you're just an emotional cripple.'

And then she leaves the room.

I can hear everything: her footsteps on the stairs,

I'm struggling to stand, my muscles trembling.

the front door opening,

I'm fighting to keep my balance.

her key turning in the lock of her car,

I'm willing my left foot to move forward.

the dull thump as the suitcases hit the floor of the car boot,

It moves for me. My first step.

the rustle of her dress as she climbs into the driver's seat.

My teeth are piercing my lip in concentration. I taste the blood in my mouth as I take a second step.

I hear the engine start on Kate's car.

I begin to lose balance as I take the third step.

I hear the tyres spin on the gravel of my drive.

'*Kate! I love you!*' I shout, as my legs give way and my face hits the floor.

The sound of her car fades to be replaced by the cry of my own anguish.

28

I've been locked in my office for three days, thinking and brooding or raging and crying. Three days of not eating, three nights of not sleeping.

I have been surprised at how physical the ache of losing Kate has been. A gnawing, turning, stabbing, ceaseless pain that adds to the mental and emotional trauma. The love of my life has left me.

I can't write. For the first time in my life I couldn't give a damn about my work. I don't care if I never work again. I've lost the desire to create.

What is the point? Life isn't about careers or money, or big fuck-you houses and expensive cars. It's not about drinking, or drugs, or wild parties at nightclubs. Neither is it about the ordinary things like watching television, or paying bills, or going to the supermarket.

Life for me is about Kate. It's about making love to your soul-mate. It's about wanting to make her happy when she's sad, better when she's sick. It's about wanting her help in difficult times, and wanting to share all your good times because they mean absolutely nothing without her. It's about being proud to be with her: It's about wanting to speak to her, just to hear the sound of her voice, about finding excuses to look at her.

It's about being near her as often as you can, because – I don't know – you just fucking love being with her.

Oh, God, why won't the pain go away? Why can't I think of something else? I can't stop running the events that led to this through my head, over and over again, searching for mistakes I made. I'm trying to understand how she could have thought such dreadful things about me.

Because I didn't do anything wrong.

I'm emerging from my isolation. I have to talk to Caroline, put things straight. I slide myself into my old wheelchair and make my way slowly down to her bedroom.

I have been reliably informed by Eugene that Caroline has been mirroring my hermit-like behaviour.

I knock politely on the door.

'Who is it?'

'It's Max, Caroline. I thought we should speak. May I come in?'

'Okay.'

I wheel myself in. It's like watching Sky TV. Another repeat, a rerun of a programme you didn't like the first time round.

Caroline is packing her suitcases.

'Going somewhere?' I ask.

'Mmmm,' she replies weakly.

'Want to tell me where?'

She goes to her wardrobe and removes another two or three items of clothing. 'We're going back to England, Max. It's the end of the holidays and it's time to go back to school.'

I shake my head. 'With everything that's happened, I completely forgot. I'm sorry.'

She shrugs. 'That's okay. We miss our friends, anyway. I think it's probably for the best,' she says, neatly folding the clothes and laying them on top of others.

I sigh. 'Our friends. I take it Nigel's going with you, then?'

'I told him he didn't have to. He said he wouldn't stay here without me.'

'I see.'

She shuts the suitcase, and the sound of the zip closing around its perimeter seems to echo around her bedroom. 'Max,' she speaks softly, 'I feel awful about this but—'

'It's okay, Caroline. Of course I'll pay the fees.' I read the embarrassment in her eyes. 'You don't have to leave. Please don't go.'

For the second time in a matter of days, a woman cries as she prepares to leave me.

'The only reason I thought about going to school in Ireland was to be near you. I can't stay here, Max. Not now. Not after all I've done.'

'Yes, you can. You fell for your teacher, your boss, your . . . circumstantial fantasy. It wasn't real. It's not your fault, Caroline.'

'Yes, it is!' she shouts. 'I did something terrible and there's no one else to blame but myself. I made Kate go away, Max. Not you, me.' She is sobbing. 'I can't forgive myself.'

'When will you leave?'

'There's a flight tomorrow morning.'

'Let's talk about this, Caroline. I honestly think you're being a bit hasty.'

'No, I'm not, Max.' She smiles at me feebly. 'The problem is, I meant what I said. I do love you. And I know you'll never forgive me for driving Kate away.'

The truth is, she's probably right. I stare at her with a mixture of sadness and desperation. I simply haven't the strength left to argue against her.

'Okay. I'll book your flights. Then I'll speak to your headmaster and sort everything out. You're not to worry, you hear?' I reverse my chair and wheel myself out of her room.

The door opposite is ajar. A small, spectacled face peeps around its edge.

'Are you sure you want to go back to school as well, Nigel?' I ask.

He nods and shuts the door in my face.

Caroline and Nigel are leaving. We're on the drive. Eugene has just brought the Range Rover to the front of the house and loaded their suitcases into it.

Caroline is weeping. 'I love you, Max,' she says.

'And I – I care for you, too, Caroline. But just as a godfather.'

'I know.'

I turn to Nigel and ruffle his hair. 'Do us a favour, Nigel. No more moonlight flits, eh? You've given me enough grey hairs as it is.'

'I promise,' he replies stiffly.

'Go on, get back to school and see your friends. Maybe you could come over and see me at half-term, if you'd like? Remember to telephone and keep in touch. Okay?'

Nods, shrugs, then they clamber into the car.

Eugene closes the doors after them, and walks back over to me. 'You shouldn't be letting them go, Max,' he declares.

'What the hell can I offer them here, Eugene?'

'More than you realise, you dozy great fecker,' he states, before walking back to the car and closing the door. The car moves off down the drive.

Nobody waves goodbye, or looks back.

Silence.

Emptiness.

I must stop this crying game. I'm so tired. I'm also racked with guilt. I've failed. I've let Jamie and Marcia down. I've let Caroline and Nigel down. I've let myself down.

The only person I have never betrayed is Kate. And she'll never believe me.

'The Man in Black. He lives alone.'

29

It's been a month since the kids followed Kate out of the door and I wish I could say I feel better. But I don't. I feel bitter, cynical and disturbed.

Losing Kate is the most terrible thing that has ever happened to me. It's worse than Jamie's accident or Maeve passing away, and even more painful than my mother's terrible death.

It's just after eleven and I'm sitting in the drawing room, nipping at the whiskey. Alcohol doesn't help either. Since Kate and the kids left, I have tried to drink Ireland dry, and I have yet to feel even slightly tipsy, let alone drunk.

I haven't heard a single word from her. Not a phone call, a fax, a letter. Nothing.

Many of her clothes and possessions and some of the things I bought for her are still here. I wanted to burn them at first. Now I find myself wandering into the Medieval Room to sit among them. I punish myself as I inhale her scent and remember how we would lie wrapped in each other's arms, as we talked about the days ahead.

Minutes ago, it seems, I was a man who had everything. Now I'm back in my shell.

Max Patterson is now incapable of love once again.

It's just after ten the following morning and Eugene and I are having a late breakfast together in the kitchen.

Eugene looks around at the disarray. 'This place is a tip. There's packets half open all over the place, tea-stains all over the work-surfaces and the floor's so dirty my shoes are sticking to it. What's this?' he continues, waving a dirty cup under my nose. 'Would you look at the mould on the inside of that cup? Another couple of days and there'll be enough penicillin in it to cure my asthma. I hate to mention this, boy –'

'Then fucking don't,' I bark.

'– but we need some help. We're going to have to replace Maeve, or Kate, or both. I'm only talking practically now, you understand?'

I look into his kind green eyes. 'Except we can't replace them, can we Eugene? You can't replace Maeve, and I'll never be able to replace Kate.'

'No. No, that we won't, Max,' he says, as he stands, and I sense the pain I have caused him.

'Sorry. I hear what you're saying. I'll make a call this morning. Perhaps we'll play safe and go for a man, eh? All boys marooned together. What do you say?'

He smiles. 'A gentleman's club, Max. And why not, indeed?'

The familiar sound of the postman opening the front door and hurling the mail into the hall distracts us.

'I'll go see what little bundles of joy he's brought this morning, will I?' He walks slowly out of the kitchen.

I make a half-hearted attempt to clear some of the detritus from the table.

'Oh, God, *oh*, *God*,' I hear Eugene cry from the hall.

'Eugene? What's wrong?'

'OH, GOD!

259

'Eugene?'

He comes running back. His face is pale, and he is holding a single letter in his trembling hand.

'Holy Mother of God, Max, I can't open this. I can't.'

'What is it?' I ask urgently.

'Here. Will you be after opening it? I can't bear to look. It's too desperate.'

I try to take the offered letter from his hand, but it's twitching so badly that I keep missing it. 'Keep still, man,' I shout at him.

Eventually I snatch the letter from his hands. The envelope is all too familiar.

I look up at him. 'This is a letter from my publishers.'

'I know, I know.'

I examine it more closely. 'From my publishers, yet they've addressed it to you.'

He's nodding.

'I don't understand. Why have they addressed it to you?'

'For feck's sake, Max, would you put a man out of his agony and just – just open the fecking thing!'

'All right, all right.' I tear open the envelope, fish out the letter and read it aloud.

Dear Mr MacEoin,

I am delighted to inform you that I am in a position to make you an offer of £25,000 for your manuscript, *American Tans*.

We propose to publish in the summer of next year.

I think it would be in your best interests, at this stage, to appoint an agent to handle all matters of contract. I recommend Julian Floyd of the Durgess Black literary agency. You can contact him on 0171 325 8910. Perhaps when you have spoken to him you could contact me on the above number and let me know if you wish to accept the offer.

Congratulations on writing a superbly original crime novel! We are all very excited by it here.

I look forward to speaking to you,

Yours sincerely,

Joan Timber.

'*Yeee-hah!*' Eugene screams, as he dances a jig around the kitchen table.

I am flabbergasted. 'Joan Timber! But she's my editor.'

'*Wooo-hah!*'

'From my publishing house!'

'*Yippee!*'

'She's even set you up with my agent!'

'*Yes, yes, yes!*'

I don't believe this. I should be delighted for him, but my godchildren have deserted me, the love of my life has disappeared, and now I'm about to have my professional thunder stolen by my bloody odd-job man.

'Why did you call it *American Tans*, Eugene? I mean, after we took all the business with the tights out and substituted—'

'Ah, well, you see, Max,' he interrupts, 'I took an artistic gamble on that one. The idea you had about the crucifix written in blood was brilliant, I cannot deny it. But I just had a sneaky feeling – call it a writer's instinct – that I was on the right lines with the ol' ten denier.'

'But why did you send your manuscript to my publishers?'

'I'd no idea where else to send it, so.'

I scratch my head tensely. 'Why didn't you tell me? Why didn't you ask me?'

'I wanted the book to live or die on its own merits now.'

I stare at him, eyes narrowed. 'Eugene, you've just been

pulled off the slush pile and paid twenty-five grand. That just doesn't happen any more.'

'Well.' He has the decency to blush. 'I might have dropped your name and my position in your household in the letter I sent them, come to think of it.'

'You surprise me,' I say sarcastically.

'Max, me ol' friend, aren't you delighted for me?'

Of course I am. *No!* I'm pissed off.

'I'm thrilled for you,' I tell him.

'Oh, Max! Isn't it a pity my Maeve can't be here to share this with me, now?'

The big feller's eyes fill with tears.

'She'd have been really proud of you today, Eugene.'

'Do you think so, Max? I could have told her, and then I could have asked what she'd like me to buy her out of the cheque. I could have bought her anything, anything she wanted. And then I could have told her how much I loved her.'

His head is slumped on his forearms, and he is weeping openly.

'I never told Kate I loved her, Eugene.'

He looks up at me.

'I tried. But I just got scared, didn't want to frighten her off. Isn't that ironic? I was going to tell her when . . . I had a plan. But I left it too late.'

'Well, boy, that's something we'll both have to live with.'

Now I'm crying too. Two men are sitting at the kitchen table weeping for their lost loves. And neither of us is able to bring them back.

It's a week or more since Eugene became a star and, to add insult to injury, West Cork's answer to Ruth Rendell is slowly becoming insufferable.

I'll give you an example. The telephone rings an hour ago. I can't expect the celebrity of the house to demean himself by answering, so I do it myself. 'Hello. Max Patterson here.'

'Oh, hello. This is Ciara Scully from the *Cork Examiner*. We were wondering if it might be possible to arrange an interview some time this week?'

'I don't really do much in the way of interviews,' I replied.

'Oh, sorry for the misunderstanding now, Mr Patterson. But it's Eugene MacEoin we were wanting to talk to, though thinking about it, it would be a lovely angle to get the two of you together. That's if you wouldn't mind?'

Mind? Mind? Why the fuck should I mind? 'How do you know about Eugene's book anyway?'

'Oh, he rang us with the good news. We're always glad to hear of a local success story. He sent me a copy of the manuscript as well. I'm only half-way through, but it's awfully good, don't you think?'

'Terrific.' I sighed.

It appears our hot-shot author is also a great self-publicist. Then, just to make my day a little sunnier, I get a letter from Caroline stating that neither she nor Nigel will be coming home for half-term. They are both staying with friends. I call the headmaster and he confirms this. He gives me the numbers of the friends' respective parents and they confirm it too.

I was so depressed I phoned my editor and my agent and gave them both a bollocking, which made me feel so guilty and selfish that I ended up agreeing to do a book tour to promote the latest hardback. I hate book tours, I hardly ever do them. Under the circumstances, though, it might fill in time and keep me occupied.

Anyway, the gym's the thing. At least in the gym I have a sense of purpose, of something I need to achieve, so I've been concentrating on killing myself and making my sweat glands work overtime so that, with a bit of luck, I'll go brain dead and I won't even be able to remember Kate. At least, that's my theory.

Failing that, I'll have another drink. That's why I've escaped for an hour. I thought it was time I faced the tiniest segment of the outside world.

I've driven myself down to the pub in Ring, and am now supping the first pint of Guinness I can remember imbibing in ages.

A very fine, soft, shapely thigh has just eased its way on to the corner of my table. The skirt, bunched at its uppermost limit, is short, and a pair of brief, transparent, lacy knickers are visible. I tear my eyes away and look up.

'Hello, Max. Long, long time no see.'

'Hello, Justine.' I force a smile.

'Well? No news, so?'

'Oh, Justine, the Third World War has come and gone since we last met.' I feel embarrassed.

'Haven't you missed me at all, now, Max?' she asks.

I swallow some more of my pint guiltily.

'I've missed you, Max,' she whispers. 'And you, you bastard, haven't even bothered to ring me. I know I got cross. But you didn't even tell me you were related to the girl. I had to find out from someone else.'

Misunderstandings. I flinch at how costly they can be.

'I'm sorry, Justine.' And I am.

'How will you make it up to me, then?' she asks, dipping her finger into the head of my Guinness then placing it briefly in her mouth. 'I'm not working. You could drive me home now. Finish what you started?'

There's a pause while we look at each other. Sex, lust, passion, it's all here. On the proverbial plate.

Justine is lovely. She has a beautiful face, stunning body, strong personality and is deceptively bright. I can have her and she may take away my pain for a few short pleasant minutes. But what is the point if it isn't Kate? And I'm not quite ready for 'just sex' again.

'I'm sorry, Justine. I could tell you it's nothing to do with you, which is true, but you'll never believe me. I could lie and say I don't fancy you. Or, worst of all, I could say yes, take advantage and let the truth come out later. I'm not really up for any of those at the moment.'

'Okay. See you around, Max.' Her mouth smiles, yet her eyes tell me I've hurt her as the thigh slips away from my table.

I've just arrived home to find Eugene in the kitchen. He's hovering, waiting for my return.

'Everything all right?' I say, disturbed by the expression on his face.

'I meant to catch you before you left. Honest I did.'

'What's wrong?'

'There's a letter for you, boy. I picked it up off the mat this morning. I was going to put it with the rest in your office—'

'Don't worry, Eugene. It's not your job. I'll give the agency another ring this afternoon. Tell them any useless twerp will do as long as we get some extra hands around here.'

'You'd best be reading it. I recognised the handwriting, you see.'

He's passed me the letter.

It's from Kate. I breathe deeply, then tear open the envelope.

'Get us a whiskey, will you, Eugene?' I open the folded page and read,

Dear Mr Patterson,

I am writing on behalf of Kate Mayle.

I believe there are still many items of clothes and belongings of Kate in the house you shared. We would be grateful if you returned them to the above address.

Yours faithfully

Richard

It's a London address. She's back in England. I check, but there's no telephone number.

Richard. There's a sort of squiggle where the surname should be. It looks as if it's been written by a two-year-old, or a doctor who's signed a prescription when he's pissed as a fart. It's completely illegible. So 'Richard' is supposed to be enough, is it? We're just supposed to know, are we? Like this guy is *so* famous.

I didn't think it could get any worse. But the thought of my Kate with another man sinks me to greater depths.

I don't want these pictures. Please can someone switch off the screen in my head.

30

It's a week later and we're in the drawing room. That's yours truly, Eugene mega-star MacEoin, and the journalist from the *Cork Examiner*.

We've shaken hands, we've had the How-was-your-journey? and the Amazing-house-you-have-here speeches. Why do people always say, 'Wow! Where did you find this?' It seems pretty obvious to me that I found it right here where it is, isn't it? Do people really presume I found it near Clapham Common and had it shipped over brick by brick? Or that I discovered bits of it in different places. 'Well, actually I found the west wing in a warehouse sale in Dublin,' I long to tell them. 'And I found the roof just lying in the road after those howling storms we had last Christmas. Nobody claimed it, so I carried it up here and stuck it on.'

You wouldn't recognise Eugene. His hair is slicked back and he's washed the grease off his hands. He's also wearing a suit, and for once not one that can be prefixed with the word 'boiler'. 'Ancient', possibly, 'tatty', certainly, 'moth-eaten', perhaps, but definitely not 'boiler'.

She's taken out her pen and pad, has Ms Ciara Scully.

'Right, where do you want to begin?' I ask, itching to move proceedings along as quickly as possible.

'Well, if it's all one to you, Mr Patterson, I'd thought I'd start by having a quick word with Eugene here.'

'Right. Fine. No problem. I'll make the tea, then, shall I?'

'Ooh, that would be lovely,' Ms Scully replies.

'Two sugars in mine, please, Max.' This from Eugene. 'He's a good lad, so. Heart of gold, despite what you might have heard,' I hear spill from his dangerously loaded gob as I leave the room in search of the kettle.

'So,' Ms Scully continues, 'Max.' (She's calling me Max, now.) 'Were you a big help to Eugene while he was working away on the book?'

'He was some help, yes, though you have to understand he's a very busy author himself,' Eugene answers for me, and not for the first time.

'What about the murder of the priest?' Ms Scully enquires further. 'You're an acknowledged master of terrifying death, Max. Did you contribute to the writing of his demise, now?'

'Good grief, girl!' Eugene declaims on my behalf. 'I just wanted him stabbed. I didn't want the murderer to remove the poor man's testicles, spray them in gold paint and wear them to a dinner party as dangly earrings! Which is the sort of thing this young whipper-snapper writes, so it is.'

'Well, Max, did you advise your man here on how to write the spicier scenes in *American Tans*?'

'Ah, come on, Ciara,' Eugene ignores the direction of the question again, 'I might not be a five-times-a-night man like I was in my prime but I still have my memories.'

Five times a night! With Maeve? Five times a year more likely.

'No,' Eugene continues, 'I couldn't have broached Max on

that subject. We had a few chats, so. He gave me technical advice more than anything. Although if I had listened to him altogether there's a chance the book would never have been published at all. And it certainly would have had a different title, now.'

'Really?' Ms Scully says, her eyes lighting up. 'Do tell.'

And he does, the bastard.

I'm going to kill him.

'That's amazing,' Ms Scully remarks, as Eugene finishes his Judas tale. 'So, Max, you must be very proud of your old friend. Sure aren't you just delighted for him?'

Eugene looks at me grinning, like the school swot who has just been made head prefect.

'I'll make some more tea, shall I?' I say as I wheel myself out of the room.

It's four days later, and Eugene and I have only just started speaking to each other again.

Oh, we now have staff: a secretary – John, who's Irish, male, efficient, ambitious and drives me up the bloody wall, he's so unrelaxing. And we have a cook-cum-cleaner – Marika, who's Dutch, female, and has lived here for years. She's not one for conversation, is Marika. Not even one for asking if you have any particular preference as to what you might like for lunch. Still, at least I don't have to make the bloody tea when His Majesty's legions of fans come calling.

Neither employee lives in. I didn't want that.

It's into October and I'm heading towards my own personal winter of discontent. I have tried to write, but my publicist is on the phone about the book tour every five minutes asking me to agree to this and that, and John the secretary is determined to disturb me with something irritatingly petty every thirty seconds. I've come downstairs to grab a coffee just to get away from him.

I've rolled silently into the kitchen. Marika is in a world of her own, chopping up some completely unrecognisable vegetable. By the look and smell of it, we should really be smoking rather than eating it, but it should liven up whatever ghastly casserole she's throwing together for tonight.

Eugene is on the telephone, his back to me.

'Well, he's going to be heartbroken when I tell him, so,' I hear him utter. 'What can I say? He's been a miserable fecker ever since you left. I mean, since she went, he's had a face shaped like an ironing-board. Talk about long!'

'Would you care to tell me who you're speaking to, Eugene?' I butt in. 'Or would you prefer to toss your shirt over my phiz and give it a quick press?'

He spins round to face me, nearly garotting himself with the telephone lead in the process. 'Well, now, talk of the devil. He's snuck up behind me like a cat after a mouse and is waggling his ears at my private conversation.'

'And would you have liked to have walked into this room and heard me telling someone what a cocky old git you'd become since finding fame and fortune?'

'That's another thing,' he says, grinning into the handset. 'He can't stand a bit of healthy competition.'

'Eugene, would you mind telling me exactly who you're assassinating my character to?'

Eugene speaks into the handset again.

'Would you like to have a word with Mr Bitter and Twisted yourself, now? And be sure to have your tape-recorder turned on, he's bound to let something juicy slip, the mood he's in.'

He gives me the phone and strolls out of the kitchen.

I am suddenly irritated by the sound of Marika decimating the vegetables. 'Marika, could you find something else to do for five minutes, please?' I ask.

She shrugs, pretty much the way the kids used to, wipes her hands on a tea-towel, then shuffles out of the room whistling some turgid Dutch folk-song.

'Hello? Who is this?' I enquire tersely.

'It's me. I mean it's Nigel, Max.'

'Nigel? I didn't recognise you there for a minute.'

'I know. That's because my voice has broken.' And in one sentence he sings an entire operetta solo with all the parts, from basso-profundo to soprano.

'I remember the feeling well,' I tell him. 'I can sympathise. My voice didn't so much break as shatter.'

'Thanks,' he says.

'It's nice to hear from you. How are you?'

'I'm fine, Max. I'm really enjoying school.'

'Oh, good, I'm glad.' Except I'm not, really.

'And Caroline?'

'She's . . . okay.'

'Okay? Anything I should know about, Nigel?'

'No. Did you get our letter?'

'Yes, I did.'

I can hear him fidgeting uncomfortably. 'Is that okay?'

'I suppose so,' I reply sulkily.

There's an awkward silence.

'Have you heard from her, Max?'

'From who?'

'Kate.'

All my feelings of despair return. 'Yeah. She sent for her things from an address in London.'

There's a second pause. 'You love her, don't you, Max?'

I cannot believe my thirteen-year-old godson just asked me that. It's not the sort of question a young boy asks, is it? What do

I do? Lie? Tell him to mind his own bloody business? 'Yes, I do, Nigel. More than life itself, mate,' I say instead.

'Then why don't you go and get her? Ask her to come back?'

'It's not that simple. I told you Kate sent for her things, but that wasn't quite true. Somebody called Richard wrote to me.'

'Richard?'

'Yes, Richard.' I'm galled by the pain that mentioning his name brings me.

'But that's Kate's father.'

I try to let this sink in. 'How do you know that?'

'She told me. It was when I was feeling down about my parents during the summer. I asked her if her mother and father were still alive and she told me about them.'

'And you remember their names?'

'Yes. Dunno why. Just do. Max?'

'Yes?'

'You know why Caroline won't come home, don't you? She thinks it's all her fault. She feels terribly guilty.'

'That's nonsense. I don't blame Caroline,' I say, with my fingers partially crossed.

'She told me what she did, Max. It was pretty stupid of her. Actually, I feel a bit responsible for all this, too.'

'You?' I say, tugging my hair in frustration. 'Now that *is* ridiculous.'

'It was me who told Caroline that you and Kate were . . . you know, together. If she'd found out a bit later, it might never have happened.'

'Honestly, Nigel, it wasn't your fault. There were things I should have said to Kate and never did.'

'All I'm saying really,' Nigel continues, 'is that either it's everyone's fault or no one's. I know I'm only thirteen and I don't know much about all this stuff, but I just think everyone's being a bit daft. That's all I want to say, really.'

I sigh heavily. 'You might have a point there. Tragic, isn't it?'

'Listen, Max, I've got to go.'

'Okay, Nigel, thanks for calling. Keep in touch, please.'

'I will. One last thing.'

'Yes?'

'I never really . . . well, I couldn't at the time, I just wanted to forget it. But, you know . . . the cliff thing. I just wanted to say thanks for saving my life. I owe you one.'

'Don't mention it. Buy me a pint the next time you see me. Oh, hang on! Where is it you're spending half-term?'

'With Pick-it Pickering.'

'Not "who", "where". And why do they call him Pick-it Pickering?'

'You don't want to know. And he lives in Richmond.'

'I'm doing some signings in London during that week, seeing neither of you is coming here. Why don't we go for a spot of lunch afterwards?'

'Yeah, okay. I'd like that.'

'Bring your friend if you want. Come along to Hatchard's in Piccadilly. I'll dig out the date and time, and drop you a line.'

'Thanks, Max. See you, then.'

'I'll look forward to it. 'Bye for now.'

He's smarter than he looks, is Nigel. Doesn't say much, but obviously nothing slips past him. He takes it all in like a sponge.

And he's right. I should own up to the part *I* have played in my own downfall.

Kate believed what she saw, simply because of the way I had previously lived my life. Until I met her, I could not deal with maturity. I handled girls, and ran from women, emotion and love.

That's why Kate didn't believe me. I provided the evidence, prosecuted myself and got a conviction.

Now I have to settle down to my life sentence.

31

It's mid-October and I'm at the signing at Hatchard's. It's a wonderful old-fashioned bookshop, with creaking stairs, beams, the smell of well-cared-for books and a delightfully Dickensian atmosphere. A queue of people stretches out before me, all holding a copy of my latest book *A Twisted Imagination*, ready for me to sign before they buy it.

And am I happy? No. In fact, I'm sulking because Nigel hasn't shown up. Obviously he and Pick-it Pickering have found something more exciting to do, but he might have let me know. I was looking forward to seeing him, and I'd been half hoping that he'd persuade Caroline to come along too.

Anyway, that's why I'm sitting here sporting a pouty face, grunting and keeping my head down. At least the hat makes it difficult for people to see my expression.

'Could you write "from the Queen of mental cruelty", please, Mr Patterson,' a female voice requests.

I begin to write in the book.

'It's a joke you see,' the voice speaks again.

I peek from under my hat. It must be. This woman looks so

timid that, next to her, Miss Marple would seem like a vicious bitch.

'I'm buying this for my husband,' she explains, as I hand her back the book. 'Our decree absolute comes through next week.'

And so they keep coming.

'Sign it, "to Tony, the terror of Tooting".'

Very droll.

'"To the Black Widow, love Max".'

That's it, bring spiders into my day, why not?

'"To Laura. You drive *me* crazy, baby. Love Max".'

'"To Mad Mike, The mind bender".'

Sure, anything. Just keep 'em moving.

'"To Kate, I love you, Max".'

I start to scrawl her name and . . . It's the hands I recognise as they grasp the book. My own are still holding the other half. I release my grip as I look up at her. Her beauty is almost too painful to bear. 'Kate,' I mouth.

'Hello, Max.'

'How are you?' I feel the beginning of tears in my eyes.

'I'm . . . okay,' she replies, but I think she's lying.

'How have you been?'

'Miserable.'

'Why?'

I shrug. 'Read what you asked me to write in the book.'

'Is it true, Max?'

I blow air gently from my lungs and steel myself for my confession. Then I nod, slowly.

'But it makes you miserable?'

'Yes. Because you're not there.'

She shakes her head in irritation, or frustration, or maybe both. 'Why didn't you tell me, Max? Why couldn't you?'

'I meant to, I wanted to, I just – I thought it might frighten you away. I didn't think you could feel the same way about me.'

She looks at me. 'Well?' She looks down to the book and she reads my writing once again. 'Thanks, anyway,' she says. 'It's nice to know.' She turns away, and makes for the door. The woman I love is walking out of my life again.

The blood is roaring around my head, my stomach is shrinking and contracting. '*Kate, wait!*' I shout, and she stops at the door. 'Don't go, Kate, please don't go.'

She turns to face me.

The shop is heaving with people, all of whom have fallen silent. They are all looking at Kate.

'You can't walk out again. I'm desperate, Kate. I miss you so much I can't eat, sleep, think. I need you. I'm hopeless without you. Christ, I've been suicidal!'

'You're missing the point,' she says, turning away.

'You two,' I point at two sales staff loitering by the door, 'don't let that woman leave.'

'We can't stop her.'

'Yes, you can. She hasn't paid for that book!'

'*Max!*' Kate snaps, turning back to face me.

'You are my world, Kate. My life means nothing without you. I cannot let you go.'

'Why, Max? Please, *tell me why!*'

Seventy-odd people are holding their breath in anticipation.

Then I remember I had promised myself something. 'Wait there,' I tell her. I stand up and walk slowly round the table. I've been cheating. Using the table for support. It's a good six to eight steps to get to her. I'm not sure if I can make it.

I look at her and in my mind I see her dancing for me, dancing in my beautiful garden. And I start to walk.

Kate looks astonished. 'Max, what are you doing?' she gasps.

I keep moving as I speak to her. I must.

'I'm walking for you, Kate.'

'But how—?'

Two steps.

'Caroline helped. That's why she was in the gym.'

Four steps.

I stumble, and she begins to come towards me.

'Stay there,' I say, recovering my balance. I've lost count of the steps. Six? Seven? I concentrate on moving forward.

'I'm walking because you said you would help me walk again and you did. Your love made me able to walk again.' I reach her and I take her hands in mine. 'And I love you.'

There. I told her. Like I promised.

'Oh, Max.' Her eyes fill with tears.

'And there's something else. Forgive me if I don't get down on one knee, but please agree to marry me before I fall over?'

'Yes, Max. I will,' she replies, and my soul leaps a somersault my body could never equal.

It's mayhem at Hatchard's. Carnival time.

Cheers, roar and applause. Pats on shoulders, hugs, laughter and the hubbub of conversation.

'I am here, O Great Sultan Schahriar,' she says, putting her hands together in prayer. 'What story should Scheherazade tell you tonight?'

'The one about Max and Kate living happily ever after. I love you, Kate,' I tell her. 'I have loved you since the first moment I saw you.'

'And I love you,' she says.

I drink in her scent as she strokes my hair. We stay holding on to each other for a long, long time. By the time I look up the bookshop has more or less emptied.

In the corner I see the unmistakable figure of a young lad in glasses.

Nigel is smiling at me, and next to him stands Caroline, who wipes her eyes and winks at me.

Nigel gives me a thumbs-up sign, then takes his sister's hand and they go through the door into the noisy street outside.

I know now that Nigel told Kate I was here today. He was the one who persuaded her to come. He's paid me back. The debt is squared.

Kate's beautiful eyes are shining with happiness.

'I want to take you home, Kate. And I never ever want to lose you again. You see,' I say as I hold her tight. 'I can't love without you.'

Epilogue

One Year Later

Somebody has just delivered before their deadline. A week early, in fact, and it wasn't me.

Kate was amazing. She had no pain-killers, no epidural, not a whiff of gas and air. I, on the other hand, gulped as though my life depended on it every time the midwife left the room.

In the whole time I've known Kate, I don't think I've heard her utter the f-word before. Well, she's used it enough over the last eleven hours to make up for a lifetime of abstinence. And most of the expletives were directed at me.

They've taken her away to give her a bath and clean her up, and I sit here with my children in my arms.

We have twins: a boy and a girl.

I wonder how Caroline and Nigel will feel about being godparents? It's a dodgy job, I can tell them.

I remember back to how I felt when Caroline was placed in my arms at her christening, how awkward and uncomfortable and embarrassed I was.

I'm amazed at the difference: holding my own flesh and blood feels so right and I have Kate to thank for that.

We were married last Christmas. Twelve months on I'm a father. God knows what we'll have to do to top this next year!

I look at my children. *My* children. 'I promise you both,' I tell them, 'I will always be there for you. I will always look after you for as long as I live. But, above all, I will always love you.'

And how do they respond?

My son has screwed up his face and howled. And my daughter has just pissed down the front of my shirt.